*Baby, did you fall from Heaven?*

Being the deity of intoxication and ecstasy might just be the best job in the Cosmos. It certainly feels that way to Bacchus after he gets booted out of it. Mortal life is nothing but a complicated, emotional, pain-riddled struggle. If he can't reclaim his divinity, he'll settle for drowning his mortality in the pleasures of wine and women—especially women.

Until he meets Ariana, that is. She's just as beautiful as the other lovelies Bacchus plays with, but her beauty comes right from her soul, and it's muffled by profound sadness. Bacchus burns with the need to heal it, and help her—and that might be exactly the trick to getting himself lifted back into the Pantheon. Too bad he knows a lot more about pleasure than love…

# Books by Cindy Jacks

Desire

**Published by Kensington Publishing Corporation**

# Desire

## Cindy Jacks

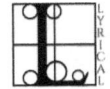

**LYRICAL PRESS**
Kensington Publishing Corp.
www.kensingtonbooks.com

*To Napo, here's hoping you are always young at heart.*

# Acknowledgements

There are so many people I want to thank for their hard work, input, and support:

Denysé, who has more faith in my talent and abilities than I have ever had.
Stacey, my beta reader who is always generous with her time and insight.
Penny, my Kensington editor whose constructive criticism shaped a good manuscript into a novel I can be proud of.
All the wonderful folks at Kensington/Lyrical for taking a chance on my quirky little book.
Arnold, for always allowing me to bounce ideas off of him and for being part of The Village.
Eva and the whole Elliott family, just for being wonderful.
Kelly, for holding my hand (and pouring the wine) while I awaited a response to my submission.
Nannette, for checking on me when I've been quiet for too long.
And of course my parents, my son and the love of my life, Napo.
Without all of your support and love I'd be a neurotic and unproductive puddle of goo.

# Author's Foreword

My greatest wish is that you enjoy this work of fiction. And it is just that—a work of fiction. I know I've taken considerable liberties with names, forms, and behaviors of deities from the pantheons of many world religions—some active, some not. For example, in traditional Greek mythology, Silenus is Bacchus' mentor and companion. However, I felt Pan was a more recognizable figure and therefore cast him in Silenus' role for this book.

As for all of Bacchus' colorful friends, I believe incorporating gods and goddesses from India, Egypt, ancient Sumeria, and even the UK is entirely appropriate in the telling of this tale. The god of intoxication and ecstasy was purported to travel widely, recruiting followers and bringing the gift of wine to foreign lands.

I also realize the tone of this manuscript is at times flippant and playful. Again these departures from more traditional piety are in no way meant to offend or tread on religious beliefs. Please take these words as they are intended—a joyful celebration of the sorrows of the world and the indomitable qualities of the human soul.

To quote the great bard himself:

"If we shadows have offended,
Think but this, and all is mended,
That you have but slumbered here
While these visions did appear.
And this weak and idle theme,
No more yielding than a dream."
– William Shakespeare, A Midsummer's Night Dream

Namaste,
Cindy

# Chapter 1

*Fall from Grace*

The scroll belonged to another god. Granted, the address read *To Bacchus*, but this foolish human had prayed to the wrong deity. It was one thing to address him by his given name, Dionysus, as opposed to the Roman name he preferred. It was quite another to mix up the god of intoxication and ecstasy with the god of viniculture and wine. "Pan," he called to his steward, "this is for Liber. How I tire of being confused with that pompous windbag."

"My apologies, sire. I shall see he gets this."

Bacchus drained his seventh wineskin of the day. Or was it eighth? "Please do. I would take it myself, but last month's lecture on the qualities of genuine cork will hold me over for a lifetime."

"Of course, sire."

"Also, make sure the nymphs are oiled up for the festivities this evening. Are the accommodations ready for our visitor from Hawaii?"

"Yes, sire. Pele's suite is ready. I inspected it myself."

"Good, I wouldn't want a repeat of the last time she visited. I hear they're still unearthing charred remains in Pompeii."

From the bottom of the pile, a gold scroll twinkled, smug in its self-importance. Bacchus bolted upright. "Pan, am I hallucinating, or is a scroll from the Council thrown in with common post?"

The squat goat-man flushed deep red, apparent even through his silver facial fur. "I-I-I, sire, I think, maybe…"

Cloven hooves echoed in Bacchus's private hall as Pan scurried to the heap. Eyes wide, mouth agape, Pan snatched the Council communiqué and ferried it to Bacchus.

"Just read it to me, Panny boy. It's probably for Liber anyway." Bacchus laughed. How very clever. Probably for Liber anyway. Good one.

Stubby fingers worked at the crystal seal. He'd barely fixed his beady gaze upon the text when a trumpeter flew into the gilded chamber and blasted a hurried version of *Hail to the Father*.

Guards, nymphs, and courtiers snapped to rigid attention. Bacchus knew he should've moved faster to pay his respects to the god of all gods, to whom Bacchus's own father, and every other deity, bowed. The room spun. Reaching out, he steadied himself. Yes, he definitely had finished eight wineskins. Still, a cold tingle ran up Bacchus's spine. Lightning flashed, thunder shook him to the core. His breath caught in his throat. Sniffing the air, he noted the scent of frankincense and sandalwood. As if greatness had a smell. Then again, maybe it did.

The Father's union with the Mother created every living thing in the Universe. In a tidal wave of snowy robes and untamed, silver hair, He flowed into Bacchus's great room. At the flick of His hand, the fanfare silenced.

Bacchus executed a deep bow, and as he rose, listed to one side. He caught himself against the arm of his throne. Curses. He'd chipped a nail. "And to what do we owe this great honor, my lord?"

"Good afternoon, Bacchus." The Father glanced around the scattered floor pillows and the sycophants lounging on them. "I need a few moments of your time. Alone."

"So you aren't here to see Liber, then?" Bacchus turned to dismiss his entourage, but no one had waited for the mere god of intoxication's permission to disperse. An implied request from the Father carried more weight than a direct order from anyone else in the Palace of Light. Oh sure, when she felt ornery, the Mother could contradict the Father, but only She dared to do so. Bacchus gave the standard answer, "Thy will be done."

The wizened deity motioned to a chaise. "Please, have a seat."

Bacchus staggered to the lounge.

Storm clouds above the Father's usually glowing brow made a poor show of hiding a scowl. He paced, a very human compulsion no god engaged in, much less The Lord of All Lords. "I trust you received the scroll from the Council."

"About that." Bacchus swallowed the lump in his throat. "There was a bit of a mix up with the post this morning."

"No matter. I would rather tell you this in person anyhow." The Father clasped his hands.

It must be very bad news, then. A heaviness in his core rooted him to the spot. Words failed him, and his mouth ran dry. He reached for his wineskin. Gods damn it. It was empty.

The Father's chest heaved. "I will not insult you by being indirect. Since Siddhartha joined the Council, he has done some excellent thinking on the sorrows of the world. Please understand he didn't target you specifically."

"Target me?" Bacchus rolled his eyes. "Am I being summoned before a firing squad?"

The Father furrowed his brow. "No, no. Not literally, anyway. Has Siddhartha talked to you about his premises regarding the sorrows?"

Bacchus waved. "Yes, he's tried several times, bless him. His manner of thinking is so far beyond me. My lord, you know I do whatever I can do to ease the sorrows of the world. I will admit I'm limited by my inferior mind, but I do try."

"No one questions your dedication, Bacchus. The debate has arisen over your methods."

"But my methods have withstood millennia, and believe me, the Puritan Era was no walk in the park for me and my devotees, but we've endured. I have my purpose. Human life is fraught with misery. My gifts provide respite from that misery."

"I understand. No one entered into this decision lightly. Mother is on the warpath. She has always been fond of your company."

Since Bacchus's birth, there had been those who argued he was not a proper god, but a demigod, since his mother had been mortal. Though, did he not deserve the status of god? Erupting out of Zeus's thigh had been no romp through Elysium for the newborn Bacchus. "Am I finally being demoted?"

The Father exhaled, white eyebrows knitted, and sat next to Bacchus. "It is worse than that, my child. The Council has decided Desire does indeed seem to be the root of all suffering. Siddhartha has proven his assertion beyond a shadow of a doubt. Since Desire—well, it is central to everything you do. Therefore, we have decided we must revoke your divine power and disband your following. There is no way around it."

Bacchus reeled. How dare the Council do this to him and behind his back? He hadn't heard a word about these discussions. True, he held the rank of lesser god, but a god of any rank was still a god. Why had no one come to him? "So just like that I'm out on my ear?"

"We did debate this for over two centuries. It was not a snap decision; I assure you. And Siddhartha argued for you hardest of all. He deems you necessary to 'the joyful participation in the sorrows of the world.'"

"Who argued against me?"

"We shouldn't get into that." The Father shook a hand, his snowy locks spilling over his shoulders.

"It was Discordia, wasn't it?" Well that smarmy, contrary, scheming little bitch had better not cross his path anytime soon. "She could use a good buggering to loosen up that tight ass of hers."

"Easy, now."

Bacchus wanted to scream at the Father, but he dare not. He reached for his wineskin, remembered it was empty, jumped up, and dashed to the banquet table. With shaky hands, he threw aside platters of grapes, a half-consumed roasted suckling pig, and a pudding of figs and ambrosia before he found a wineskin. He drank greedily.

Ages had passed since anyone had attacked Bacchus outright, and he'd always managed to pull his pretty, fleshy bottom out of the fire. Once he had invoked his female form, Bacchus draped herself across the Father's lap with feline grace. Her golden hair spilled over masculine thighs. She wound a long, slender finger around a lock of the Father's beard. "Isn't there anything you can do to help me, my lord?"

A flash of craving broke the Lord of All Lord's mask of gravity.

Silently, Bacchus summoned her two most fetching nymphs, Maia and Saraesa. The lithe women fell at the Father's feet and stroked Bacchus's voluptuous curves. Tinkling strains of laughter resonated in a seductive chorus, curling around the would-be lovers. Maia and Saraesa leaned into each other, and their lips melted together.

The Father licked his lips, breath quickening. Bacchus had Him enthralled. Saraesa stripped off Maia's gauzy wrap and pulled the nymph's pert breasts to her mouth.

A low growl rumbled in the Father's throat. "Enough."

The nymphs disappeared in a flash of stardust, leaving silence in their wake. Bacchus reverted at once to his male body.

"This is exactly to what the Council refers. There has to be more to life than pleasures of the flesh."

Chastened, Bacchus hung his head. "I agree, my lord, but life cannot flourish either without passion or ecstasy."

"I used to believe that, but now I see this is where we have gone wrong. Many of our children lead happy lives of sobriety and abstinence."

"Happy or uneventful? There is a difference."

The Father rose. "I am truly sorry, Bacchus, my love."

"There's nothing you can do to help me?"

"It is not my decision to make. The Council has spoken."

"Every decision is yours to make."

"You know as well as I, that is not how it works. As of now, your powers have been revoked. I am sorry. I will leave you to your packing." The Father turned toward the grand hall exit.

Bacchus caught a glimpse of himself in a mirror. As usual, his reflection drew his attention, but he hardly recognized the person peering back. A sneer tugged at his cherubic face. Perfectly arched eyebrows furrowed. Fear, worry, anger, he had no way to calm the storm raging inside. "Some all-powerful lord you are."

The Father froze. His ire ignited a ring of flames around him, but he doused them with a single flick of his wrist. Without facing Bacchus, he replied, "I shall ignore your blasphemy this once. Wounded feelings have clouded your judgment." The Father disappeared.

The gilded chamber fell dark, cold, and silent. Darkness and chill would rule the rest of his life if he failed to think of a solution.

# Chapter 2

*Once Was Lost*

*Six months after exile…*

"Sire, wakey wakey," a gruff voice intruded on Bacchus's slumber.

"Mmm, Angela." Swimming up through the fog of sleep, he wrapped his arms around the person trying to rouse him. "Where have you been, you naughty girl?"

The shock of pain to his shin jolted Bacchus upright. He rubbed his throbbing leg, which bore the imprint of a cloven hoof.

"Hey, what do you mean waking me up like that?"

Pan struggled to his feet. "I do so apologize, sire. But you know how hands-y you get when you're half asleep."

"Sorry, my friend." Waking in Athens, Greece and not Olympus, still confused the former god. The beach? How in the world had he wound up on the beach? The sun intensified the pounding in his head. "Ugh, what time is it?"

"Three in the afternoon, sire."

"Already? Damn, I feel as though I just fell asleep."

Pan helped Bacchus stand and strained to brush sand from his broad shoulders. "You need to start taking care of yourself, sire. You are mortal. You're killing yourself."

"I don't care if I am. What have I got to live for?"

"Please, don't talk that way. We'll get you reinstated. I've been reading about Siddhartha's earthly philosophies. I think the Father gave you the clue you need to appeal the decision."

"You're a loyal friend. A fool, but a loyal friend." Each breath took effort to force from his aching chest. Nothing could reverse their decision.

A breeze stirred the palm overhead, and sand attacked his skin. Fiery, raw agony shot through his feet, lobster red against the pallor of his legs. "By the gods, what happened here?"

"Ah, well, sire, maybe next time you pass out on the beach you should do it under a tree large enough to shade your entire body."

One more betrayal by this frail form. Sunburn, indeed. He used to sup with Apollo and Ra on a regular basis, and now a few hours without shade scorched his skin. Pathetic.

Though Pan had offered to carry his lordship, Bacchus endured the walk to his villa, wincing with every step.

Naked and wet, after a quick shower, Bacchus trotted to the kitchen, opened a beer, and washed down an assortment of over-the-counter medication, some to relieve his sunburned feet pain and some just because he liked the way they mixed with alcohol. The refrigerator held little of interest, but he rejoiced in finding a wilting fig and small piece of feta. "You know"—Bacchus took a bite of fruit—"I think I've lost some weight since I haven't had ambrosia to gorge myself on."

"Yes, sire, you're looking very svelte."

Overflowing trashcans, garbage heaps, buzzing flies, and toppled liquor bottles had replaced the overflowing flower urns, delicate chocolate heaps, winged dark faeries, and silken floor pillows that once surrounded him. "I might have company again tonight. Could you straighten up a bit?"

"Of course, sire."

Pan picked up a soggy dishtowel, more putrid than the surfaces he wiped. With a grimace, he clucked his tongue and abandoned his efforts. Stepping carefully, he avoided a pair of panties and a small marijuana pipe. "Safe to assume these aren't yours, sire?"

"Those are from my friend last night. Amy? Anna?"

"Angela?"

"Yes, that's it. How did you know?"

"You called me that name this morning when you tried to spoon me, sire." Pan picked up the undies. "I'll be sure these get back to her, unless you would like to keep the pipe."

"No, thank you." True, Bacchus had dabbled with human pharmaceuticals, but he preferred the usual sacraments—women, wine, and song. Really, he could do without the song if need be. During the first few months after his fall, he'd nearly murdered his mortal form with booze and an endless parade of strumpets. After his first case of the clap, he'd re-evaluated his lifestyle. Pissing razor blades had that effect on a fellow. Not that he'd slowed down much, but at least he'd taken the healer's advice and started using a penis sheath called a condom.

Bacchus left his steward to the cleaning. In the master suite, he tried to decide what to wear from rows and rows of clothing in his walk-in closet. The ridiculous riches the Council had bestowed upon him as a sort of severance package had easily funded his copious shopping trips. He owned labels from every top European designer, but none of the clothes pleased him as much as a fine linen tunic would have. He chose charcoal Hugo Boss slacks and a beige cashmere sweater then emerged to find the place sparkling clean. "Pan—"

"Before you fly off the handle, sire—"

"Frivolous magic when visiting Earth is forbidden, Pan."

"It wasn't a frivolous use of my powers."

"It's in the Code of Divine Ethics. 'No divine being shall alter the natural course of events unless for a higher purpose.' You know as well as I do what that means."

"Sire, how often is that rule actually enforced? Besides, one could argue saving a god's domicile from complete and total putrefaction is indeed a higher purpose."

Bacchus took his friend's hand. "One day you're going to have to accept I am not a god anymore."

"I'll never accept that. They'll have to render me inert first."

"By the gods, I couldn't survive without you, but the thing is, Panny, if you don't accept it, then I never will, either."

# Chapter 3

*Lost at Sea*

*One year after exile…*

Laughter jolted Bacchus awake. Why was the earth moving? His brain sloshed around his head, or maybe it had been pureed. Once his eyes adjusted to the sunlight streaming through a picture window, he found himself in a strange bedroom.

When he reached for the brass and ceramic lamp, another wave of dizziness hit him, and he tumbled out of bed. His hands and knees sunk into plush ivory carpeting. Desperate to steady himself, he reached for a column of polished wood to no avail.

He listed forward and smacked his forehead into a rum bottle. By Zeus, that's where he'd put it. A vague memory of playing a game called *Find the Rum Bottle* swam around his liquefied mind. He uncorked the bottle and swigged. Brown sugar, sweet and smooth, the liquor warmed his throat and chest. He struggled to his feet, walked to the window, and squinted to focus on the scene outside. Tears stung his eyes.

Water the color of Neptune's limpid eyes sparkled in the sun. A pod of dolphins swam along side the vessel, arching in and out of the wake. How the hell had he wound up on a yacht?

Laughter rang out from another room. Simone. Oh, yes, Simone. Wild, golden hair encircled her head like a mandorla. Eyes black as the night sea trimmed in long, arched lashes. Her cappuccino satin skin had captivated him. He longed to run his hands, his fingertips, and his tongue over every inch of her. He had done just that in the last forty-eight hours. What a lovely, giving creature.

He'd met the young woman in the streets of New Orleans, at a festival known as Mardi Gras. It was the only party on Earth that came anywhere near a proper Bacchanal, though Vegas used to be crazy fun before it went all corporate.

The trip to the territory known as New Orleans had been a wild one. When he'd first landed on Earth, he'd planned to stay in his beloved Greece until old age and death allowed him to return to the Elysian Fields, but the best laid schemes of mice and defrocked gods often went astray.

First, he'd met a belly dancer named Kristina—an exotic tattooed beauty—who'd taken him to Paris to be something that translated roughly into "boy toy." And when she'd tired of him, he'd taken up with a stunning young German woman who was backpacking through Europe. In the British Isles, now known as the UK, he parted ways with Dieta and met an American writer on vacation. Laney said she hailed from a town known as the Big Easy, and she invited him to come home with her.

How Bacchus had come to love New Orleans, and he loved it even more once Mardi Gras began. Which was where he met *la belle* Simone. On the solemn Wednesday that marked the abrupt end to the festivities, Simone made Bacchus an offer he couldn't refuse. Her friend owned a yacht and would be in port the next day to pick her up. The boat turned out to be a floating palace of debauchery.

More giggling in the hall drew his attention. Now, where had the little minx gone?

Rum bottle in tow, he trotted out of his stateroom. The laughter grew louder. At a room farther up the passageway to his left, he knocked and called, "May I gain entry, pretty please?"

An athletic woman with dark chocolate curls and skin to match opened the door and grinned at him. "What?"

"May I come in?"

"Oh sure." She pulled him by his neck and murmured, "Aren't you a tall drink of water, sailor?"

"Funny you mention that. I spent quite a lot of time sailing around the Mediterranean. This was back in 500 BC when—" A kiss cut off his mindless rambling.

Oddly enough, the woman tasted like chocolate, too. She broke away from his lips and offered him a cocoa-colored drink garnished with three white chocolate truffles on a toothpick. "Godiva martini?"

Well, that explained that. A beautiful woman with a beautiful drink. Was there a more fantastic sight in all the world? "Thank you, love." He winked, accepted the glass, and threw the rum bottle aside. "Seems we won't be needing this."

Another nubile woman appeared beside the ebony-skinned beauty. They looked at him as though he were the prime rib at an all-you-can-eat buffet. Two beautiful women and a beautiful drink. Indeed, he had found a more fantastic sight. Bacchus stood corrected.

"I'm Billie," the dark woman said. "This is my friend Layla."

Layla fluttered her fingers to say hello. She was tall with legs that stretched into the Afterlife, hair the color of harvested wheat, and so many dangerous curves.

He tossed back the martini in one gulp.

Giggling, Layla pushed him onto the bed and knelt beside him.

His lips crushed against hers.

Laughter rose from Billie, and she settled on the other side of him. Hot flesh pressed against him, the women stroking his skin.

His body melted against the mattress. What sweet surrender. Dizziness slowed reality, not the heavy, sickening dizziness he'd awoken with. This reeling was airy. Disconnected. Pleasant.

In slow motion, Billie slipped the spaghetti straps of Layla's babydoll nightie down milky shoulders. For a moment, the garment fluttered to the ground. Or had an hour passed, the nightgown rippling mid-air?

The soft smack of someone's lips became loud as Billie suckled Layla's breast while removing her own bra and panties. Their laughter echoed as they reached for Bacchus.

One removed his shirt as another stripped his pants and underwear.

He felt fuzzy and light as a feather, as if he were hovering near the ceiling. But he must still be on the bed, because the satin sheets felt like a river of liquid silk.

He rubbed the nearest woman's backside and chuckled. "What was in that drink?"

"Something to make you feel good all over," Billie murmured.

That he did. Not that he needed any help to enjoy sex, but still, it was thoughtful of the women to heighten the experience. Pleasure coursed through his veins.

The dark-skinned beauty worked her way up his body and straddled his face Her musk ignited his loins and drew his core tight. Bacchus held her hips, devoured her clit and labia, and gorged himself on her tart juices. Her moans sounded like the music of angels.

Layla straddled his lap, rolled a condom over his hard cock, and slipped him inside her. Bacchus groaned. Finding Simone would have to wait.

* * * *

Bacchus awoke parched in a way he'd never before experienced. Olympus help him, he might have to resort to a glass of water. A sad state of affairs indeed.

He disentangled himself from…oh dear, what were the lovely ladies' names? No matter. He kissed each of them on the cheek and bade them goodbye, though neither stirred from their slumber to return the farewell.

Staggering around the room, he sorted through the scattered clothing and found his. His head felt as though it'd been wrapped in freshly sheared wool and then encased in a ceramic urn. His thoughts echoed with alarming volume. *Shh*, he told himself to no avail.

Bacchus had been to the dining room on the yacht only once, when he'd first arrived. And he hadn't had time to explore the various levels the ship offered. In fact, his venture into the Nubian princess' room was the first time he'd left his cabin since Simone had pulled him below decks three nights ago. Was it three nights ago? It felt like only three, but it could've been a year for all that time and space had melded together.

He trudged into the glass-paneled elevator and slapped the buttons. One of the levels had to have an eatery of some type. Food, yes. That was what he needed. Food and water. Maybe a bottle of Pinot Grigio. Something nice and light. He swayed as the glass box halted, and the doors dinged open.

Emerging from the elevator, he wandered into yet another party that encompassed the entire deck. A glistening pool filled with revelers surrounded a bar shaped like the front end of a speedboat. Scantily clad waiters and waitresses ferried drinks on lifesavers-turned-serving-trays. With every passing moment, Bacchus gained more and more respect for the owner of this floating den of iniquity.

Every fiber of his being begged him to stay, to take part in the festivities, but his mortal needs won out. He stooped, yelling over the blaring music, and asked a waiter in the pool where he could find a meal. The young man, chest glistening with droplets of oil in his sparse chest hair, barked vague directions and pointed at a passageway to the right. Bacchus thanked him and headed down the corridor.

Unmarked doorways lined the hallway. None led to a room large enough to accommodate diners. He walked to the end, testing entryways as he went. The hall dragged on and on, but at last ended outside double doors covered in cream leather and brass studs. A porthole showed a group of men seated around a felt covered table.

He stepped through the swinging doors.

Three men with arms as thick as Bacchus's two legs put together set upon him like Cererbus upon the souls of the damned. Lips drawn into flat lines, chests puffed out, the men formed a wall in front of Bacchus. Gone were the days when he could drive men to the brink of insanity with rage and passion. Best not to engage them.

"Did I interrupt something?" Bacchus threw in a smile for good measure.

"This party is invitation only," said the shortest. A Spanish accent of some kind thickened his pronunciation of English vowels.

"My apologies, I'm looking for somewhere I might get to eat."

A man, whose short-sleeved silk shirt hung off him in volumes of fabric, stood and walked over to Bacchus. Narrowing one golden eye, he gave Bacchus a once-over and nodded. "You lost, pretty boy?"

Bacchus arched an eyebrow. "Apparently."

He spoke with the same accent as the other man. "You think you're funny? What're you doing on my boat?"

"This is your boat? I have to say, you, sir, know how to throw a party. And believe me, that's a lot coming from me."

"I didn't ask what you thought of my entertaining skills. I asked what the fuck you're doing on my boat."

"Well, lots of things, but a gentleman doesn't kiss and tell. Simone invited me."

She waved from the lap of a man seated at the table.

"Oh, Simone, there you are." Bacchus returned the wave. "I've been looking for you all over. So, I suppose, then, I'm not lost at all."

Silk shirt shook his head and ran a hand through wisps of curly gray hair. "You know this *maricon*, Simone?"

She nodded and grinned. "He's all right, Santos. This da one I been tellin' you 'bout."

Santos relaxed and gave a yellowed smile. "'*Ta bien, muchachos,*'" he said to his bodyguards who released Bacchus. "I think our new friend here should join our game. Everyone good with that?"

The men at the table nodded and chuckled.

"Are you gentlemen engaged in a game of chance? I'm just learning this game. It's called Texas Hold 'Em, isn't it?" asked Bacchus. "You know I'd love to join you after I get a bite and something to drink."

With surprising strength for a man of such slight stature, Santos pressed Bacchus into an empty chair. He snapped his fingers. "We can take care of that here."

A young woman hurried to his side. Silken black hair hung down to her waist. Clad in a bra and skirt uniform, she jiggled in all the right places.

Despite the vulgarity of her outfit, Bacchus was taken with her elegance.

Yes, elegance. Perhaps it came from her aquiline nose or the curve of her neck into her delicate collarbone. Her eyes, too—dark and complicated—showed a defiance for her current situation. Springtime emanated from her aura.

A white linen *stola* would dazzle against her skin the color of fine bourbon, nearly as bright as diamonds woven into her raven hair. The opulence of his former palace would dim compared to her, if only he could take her there.

"Maybe you ain't no *maricon* after all. You gonna answer the woman?" Santos laughed without humor.

"I'm sorry?" Had the man just called him queer?

"What would you like to order?" Her voice tinkled soft as silver bells.

Thoughts about food had escaped him. "Please, bring me whatever the kitchen is serving and a bottle of white wine."

"Yes, sir." She gave him a curt nod and glided out of the room.

"So." Santos took his seat. "What's your name?"

"Bacch—" He caught himself. How difficult it had been to adjust to his mortal pseudonym, to be burdened with a surname. Couldn't he be known by only one moniker like Cher or Madonna. Or perhaps, The Former-God-Formerly-Known-As-Bacchus. Oh well. Pan had advised he blend in as best as possible. "I'm Bach Sabazios."

"*Mucho gusto,* Mr. Sabazios. I'm Santos. This is Pops, Nakamura, Tito, Billy, and Jean-Claude."

Men of different ethnic and cultural backgrounds flipped a brief wave or head nod. "Nice to meet all of you as well."

"We do this game a few times a year. We start in Miami, cruise around Florida and the Gulf, picking up players. Once we're in international waters, we can do what we like, right?" Santos gave a savage laugh. "You enjoy yourself this time, maybe you come back next time, ey?"

"I might just do that," said Bacchus.

"*'Ta bien.* All right, enough talk. Let's play some cards, *muchachos.*"

Bacchus laid paper currency bearing the image of some mortal named Ben Franklin on the table. "Is this enough to get started?"

"Put your cash away, Mr. Sabazios. Simone mentioned you are good for a lot more." Santos nodded to the dealer.

The dealer gave Bacchus twenty-five grand in chips. The table buy-in was a hundred dollars, which didn't seem like a lot, but what did he know about money? He'd had the hardest time figuring out monetary denominations. A fifty looked so much like a five except for the little circle at the end of the number. Who had time for such details?

Speaking of details, Bacchus peered at his cards and the flop or the river or whatever in Hades the features of this game were called. Not like a simple game of Tabula or Knucklebones. Eager to learn, he bet with abandon. His first defeat cost him fifteen hundred dollars.

The second hand he lost because he was more interested in wolfing down the pork sandwich his dark beauty had brought him than keeping his head in the game. "What is this delicious wine?"

She presented the label to him. Bacchus ordered two more bottles.

When she brought his drink order, he took her hand and asked her name. The meanest-looking of Santos's thugs bristled and glared at Bacchus, but Santos waved off the man's annoyance.

"Ariana," she replied.

*Ariana*. Her name washed over him, a gentle wave cooling hot sands. "Lovely to meet you, Ariana."

She nodded and disappeared behind the galley door.

By the last hand of the night, Bacchus was nearly a hundred grand in the hole. Not that it mattered to him in the slightest. Every time Ariana entered the room, all he could think of were dandelions and buttercups, her red lips puckered, white fluffy seedpods spinning in the wind, and yellow flowers braided in her hair.

While most of his godly powers were lost to him, he could still read the aura and memories written on the human soul. Perhaps his retained skill had been an oversight on the Mother and Father's part, but Bacchus doubted this was so. He suspected they'd allowed him this gift as protection in the unfamiliar world he inhabited. Humanity could be surprisingly deceptive and cruel. At times, more evil than Lucifer himself.

For instance, the stocky thug in the far corner had taken a special dislike to Bacchus. He had a gaping hole where his spirit should be, yawning like an open grave, sucking light and happiness from auras around him. Sure, he was handsome—chiseled jaw, stylish black waves, striking emerald eyes. No doubt, the man had begun as an innocent baby boy, but life had decayed him. A legacy of pain had stolen the man's soul, twisted him into something grotesque. No amount of physical beauty could cloak it.

The last hand ended as the first had, in disaster. A small price to pay for the pleasure of her company.

As though the aged man had read Bacchus's mind, Santos said, "It seems lady luck was not with you tonight, *muchacho*. I've never seen a man so happily lose this large a sum of money."

Bacchus drained the last of his wine. "Good drink, good company. It makes the loss more bearable, don't you think?"

"*Sí*, I do. Maybe you could use a little more company tonight? Maybe in your private quarters to help ease the pain of your loss?"

"I'm always up for some private amusement."

For the umpteenth time, the shortest henchman set his jaw, eyes narrowed, hands clenched in fists. Nonetheless, no objections spilled from his thin, tight lips.

"What do you say, *mi'ja*?" Santos asked Ariana. "Does Mr. Sabazios deserve some tender, loving care?"

"Yes, sir. Of course."

How wonderful, the night had not been a complete wash after all. Excitement rippled through his abdomen, and Bacchus tried to catch the woman's eye.

She focused on clearing away the men's glasses.

One by one, the poker players dispersed. Santos headed to his stateroom with a lovely lady on each arm. Bacchus lingered. Pouring himself a drink from the rum left on the card table, he waited for his dark beauty to emerge from the galley again, but she didn't. The only person he saw on the way back to his berth was the man with the void inside. Arms crossed, the minion stood immobile in the second deck passageway. Bacchus flipped the man a friendly wave. The soulless one didn't return the greeting.

# Chapter 4

*Once Was Blind*

Had Bacchus not been listening for it, he might not have heard the timid knock. Running his fingers through his hair, he checked his reflection before he opened the door. Perfection, as usual. He opened the cabin door.

Ariana wavered in the doorway. Her once radiant skin bore a pale green tinge. Her eyes glistened with vacant glassiness.

"Are you all right, love?" He took her hand and escorted her inside.

"I'm fine." She shrugged. "Why?"

"No reason." He settled her into a barrel back chair. "Would you like a cocktail?"

"Sure."

He skittered over to the wet bar and selected a lead crystal tumbler.

"No need to dirty a glass." She bounded up behind him, plucked the rum bottle from his hand, and took a swig.

Ah, a woman after his own heart. He gathered Ariana in his arms and swept her hair from her face. His next move would've been a sensual kiss followed by long, meandering caresses, but her lifeless eyes stopped him cold.

Though her body showed no resistance, no attraction burned in her gaze. Bacchus had never been in such a situation before, but it seemed possible she wasn't there of her own accord. Oh no. That wouldn't do. He released her.

She stumbled to the bed and took another drink. "Come on. Let's get to it."

The heat in his loins and torso vanished. Tickles in the pit of his stomach ebbed. Bacchus sat down next to her and took her hand in his. "As appealing as that offer is, why don't we forgo this charade? You don't have to do this, love."

Frowning, she shook her head and swallowed another mouthful of rum. "But really I do." Bottle raised to her lips, she started to take another drink.

Though it went against every instinct in his body, Bacchus took the bottle and set it aside. "Please, stop. Let's give the rum a break for a while."

She studied her lap. "You don't think I'm pretty?"

"That's not it at all. I find you quite lovely. More than lovely, you're beautiful." He tucked a lock of hair behind her ear. "It's just that I'm not in the habit of forcing myself on anyone."

"You're not? You didn't seem to object in the game room."

He'd believed Ariana's agreement to be genuine, that she'd wanted to come to him tonight. That Santos had offered her without her consent incensed Bacchus. "Ariana, my dear. I'm afraid I've put you in a terrible position." He tried to convey with his expression his sincerest apology, but she wouldn't look at him. "If you have to get this intoxicated to give yourself to a lover, it's not worth doing. Intoxication and lovemaking should be purely pleasurable experiences, not a means to an end. Do you understand what I'm trying to tell you?"

"I'm not intoxicat—" She vomited on the carpet.

A bit splashed on Bacchus's leg. He tensed and fought the spasms of his own belly. "Of course you aren't, dear."

She ran for the bathroom.

Not the way he'd thought this evening would go, to say the least. Bacchus summoned Pan.

He appeared in a puff of light and goat hair. "Sire, you called?" Pan surveyed the mess. "Oh my."

"Yes, my lady friend has had a bit too much to drink. Could you?" He motioned to the vomit.

"But of course." A flick of Pan's wrist swept away the regurgitated food and alcohol. "Do you need help for your sick friend?"

"A restorative potion from Panakeia would be great."

"Right away, sire." Pan disappeared, shedding more fur as he did.

The woman had fallen silent.

Bacchus put his ear to the door. No more retching or gagging. He knocked then opened the door.

She lay, hair fanned out around her face, supine on the floor.

"Ariana, love?"

She gave no reply. Poor dear. She'd done this to herself to work up the will to spend the night with him.

He'd never meant to cause her distress. Saddened, he scooped her up and carried her to the bed. After getting her comfortable, a pillow tucked beneath her head, he fetched a cool washcloth from the restroom.

Pan returned, helped administer the curative tincture then vanished.

Bacchus settled next to Ariana and mopped her brow. Unlined cinnamon skin stretched taut over high cheekbones. Black hair and eyelashes contrasted the warmth of her complexion.

He touched the cloth again to her forehead and closed his eyes. Visions of yellow flowers, green grass, and a deep blue ocean marked her spirit. True, a dark storm pushed in over her aquamarine sea, but the storm did not belong to her.

Her aura painted pictures of a child who did cartwheels along the beach and drew happy faces in the sand. Laughter, so much laughter. Something changed when she became an adolescent, something she guarded and sealed away, but it wasn't the only darkness. Drudgery, pain, a sense of feeling trapped. Of the memories open to him, these made up the dark cloud on the horizon. She fought the darkness, held it away from her soul.

The more Bacchus saw of her inner beauty, the more he regretted causing her this distress. "Who troubles your placid waters?" He leaned forward and kissed her forehead. "I am so very, truly sorry, love."

\* \* \* \*

All night long, Bacchus had visions of lying in a field of flowers, and though in the dream it was day, he could see the stars. He felt at peace and at home, but sensed something missing. A gentle breeze ruffled his hair, sweeping the crown from his head and carrying it into the sky.

His half-brother, Heracles, spoke to him. "It is not your crown I seek. Find her crown."

Consciousness crept over him and dissolved the strange dream. For the second time in three days, the sound of a woman's laughter woke him. At least he'd thought it was laughter until he opened his eyes.

Sobbing, Ariana sat in a ball on the loveseat, her knees pulled up to her chin.

Bacchus rushed to her, the cool cabin air chilling his bare body. He'd never seen the point of pajamas, but his naked presence seemed only to incense her cries. After securing a towel around his waist, he sat down next to her. "What's wrong, Ariana?"

She squealed out a few unintelligible words.

Bacchus smoothed her hair. "Nothing happened last night, love."

His assurance spurred on her hysteria.

He froze. What was he supposed to do? Hold her? No, she didn't want him anywhere near her. Slap her? Decidedly not. He had half a mind to start wailing with her. He went with the only offer of comfort he understood. "A drink?" he asked. "Should I get you a drink?"

She shook her head.

"A glass of water, maybe?"

She hiccupped another cry.

"Ariana, you have to help me here. I don't know what to do."

"There's nothing you can do."

He took her hand. "Perhaps if you tell me what the problem is…"

She jerked away. "I'm screwed. So seriously screwed."

Frustrated, Bacchus got to his feet and went to the bathroom. If she wouldn't make the effort to calm down, he could at least splash some water on his face. Human women had proven so much more emotionally unstable than goddesses or nymphs. Deities never cried. Really, what was the purpose of blubbering and howling like a banshee? For the gods' sakes, he hadn't even touched her last night. He thought he'd done the right thing. For once in his existence, he'd exercised some semblance of a moral compass, and this was his reward? Emerging from the loo, he took a few deep breaths.

"So listen," he said. "I'm sorry I didn't, uh, make love with you last night. I didn't mean to hurt your feelings or anything. I was trying to be a gentleman, and believe me, being a gentleman is something I'd usually avoid. You seemed so forlorn. And you did throw up on me so—"

She huffed, rolling her eyes. "I'm in trouble either way. Damned if you did, damned if you didn't."

"What do you mean?" He sat next to her.

"Don't worry about it." She narrowed her eyes. "I have to go."

Bacchus caught her hand. "Wait. Tell me what's going on. Maybe I can help."

"*Coño*," she swore. "Look, I'm sorry I threw up on you last night and wigged out just now, but don't. Please, don't." She pulled away, stood, and slipped on her shoes. Without another look backward, Ariana marched out the cabin door.

He stood, compelled to follow her, but he remained frozen in place, like every statue that had ever been made of him.

# Chapter 5

*Big Blind*

Copious amounts of rum restored Bacchus to his senses. The yacht had an ample supply, and he was grateful. Rum also made Pan's hours of poker instruction more bearable.

"You're sure you can remember all this, sire?" Pan planted his haunches on the dense carpet.

"If I could, as a youth, turn fermented grapes into the beauty that is wine, I can surely master one insignificant card game." Still, this insignificant card game stood between him and his beautiful Ariana. Best to keep practicing though a diligent student Bacchus had never been.

"I miss the days when we could unleash the *maenads* on an enemy and be done with it."

"As do I, but I no longer have those sort of resources at my command. So, I must work with what I've got. Thanks for bringing some of my special brew. How did you sneak this out of the palace?"

He stamped a hoof as his lips twisted into a sly grin. "I have my ways, sire."

"After a nip of this, my gaming skill won't really matter. They'll hardly be able to hold their cards, much less best me. I'll wrest her from his clutches one way or another."

"This woman is that extraordinary?"

"She's extra extraordinary, Panny. She doesn't deserve to be used as a common whore. Not that there's anything wrong with prostitution, mind you, but it should be a lady's choice to profit from her skills, not something forced upon her."

"Of course, sire."

Bacchus smoothed a burgundy dress shirt over his muscular abdomen. "How's this one?"

Pan brushed a bit of lint off his lord's shoulder. "You always look smashing in anything wine-colored."

Bacchus secured the cuffs with a pair of diamond links. "It's going to be a late night. Don't wait up."

"Summon me if you need me, sire."

Bacchus bid Pan good night and trotted up to the game room.

Santos smiled, more a baring of fangs than a greeting. "Mr. Sabazios. How are you this evening? Please, have a seat."

"I'm well, thank you. How are you?"

"Good. Thanks." He wiped his mustache and sat across the table from Bacchus. "You had a good night then?"

"I did. Thanks."

"You found your visitor…adequate, no?"

"Sr. Santos, I'm loath to admit this, but I'd had a lot to drink last night, and I'm afraid…well, let's just say I was inadequate." Bacchus glanced at Ariana and hoped his lie had helped ease whatever predicament had distressed her this morning. Though she gave no reaction, the other men at the table snickered. Not that Bacchus cared what they thought of him and his manhood.

"*Que maricon, qué le dije.*" The soulless man sneered.

Santos smoked his cigar. A gleam flashed in his otherwise guarded eyes. In Spanish, he ordered Ariana to get Mr. Sabazios a drink.

"*Vino blanco, por favor, como la ultima vez. Gracias,*" Bacchus said. If their intention had been to cut him out of the conversation, they had another thing coming.

Santos licked his lips, fixing his gaze on Bacchus. "You speak Spanish?"

"I do. I also speak French, Portuguese, Russian, Greek—both ancient and modern—Hindi, Babylonian, Latin—though no one really speaks Latin any more, do they?"

A chuckle from Santos flashed another predatory smile. "Is there any language you don't speak?"

Bacchus scratched his chin, shrugging. "Well, I've never quite gotten the hang of Mandarin Chinese. Or Szechuan for that matter."

Santos raised one eyebrow.

Around the table, men exchanged looks and chatted amongst themselves, but none spoke directly to Bacchus. He felt their contempt of him beneath a current of desire to take him for all he was worth.

Soon enough, the game was underway, and all pretense of friendly chitchat dropped. Though the players cloaked their hostilities in joking tones, they were serious about winning. Too bad for them.

Bacchus had an ace up his sleeve. Or more accurately, a flask in his breast pocket, which he extracted. So far, he had struggled to break even, but this lackluster luck was about to change. He asked Ariana to set everyone up with shot glasses. "Gentleman, have any of you had the pleasure of traveling to Athens, Greece?"

The middle-aged man in a cowboy hat snorted. "No, but I been to Athens, Georgia."

The rest of the men chuckled.

"More's the pity." Bacchus proceeded to pass the flask to Ariana. "However, I've brought with me my family's private brew. The finest ouzo in the Universe." This was, in fact, true. The ouzo was Olympian stock. What he'd failed to mention was this particular recipe used ambrosia— food of the gods—in its distillation, which gave the concoction quite a kick. More than a few shots could kill a human, but one little drink should incapacitate the players enough to dilute their skills and allow Bacchus to claim his victory. "Since you all have been so kind as to include me in your game of chance, I'd like to return the hospitality. Who'd like to take a shot with me?"

Tito twisted his mouth in an expression of distaste. "Ouzo? Is that some chick drink or something?"

Bacchus shook his head. "I assure you it's quite potent. But if you think you can't hold your liquor and play cards at the same time, by all means, don't partake on my account."

"Bring it, fancy man." The cowboy licked his lips.

Ariana went around the table and poured shots for everyone.

Santos waved her away.

"In the words of my uncle, who's an avid seaman, 'Through the lips and over the gums, watch out stomach here it comes.'" Bacchus made a show of tossing back his portion as the other men uttered words like, "cheers," and "*salud*." Though his liver was surely up to the task of handling ouzo of the gods, the whole point was to keep his mind clearer than those of his opponents. Pan's magic made the liquor evaporate in Bacchus's mouth. He pretended to swallow, feigned a grimace, and sucked in an exaggerated breath. "Smooth, isn't it, gentlemen?"

They coughed and sputtered, trying to play off what must've felt like a river of fire racing down their throats.

"Very smooth," Jean-Claude croaked.

Within minutes, the cowboy fled toward the bathroom. He'd been drinking whiskey all night. Tough break for him. All but Santos struggled to focus on their cards. Eyes glazed over, they became giddy.

One by one, the men gambled away their chips. Hand after hand, Bacchus and Santos grew richer until they were the only men at the table still playing.

"I'd like to take a break before we go on. Are you all right with that, Mr. Sabazios?" Santos straightened his chips then offered Bacchus a cigar.

"Fine by me." Bacchus dragged in his winnings. Though he'd never been fond of the things, Bacchus had to accept the gift. He bit off the end, leaned over, and lit it from Santos's offered Zippo.

The last two stragglers cleared the room. Santos's hired muscle assisted the very drunk men.

Bacchus took a couple drags from the cigar then abandoned it in an ashtray.

Santos let the smoke roll around his mouth before blowing it out in a large gray cloud. His gaze roamed over Bacchus's face, and his lips drew together.

"That was pretty slick, taking out the competition the way you did. What was in that flask? It wasn't any ordinary liquor." Santos tapped the ash from his cigar.

"Would you like some? It's ouzo, plain and simple."

Santos broke his chips into smaller stacks, shaking his head. "Wouldn't you prefer to beat me the old-fashioned way?"

Bacchus cracked a smile. "Why whatever do you mean, Sr. Santos?"

"I don't mind that you fleeced my guests. They were stupid for underestimating you and your bottle of luck there." He chuckled, but it sounded more like a grunt. "Maybe you should walk away while you're ahead."

Bacchus picked up his cigar and rolled it between his thumb and forefinger as he studied the floor. He set his jaw.

Santos's soul radiated iciness, and his gaze unrelenting frosty blankness.

It would be a pleasure to teach this arrogant human a lesson, to strip him of what was never rightfully his. "Don't you find this whole betting money thing a little dull?"

Santos shrugged. "I don't know. Taking a quarter of a million from you doesn't seem so dull to me."

"True. You'd be a richer man for having done so. And I the same if I best you. But we are already rich men, so what really have we gained, or lost for that matter?"

Santos took the cigar from his mouth, and his gaze flicked over Bacchus's chips. "What did you have in mind, Mr. Sabazios?"

Bacchus scratched his chin. "Are you a real estate man? I have a villa in Greece I'd be willing to pit against…say, your club in Miami. And all the employees in it. If I win this hand."

"Those are some very high stakes. How do I know you'll keep up your side of the bargain?"

Bacchus extracted the deed to his villa.

The old man licked his lips then raked his teeth across them. "You want *la morena*, don't you?"

Bacchus dipped his head to the side.

"I can sell her to you for a price."

This disgusting man wasn't going to get off that easily. Santos needed to feel the loss. "Are you afraid you can't beat me in one more hand of cards?"

"Baiting me won't work, either, Mr. Sabazios. But I'll play your little game and take your villa too, since that's clearly what you want."

"Clearly."

"Then let's do this." Santos tamped out his cigar and nodded to the dealer.

The dealer pulled a fresh deck and shuffled. "Head's up rules in effect."

"Head's up?" Damn this complicated game.

"Sr. Santos is responsible for the small blind. You, Mr. Sabazios, place the big blind," the dealer said.

"No need, Ricardo." Santos pushed his chips into one large pile. "No betting this game. A winner and a loser as determined by the cards."

Ricardo nodded and dealt their hole cards.

Bacchus had a six of spades and a two of diamonds. Crap, just as he'd expected. It'd taken him the whole evening, but he'd figured out Santos's card marking method. A subtle pattern of dots blended into the ornate design on the backs, barely noticeable unless you were looking for it.

Skipping the pre-flop betting, Ricardo laid the flop, three community cards, face up. Ten of clubs, a queen of spades, and an eight of hearts. He dealt the river, the last two community cards, a six of clubs and a queen of diamonds.

Santos checked his hole cards, but kept his face neutral. "I'm an honorable man, Mr. Sabazios. I'll give you a chance to fold, one more chance to walk away. Keep your winnings, keep your villa, and walk away."

Bacchus held two pair. An unremarkable two pair. Still, he might've taken a chance, if he didn't know Santos held the queen of hearts. Three of a kind. Perhaps the dealer had stacked the deck to put him in just such a situation. A believable loss, but Bacchus wouldn't lose.

He put his hand in his pocket and dipped his fingers into the transformation dust Pan had procured for him. Pretending to check his cards, he rubbed the dust onto them and concentrated. He downed his last sip of wine. "I'll stay in."

"If you insist." Santos scooped up his cards and flipped them over.

Bacchus flipped his cards, revealing a jack of spades and a nine of hearts. A straight.

Santos's eyes grew wide, his mouth agape.

Bacchus knocked on the felt tabletop. "Looks like I'll be keeping my winnings. And my villa."

Santos slammed his fists against the table. "Not possible."

"What's not possible? That I beat you?"

Again, he slammed his fists against the table. "Not possible."

One of his goons rushed into the room, the soulless one. "*Que paso?*"

"He cheated." Santos spat as he blustered. "This *maricon* cheated."

The soulless man cocked a gun and shoved it against Bacchus's temple. "Get up."

"Now, wait. Wait a second. We can be reasonable about this. You say I cheated, I say I didn't. And in the end, if you kill me, what have you gained?"

Santos gritted his teeth. "I'll feel a hell of a lot better. No one comes onto my boat and cheats."

"I didn't cheat any more than you did." Bacchus held the gangster's stare.

"You thought you could come here and take what is mine? I'm not the kind of man you want to fuck with." Santos growled, still frothing at the mouth.

"I'm sure. Nor am I. But what if I go ahead and pay you for the property? That way, we don't have to argue about who's right and who's wrong. It's a simple business transaction."

"How about I kill you and take all your money."

Bacchus laughed. "All my money? You mean this paltry quarter of a million? Oh, it's nowhere near all my money. I'm not going to part with all of it tonight, either. But I'll give you a fair price for the club."

Santos ran a hand through his hair. Sure, the man was angry, but he wasn't stupid. Signaling for his thug to back off, he leaned down and glared at Bacchus. "How much are we talking then?"

"How about a nice even number like one million?"

"How about two? Since you're feeling so generous."

Though Bacchus could've easily paid his asking price, he would garner more respect if he negotiated. "One point one."

"One point seven."

"One point five. I've been apprised of the property values in Miami, and that's more than fair."

Santos sucked in his cheeks and rubbed his forehead. "All right, done. Keep Bach at gunpoint until the wire transfer is made."

Pan would know what to do. Bacchus need only wait for his steward to place the money into Santos's account.

The kingpin ate a pork sandwich and washed it down with a bottle of beer, of course without offering Bacchus anything. Once the man finished his meal, the call came from his accountant. The deep lines around Santos's lips softened. The waddle beneath his throat jiggled a bit as he nodded. He dismissed the thug and handed Bacchus another cigar. "Now, we can be friends again."

Not wishing to ruffle the man's freshly smoothed feathers, Bacchus took the cigar and lit it. "Thank you."

Santos took a couple drags and blew smoke rings at the ceiling. Shaking his head, he asked, "Why?"

Bacchus shrugged. "Why not?"

"*Estas loco*. You are one crazy son of a bitch." Santos turned to Ariana. "*Mi'ja*, why don't you get your new boss here another drink?"

# Chapter 6

*But Now Can See*

Pan's voice dragged Bacchus from his slumber.

"Sire, it's two in the afternoon."

Bacchus rolled over and put a pillow over his face. "One more hour."

"Sire, you have to leave by three-thirty. Now, come on. Up, up, up." Pan clopped away toward the master bath.

"No." Limbs heavy, eyes drifting shut, Bacchus gave over to the warm pull of sleep.

The covers flew away, and cold water rushed over Bacchus's bare body. He sat up, heart racing, teeth clenched. "You are the most vile, contemptible, uncivilized—"

"Cruel, heartless and unloved soul that ever existed. Yes, sire, I know. We go through this every morning."

Bacchus dried his face on his duvet. "Well, as long as you know." Pain and nausea racked his body. He rubbed his eyes and temples. "Did you bring my morning kit?"

Pan handed over a grocery bag with a sports drink, Advil, and Alka Seltzer. Bacchus dissolved the seltzer tablets in the sports drink and washed down four ibuprofen with the foul-tasting concoction. In about twenty minutes, he'd be right as rain.

Pan had researched the cause of hangover symptoms and formulated the restorative combination.

Now that Bacchus had somewhere to be every afternoon, he couldn't afford to lounge in bed all day, lamenting the night before. The club had been a positive influence in many ways. To his surprise, Bacchus enjoyed his newfound business owner status. He'd made some rookie mistakes, like placing his first order with the liquor supplier under the assumption the club goers would drink at the same rate he did. But hey, now he had back stock that would last for a couple years, so no biggie, right?

The employees were a source of endless fascination for him. All the lovely young women dressed in tight satin dresses, flirting with clients they'd rather spit on all in the name of good tips. The young men who worked security at the bar tried they're damnedest to get those same young women to leave with them each night. Few of them possessed the skills to seduce a woman. Bacchus could leave with any of them at any time, but since he dreamed nightly of the beautiful Ariana, and awoke often enough screaming her name, he forwent the pleasure of nightly company.

Ariana, Ariana—she proved a constant distraction. If only she'd acknowledge Bacchus's existence. Since their meeting on the yacht, she had barely spoken three words to him, unless he solicited conversation. Even then, she was polite, but never warm or welcoming.

Shaking away thoughts of his unrequited love, Bacchus pulled himself out of his soggy bed. "How was your night?"

"Fine, sire. Thank you for asking."

"I don't know why you don't sleep here."

Pan shook his head. "Thank you, sire. Not to complain, but it's hard for me to be so far from nature and in human form. I'm struggling enough with the long hours at the club. The last one of your employees who saw me in my true body ran screaming. The swamp suits me just fine at night."

"As you wish." Bacchus trudged into the master bath of his beachfront condo. Catching a glimpse of his torso in the mirror, he paused. With a flex left and a flex right, he admired his sculpted abs. He'd been no fatty in the many millennia he'd spent as a god—despite the manner in which that cheeky bastard, Cornelis de Vos, had portrayed him—but Bacchus's mortal form possessed an amazingly lean firmness. He'd never known the body encompassed so many individual muscles. As a god, he'd never gained, lost, or expelled anything for that matter. Urination and defecation had been adventures to master. He flexed his obliques again and marveled at his resemblance to a marble statue.

"Vanity, thy name is Bacchus." Pan appeared behind him and nudged him toward the dressing area. "Please, sire, you must get dressed."

"Right, sorry. I got caught up in my reflection. Am I very handsome?"

A sincere expression crossed the satyr's features. "You are as beautiful as I've ever known you to be, sire, which means you're stunning."

"What would I do without you, old friend?"

"Show up late every day to the club. Now hurry, hurry."

Bacchus donned a garment known as a T-shirt and a pair of jeans from some singularly talented tailor named Calvin or was it Klein? First and last names still confused him. Though the clothing lacked the grace of a *chiton*, he had to admit the vestments accentuated the positive. He checked out his buttocks in the mirror.

Satisfied with his appearance, he swept into the living room.

Pan had prepared a platter of fresh fruit, a green salad with feta cheese and honeyed walnuts, and fresh coffee.

Another result of daily hangovers, he'd developed a taste for coffee. Miraculous potion. "This looks wonderful, Panny."

"Thank you, sire. You need to replenish your body."

Munching on a fig, Bacchus mumbled his agreement.

After breakfast, Pan shaved him with a straight razor and slapped cologne on his master's baby smooth face.

Bacchus collected his wallet, keys, and a bottle of eighty-two Lafite-Rothschild he'd purchased while in Paris. No special occasion. Really, did one need a special occasion to enjoy a gorgeous vintage such as this?

Jingling the chain holding the key to his Alpha Romeo 8C Spider, Bacchus turned to Pan. "Are you ready to ride with me to the club?"

Blanching and turning a little bit green, Pan gave his lord a forlorn look but didn't object. Instead, he assumed his squat, troll-like human form and walked with his master to the parking garage.

* * * *

Going from zero to a hundred kilometers per hour in less than five seconds always gave Bacchus a rush. Even if Pan constantly questioned the wisdom of tearing down Ocean Drive at breakneck speeds.

At his club, Eliseo, the driving hip-hop beat made Bacchus want to take off his clothes and pulse around the nightclub. How the music captured his fancy remained a mystery, though he wasn't alone. Glittering, coiffed, and bejeweled revelers pulsed with him. They packed themselves in by the droves, just to flail around to the pure rhythm.

Bacchus pasted a toothy grin on his face, slinking around the steel and glass fixtures that separated the crush of bodies. Summer in Miami drew all walks of life from hookers to heiresses. Streetwise veterans of the scene to fresh-faced twinks. Every shade of skin color, every nationality represented. He watched them all come together on the burgundy leather of booth benches and scattered chaises. Flashing disco lights erased all flaws until there was nothing but music and lust and drinks. Luscious, colorful drinks that servers in the shape of nymphs and adonises ferried to patrons. A more glorious temple to his gifts had never been built, not even when he had been a god and the alter upon which the most devout worshiped, the VIP lounge.

Bacchus sauntered up to one of the counters serving the VIPs. "How's it going tonight, Fede?"

"Very good, Mr. Sabazios." The young Cubano bartender filled a tray with shot glasses.

A stream of nubile cocktail waitresses dropped off orders and ferried a rainbow of mixed drinks to clients.

Ariana. His dark beauty Ariana. She barely gave him the time of day. One would think, having thrown up on him and all, she'd feel a bit more familiar in their relationship.

"Hello there, Miss Ariana." Bacchus bowed.

"Hello, Mr. Sabazios." She avoided his gaze and focused on loading glasses on her tray.

"You're looking lovely this evening."

A simple pink, satin slip dress hugged her curves regally. "Thanks."

Bacchus leaned down and spoke into her ear. "You all right, love?"

Ariana skittered away and cast a shifty look at him. "Everything's fine." She hoisted the tray and hurried across the floor to a red velvet chaise where a predatory peacock of a man lounged, surrounded by a group of thugs.

One of Santos men, the one who'd tried to intimidate Bacchus that night on the yacht. He frequented the club and spent his time shooting dirty looks at Bacchus.

Bacchus had it on good authority his boss had forbidden him to start any trouble with the new proprietor of Eliseo. Amazing how much respect one point five million dollars could buy.

The man's hands roamed all over poor Ariana.

Bacchus's stomach churned. Motioning to a member of the VIP security team, he set his jaw.

A wall of muscle packed into a teal polo shirt appeared at his side. "What's up, Mr. Sabazios?"

Bacchus subtly pointed toward the chaise. "Cliff, warn our friend over there to keep his hands to himself, please."

"Yes, sir." Cliff strolled to Ariana's side.

Arm hooked around Ariana's thighs, the man glared at Cliff and pulled her tighter. More words were exchanged, and with a smirk, the man pushed Ariana away.

When Cliff returned, he folded his arms over his chest. "His name's Alonso Desiderio, works for Santos and thinks that makes him untouchable. He says she's his girlfriend, and she confirmed it, but I told him hands off during work hours or he's out."

"Really? He's her boyfriend?" Well, that explained a lot. He'd never have guessed a relationship existed between the two. She never seemed particularly happy to see him. And if she were his girlfriend, how could he have let his employer treat her like chattel? A vile man, indeed. "How dreadful for her."

"True, but not a security issue." The bouncer took his leave.

Still and stiff as stone, Ariana stared vacantly at the marble wall.

Slime ball continued posturing and never spared a glance beyond her shoulders.

If Ariana responded to this man at all, her quaking would indicate revulsion. And something else—fear maybe? Bacchus couldn't see her being moved by the man's looks alone.

Ariana appeared at the bar and ordered another round of drinks for her section.

Bacchus scooted next to her. "Now, I know you told me you're okay, and I don't mean to pester you, but you don't seem to be enjoying that man's company."

She wrung her hands. "No, he's fine. I'm sorry he's all over me at work. I've told him he can't do that here, but he doesn't listen."

Bacchus placed his hand in the small of her back, but she stiffened, so he pulled it away. "I'm not scolding you, Ariana. I'm concerned."

"Thanks, Mr. Sabazios. But really, I'm fine." She chewed at her bottom lip, her brow furrowed.

He opened his mouth to say more, but she turned and walked away with her tray of drinks. As soon as she approached Mr. Desiderio, he rose, shouting, and pointed at Bacchus. She shook her head, tried to talk, but her boyfriend snatched her by the wrist, spilling the entire tray of drinks. The entourage around him broke out in mocking laughter.

Pulling free, she placed a hand to her mouth and hurried toward the back stairwell.

The man stormed after her.

Cliff hurried to intervene, but Bacchus stopped him. "I got this. See housekeeping gets to that spill."

"Yes, sir." Bacchus sauntered after the pair.

Shouting resonated into the hallway leading to the back alley. Bacchus opened the door.

The weasel was inches from Ariana's face, spewing insults at her.

Though every fiber of Bacchus's being longed to flatten the man, he leaned against the wall, arms folded. The time to act would come.

"You fucking little whore." Spittle dripped from his lip onto his black Armani suit.

"Please, Dezi, calm down." She peered up at him, eyes wide, whole body trembling. "I didn't do anything. Mr. Sabazios didn't do anything. He was checking on me."

"You think I'm fucking stupid? I know you fucked him that night on the boat, and don't give me that bullshit that you didn't. And I saw him touch you now. I swear, if you're still fucking that faggot, so help me—" He grabbed her throat.

"Don't." She clawed at the hand.

Bacchus grabbed Dezi's arm. "Why don't you let her go and throttle me?"

Dezi glanced at him then cocked a fist. "Isn't that cute, your little *maricon* boyfriend is here to protect you."

Bacchus pulled himself up to his full six feet five inches, caught the hand about to crash into Ariana's cheek, and glowered at the despicable man. "I take exception to the word little. In case you're too stupid to understand what I meant, I'll make it simple for you. Let the young lady be and leave my establishment."

With a vicious shove, Dezi pushed Ariana away and turned on Bacchus. "You sure you want to get mixed up in this?"

"Quite."

"You don't know who you're messing with, pretty boy."

"Nor do you. I've sat at the dinner table with Darkness and dined with demons. I assure you, there's nothing about you that inspires fear."

"What the fuck are you talking about? You mental or something?"

"Or something."

The slime ball tried to wrest his hand free of Bacchus's grasp, but Bacchus held fast. At least The Council had blessed him with a strong, capable mortal body.

Pan appeared in the doorway. "Everything all right, sire—uh sir?"

"This man and his friends were just leaving." A drop of sweat trickled down his temple.

"Of course, sir."

The old goat, in full human form, grabbed Dezi by the neck and pushed him toward the door. "Let's get your friends and walk them out, too."

Judging from the glazed look on the greasy man's face, Bacchus could tell Pan had taken control of Dezi's mind. How Bacchus missed pulling tricks like that on his adversaries. He turned to Ariana, his heart seizing as soon as he set his gaze on her. "Are you all right, love?"

All the blood had drained from Ariana's face, and she trembled. "You don't know what you've done."

Bacchus walked over and took her by the hand. "There's nothing to worry about now." He led her into the club and to his office. After he settled her in the black leather sofa, he poured a glass of Sandeman for him and two fingers of rum for her.

"Thanks." She took the glass and twirled it between trembling hands.

He knelt in front of her. "Drink this. It'll calm you."

She took a small sip, then sputtered and coughed. "Strong."

"It's one-fifty-one rum. I find it an efficient libation."

Tears welled up, and her lower lip shook.

"Don't cry." Bacchus stroked her hair. "Please don't cry. As well you know, I'm not very good with crying women. I don't have much experience with them."

A halted chuckle shook her chest. "No one's ever stood up for me like that before. Of course, you're a dead man now."

As if. And what if he did die? Hades had always been a friend. It would be good to see him again. "There are worse things than death, love."

"No, I mean it. He's part of the Cuban mafia." She pressed a hand to her forehead, squeezing shut her eyes.

Mafia. A derivative from the Italian adjective *mafioso*, perhaps, which meant bragging. Hardly worrisome.

"What are you trying to tell me?" Bacchus studied her shifting gaze. "What is a 'mafia'?"

"Some very bad people. How can you not know that?" She threw her hands in the air then wrapped her arms around herself, rubbing her arms as if to warm a chill that could not be warmed.

He brushed a stray curl from her face. He longed to wipe away the small creases around her eyes, the one between her brows. "My apologies. I'm lacking in current events."

She blanched. "What am I going to do?"

"What do you mean?"

"Oh my God." Her voice rose an octave. "I can't go home. He'll be waiting for me."

"Don't worry. You can come home with me."

"It's not that simple."

"It is that simple. If this man is so dangerous, you need to be rid of him. Make a clean break."

"I can't—I can't." Ariana got to her feet and paced.

He stepped in front of her and clasped her hands. Breathing in the calm beneath her storm, he focused on the sweetness of spring, the golden sunshine buried beneath layers of her fear and shame. She could be reborn, reclaim her goodness and pride. It was in there somewhere, he could feel it in his very core. He had to make her see.

"You have to. You're too good a soul to be trapped by someone like that. You're coming home with me, and that's final."

"And what is it you think you know about my soul?"

Cupping her face in his hands, he met her gaze. "I can see you as a very little girl, with a sunburned nose, missing a front tooth, but you smile anyway. You liked to curl up on your mother's lap, and she would sing you songs about Cuba. Songs her mother used to sing. The fuzzy dandelions in your front yard were your favorite feature of your new home. That little girl is still inside you, and she tells me you are a good person. Perhaps one who's made some ill-advised choices, but still good."

She searched Bacchus's eyes, mouth parted. "What kind of devil are you?"

"I'm no devil I assure you. Quite the contrary. I only want to help."

"Why?"

Bacchus shrugged. "It makes me happy to lend you a hand. It reminds me of someone I used to be."

"I can't repay you, and I won't—"

"I'm not looking for payment in any form. I'll send Pan to get your stuff from your locker and take you to my place."

"What if Dezi shows up there, too?"

"Then I'll beat him down like I wanted to a few minutes ago."

"He has friends—lots of nasty, dangerous friends."

"I have a few friends of my own. Don't worry, Ariana. You're safe with me." He handed her a tissue.

She huffed, wiping tears and her nose. "You're really not afraid of him."

"Not a bit."

She leaned in and planted a kiss on his cheek. "You were very brave. *Muy macho.*"

Warmth flooded his chest. "Was I?"

"Oh yeah." She nodded. "Well, except that part about having dinner with demons. That sounded a little fruity."

"Really?" Maybe she didn't understand he was being literal. "Because that's actually true. I have. Nasty sons-a-bitches, that lot."

Ariana shook her head. "You're so strange."

He reached for his glass of port and took a long drink. "You don't know the half of it."

# Chapter 7

*Salvador*

"This is remarkable," Bacchus said around a mouthful of silky, savory ambrosia. "What do you call it again?"

"*Arroz con pollo.*" Ariana scooped some of the dish onto a plate.

"Well, I would've thought it was something much more complicated than chicken and rice."

"Thank you, Mr. Sabazios."

"You're welcome. And please, call me Bach."

"Bach? Did your mother like classical music?"

"Not in the sense that you mean 'classical.'" Bacchus smiled to himself.

"Excuse me for saying this, but you don't look like a Bach."

"I don't? What do I look like to you?"

"Christian, maybe."

He wrinkled his nose. That religion's obsession with abstinence didn't mesh with Bacchus's lifelong pursuit of pleasure. "I'm thinking not."

"Angel?"

"Definitely not."

"Salvador?"

"I'm afraid I haven't been considered a savior in a very long time."

"You were mine last night." Her dark eyes, fringed with ebony lashes, caught Bacchus's gaze.

"Well, there's a first for everything, right?" Still adjusting to human emotions, he picked up his wine goblet and washed down the lump forming in his throat. Savior? If he ever got back into the Palace of Light, the Council would have a long hard laugh about that one. Bacchus—the playboy of deities—affable slacker and divine gigolo, yes. Savior, heavens no. "I'm flattered that you think of me that way."

She planted a quick kiss on his cheek. "Should I make a plate for Pan? He was nice enough to take me to the market earlier."

"Yes, do make Panny a plate. He'd like that. I'm told my culinary talents leave something to be desired."

"Well, you had nothing at all here to cook. If you don't mind, I'd like to go tomorrow morning and stock up."

"So kind of you to offer. I'll send Pan with you to make sure no one bothers you." Bacchus fished ten hundred dollar bills from his wallet. "Will that cover it?"

"Uh, yeah. More than cover it. Unless you want me to pick up a month's worth of caviar and filet mignon while I'm out."

"Whatever you think is best."

"And that was a waste of sarcasm."

"What?"

"Oh nothing." Ariana shook her head. Once she'd stowed the leftovers in the refrigerator, she set to work on the dishes.

Her presence in his home made everything feel lighter. Had he grown so accustomed to the dark it no longer registered with him until its presence abated? What about Ariana made his skin feel warm from the inside out? He hoisted himself onto the kitchen counter. "May I ask you a personal question?"

"I suppose I owe you that much."

"How did you wind up in the clutches of someone like Dezi?"

At the very mention of the man's name, the young woman's shoulders slumped, and she hung her head. "I'm sure you wouldn't agree with my choices, but I have my reasons."

"I'd like to hear them, if I may. But if you'd rather not talk about it, that's all right, too."

She put down the wooden spoon, chewing at the inside of her cheek. "I don't know. It's all… It's all so messed up."

Her eyes glittered, ears turning red. "It's all right. I think you'll find I'm the least judgmental person you've ever met."

"But I—the things I did." She trained her gaze on the floor.

Bacchus laid down his fork and rounded the kitchen bar. "Ariana, I know you were a prostitute. To my mind, there's nothing wrong with that. Really."

Snapping up her head, she met his gaze, her jaw set, lips pinched. "I was not a prostitute. Not by choice."

"I'm sorry. I didn't mean—"

"What was I supposed to do? Let them kill my father?" Spittle gathered at the corners of her mouth, but then she blew out a sigh. "Papa was the only family I had left. After Mama died... I couldn't let them hurt him. So I let them hurt me."

"Dezi and Santos?" Bacchus reached for her arm, but she pulled away.

"Who else?"

"Why did they want to hurt your father?"

Ugly red splotches appeared on her cheeks and chest. "He was a gambler, all right? And a bad one at that. Not to mention an alcoholic. Santos was his bookie, and Dezi is Santos's enforcer. Every time Papa would dig himself out, he'd dig himself right back in again until he made a hole he couldn't get out of. Dezi beat him so badly one night Papa almost died."

A light switched on in Bacchus's mind. That was how she'd gotten into Dezi's clutches. "You paid your father's debt with your body."

Pressing her lips together, she closed her eyes, and shook her head. "Don't say it like that. It sounds so ugly like that."

A tear slipped down her cheek. Bacchus caught it with his forefinger, but again she shied way. "I meant what I said. I see nothing wrong with what you've done, especially now that I know the reason why. By Hades, I do ten worse things than that on a daily basis."

Though she pressed her lips harder together, a chuckle shook her shoulders. "No you don't. Not that I've seen."

Bacchus reached for his glass of wine and took a gulp. "You haven't been here that long. Stick around a while, you'll see."

"You're too hard on yourself."

"As are you." He cupped her face in his hand. This time, she didn't pull away. "So if you worked for Santos, how did you wind up with that son of a bitch Dezi?"

Swallowing hard, she closed her eyes. "He's always had a thing for me. An attraction I couldn't fight. If I didn't give myself to him, he threatened to pay my father another visit."

As she spoke, images of Ariana as a laughing young woman flashed through his mind. It was a smile he'd never seen from her in real life. The innocence of her first kiss, her first lover at the age of seventeen. The young man had been gentle with her. She'd known love in its sweetest form. Now that she was trapped by Dezi's sickness, Bacchus had the overwhelming urge to shelter her, protect her. Rescue her.

After a faltering breath, she opened her eyes. "I couldn't refuse the clients Santos gave me, but each time I did a job for Santos, Dezi would fly into a jealous rage and…and—"

Her voice cracked as if it refused to speak anymore on the topic.

"And beat you."

"And worse," she whispered, trembling. A tear dropped off the end of her chin. She wiped her nose.

That's what she'd meant the night on the yacht when she said she was damned if she did, damned if she didn't. Bacchus prayed his little charade had spared her Dezi's wrath. "And what does your father think of your situation?"

"Papa was rarely sober enough to walk, much less notice my 'situation,' as you say. And now, he doesn't think anything about it. Papa passed away last year."

"I'm sorry to hear your father is gone, but doesn't that release you from his debt?"

"Yes and no. Yes, Santos hasn't made me take a client in a while—not until you showed so much interest in me. And no, not in Dezi's mind. He's made it very clear if I ever break things off with him, he'll—he'll kill me." Putting a hand to her forehead, she rubbed away the beads of sweat.

"You have no other family to help you disappear?"

"I told you my mother is dead, so no, I don't." A storm brewed over her brow.

Bacchus peered into her soul and saw the grave and the tears of a forlorn child. So much tragedy. Too much for one young woman.

"Mama died when I was twelve. A brain aneurysm."

Bacchus's heart cleaved in two. She'd barely had a chance to live or experience any joy in her life. How she found the strength to weather so many trials in one short lifetime, Bacchus didn't know.

"You know, I have a good deal of money myself. I'm happy to pay off Dezi, if it means you'll be free of this evil man."

She turned away, wrapping her arms around herself. "Thank you, but I don't believe it's about the money. It never was. And he'll never let me go. He says he wants me with him forever, lavishes me with expensive gifts—jewelry, clothes, whatever I want. I think in his own psycho way, he believes he loves me."

Bridging the distance she'd created, Bacchus folded the petite woman in his arms. "I don't know much about love, but I do know that's not what it looks like."

The floral scent of her shampoo reminded him of his own childhood, countless millennia ago. The nymphs who had cared for him bathed in lavender and rosewater. Some of his earliest memories flowed along on rivers of perfumed hair cascading around his cheeks just before he faded off to sleep. Bacchus planted a kiss on her forehead.

"I promise, if it's the last thing I do on Earth, I'll put this right for you," he murmured.

"I don't know why, but I believe you."

"Good. Now, no more tears. I'll clean the kitchen." As if he had any idea how to wash dishes. "You go relax in a hot bubble bath."

Releasing her, he jostled her in the direction of the guest bathroom. She turned to face him, the worry lines at the corners of her mouth relaxing.

"No, it's all right. I'm all right." She wiped her wet cheeks and blew out a heavy breath.

Bacchus nudged her. "Don't be silly. I insist."

A grin crinkled the edges of her eyes. "Can I ask you a question?"

"Of course."

"How did you pull off that winning hand? I was watching the deal. There's no way you should've had the cards you did."

"A magician never reveals his secrets." Bacchus winked. "And Sr. Santos needs to learn, things aren't always as they seem."

"You aren't going to tell me."

"Nope."

Ariana rolled her eyes but smiled, then shuffled off to the guest suite. Bacchus watched her, unable to turn away. He imagined her in his bed, a light sheen of perspiration setting her skin aglow. Her body beneath his; her legs around his hips. Her mouth, hot and wet on his throat. A shiver darted through him.

The depth of longing he felt for this mortal woman unnerved him. Other than Pan, he'd felt very little connection to another being.

The old goat had been like a father to him since Bacchus's own father, Zeus, had been far too busy with his own divine politics to spend much time with his bastard son. Not to mention Zeus's wife had, through treachery, killed Bacchus's mother and plotted to kill him as well. So as a baby, Bacchus had been placed with the wood nymphs to grow up in their protective care.

The picturesque valleys and grottoes he'd grown up in provided an idyllic backdrop for most of his youth. Various nymphae had taken turns caring for little Bacchus, nurturing him each day with flower petals and morning dew, then reading him Homer's *Odyssey* at bedtime. The character of Penelope waiting faithfully for the return of her true love had captured the young god's heart. Romantic tales and pixyish nannies had shaped his picture of ideal femininity. Until now, Bacchus had never met anyone who embodied the spirit of Penelope. What was this feeling stirring in his chest? An ache, but at the same time a pleasurable one. Excitement and elation. These new emotions hurt, but hurt so good.

* * * *

Waves of black hair rippled out across the fallen god's lap and morphed into a deep indigo ocean. A thick mantle of stars dappled the night sky. Bacchus floated in a small boat over calm water and lay on his back. Hercules and Orphiuchus twinkled down at him, but something was missing. If only he could put his finger on what it was, but there was no time for speculation.

Six fireballs streaked across the Earth's atmosphere and plunged into the sea. A violent tidal wave carried Bacchus's vessel and hurled it ashore. His tiny boat crashed to bits against a field of jagged rocks, water swirled and beat his body. He struggled to swim to the surface. Instead, the black ocean pulled him down through a swirling underwater storm. A maelstrom sucked him into its core, but instead of drowning him, Bacchus found himself spit out into burning sunlight.

He squinted against the sudden onslaught of brilliance. Walls broke through the dried, cracked mud around him and shot toward the heavens. The walls trapped him in a corridor. He stumbled along, suddenly parched, his wineskin empty. A woman's cries—Ariana's cries—spurred him on. She sounded as though she was just on the other side of the right-hand wall, but it was too high and too slick to scale. From time to time, an animal's roar shook the wall to his left. What beast was this? And really, did it matter? As long as he found his dark beauty before it did. And he would. He swore he would, his hand to his heart.

He walked until his feet blistered, his lips cracked from the extreme temperature. Finally, a crossroads presented itself. The caress of a cool breeze stopped him. He paused and listened to the voice carried upon the wind. He recognized The Oracle's voice. The dulcimer tones of the Pythia flooded his mind.

"Rescue," the priestess murmured. "Rescue the crown."

Again, the beast growled and Ariana wept.

Though Bacchus knew not why, he put his hand to his heart and swore he would. He would save Ariana from the beast that stalked her. At this oath, the ground split open and shot out a tower of fire.

Bacchus rode the fire into the sky but remained unharmed. The flames didn't burn, in fact, they filled him with a joy the likes of which he'd never felt. Atop the tower, he found himself among the stars. Heracles gave him a hand and pulled Bacchus. Floating in the ether of the heavens, Bacchus bore a shining crown of stars upon his head. His beautiful Ariana appeared and clasped his hand in hers. He placed the crown upon her head and pulled his goddess queen to him. Their lips met for the briefest of seconds, but ecstasy rippled through the reinstated god's body. Yes, he was back on high where he belonged.

"Rescue the crown," the Pythia whispered again.

Then, Bacchus opened his eyes and found himself still earthbound, still in his own bed. His body trembled, and the fire he'd ridden in his dream seemed to sear his chest.

What in the name of Hades did it all mean? A burning thirst drove him to find out.

# Chapter 8

*Purple Haze*

A rolling cloud of violet smoke announced the arrival of his eagerly awaited visitor—the great Remover of Obstacles himself. Bacchus closed the door to the guest bedroom more out of protective reflex than concern about disturbing Ariana's slumber.

Her nerves had been so frazzled she had no luck getting to sleep. Bacchus had given her wine and an over-the-counter sleep aid, to no avail. None of the traditional cures helped her fall asleep. Finally, Pan had scrounged up a draught from Morpheus, and nothing could rouse her until the satyr administered the antidote.

Tall and lean, Bacchus's best friend in the Cosmos emerged from the cloud. The god wore a loincloth and a lei of chrysanthemums—and little else.

Coughing his way through the purple haze, Bacchus extended his hand, taking his friend's blue one. "Vighnesha, hey, thanks for showing up."

"Oh, no sweat. It's totally cool. When Pan popped in at Amarapura, I was all like 'dude, where you been, man?' But you know, at first, I didn't even know if he was really there. I'd gotten this righteous bud from the Disciples. Man, last time I got some shit from them, I woke up a century later with this elephant head on. I still haven't lived that down. So yeah, I was totally freaked by the goat-man." Vig scratched his soft, little paunch that peeked out from his beaded vest. It was the only part of the man that wasn't sculpted and muscular.

"Sorry about that."

"Nah, it's all good. So, Bacchus, dude, how have you been? It's been ages." Vig pulled Bacchus into a hug and clapped him on the back before releasing him. The gesture could be quiet painful when Vig had his other appendages, but tonight, only two arms and two legs.

"Well, aside from being stripped of my god status, I'm peachy."

"Really, man? Totally harsh. Why'd they kick you out?"

"Something about me causing more suffering than I alleviate."

Vig's powder blue skin turned a deeper shade of azure. "That's totally bogus. How'd they figure that?"

"I'm not sure. Actually, that's why I called you. I need a favor. You're one of the only beings I know, aside from Siddhartha himself, who has mastered Siddhartha's philosophies. I need you to explain something to me."

"Ah yeah, Siddhartha's got mad meaning-of-life skills. Go ahead, shoot."

"What in Hades is he talking about when he advocates 'joyful participation in the sorrows of the world'?"

"Okay, bro, it's like this—you only gotta know three things. Life's a bitch and then you die. The reason life's a bitch is because you want more than you got. But if you want life not to suck you have to stop wanting anything."

"The root of all suffering is desire," Bacchus murmured.

"Right on."

"But how can all desire be bad? There's nothing more uplifting than falling in love and joining bodies with someone else."

"True, but think about it. You ever been with a chick you really, really dug?"

"Oh yeah. Aphrodite can do this thing where she puts an ankle behind her ear and—"

"Right? I know the thing you're talking about, and somehow, she flips over and can still grab your junk. Woo, good times." Vig paused to tuck a lock of hair behind his ear. "Anyway, so what happened when Aphrodite was gone?"

"Bastet came from Egypt for a visit."

"Okay, bad example. How about this—have you ever lost something important to you?"

"Uh, hello." Bacchus waved. "One cast out god over here."

"Sorry, man, I forgot. But cool, that's the perfect example. How do you feel about all that?"

"I'm pretty miserable."

"There you go. You get what I'm saying, bro? The desire to be a god again is bringing you down. If you accept your new lot in life and go with the flow, you won't feel so fucked up."

"So wanting anything is bad?"

"Not bad. No. Siddhartha's not making it some good or bad kinda deal. He's saying the path to imperturbable happiness is to be satisfied with where you are and what you got."

"And how does all this relate to 'joyful participation'?"

"This is the best part. It's so friggin' elegant it makes me want to cry. Okay, it's about enjoying something cool while it's there to be enjoyed. Then letting it go when it's time for the experience to end."

"You mean like Aphrodite and Bastet? I enjoyed Aphrodite, but when it was time for her to go, I didn't beg her to stay or mope because she left. I turned around and enjoyed Bastet."

"Right on. The journey is the destination. Be here now."

"I think I understand. It's not intoxication and ecstasy that's feeding the sorrows. It's the desire for intoxication and ecstasy. More than that, it's weakness in the face of that desire."

"You got it, my man. So, whoever put the finger on you, did the world wrong. And you gotta get the Council to see that."

"And I have to do it before my followers lose faith or die out. Can you imagine a world devoid of strawberry margaritas?"

"I shudder to think of an existence without umbrella drinks, bro. Anything I can do to help?"

"You've done more than enough on that front. I may need some backup for some nasty business brewing down here, but I'll send Pan for you if things go bad."

"I'm totally there. Whenever and wherever. And I'll give Heracles, Cúchulainn, and Gilgamesh the heads up, too. Those dudes are itching to throw down."

"Thanks, Vig."

Vig scratched the round blue belly under his golden vest. "Hey, I hate to ask, but I got fierce munchies. You got anything to eat around here?"

"I don't." Bacchus looked for his phone. "But let me introduce you to an exquisite service the humans invented. It's called pizza delivery. You'll love it."

"Sweet, bring it on, bro. And don't forget the extra cheese." Vig licked his lips.

* * * *

At Pan's arrival in the afternoon, Bacchus met him at the door and danced a jig.

"Drunk already, sire?" Pan asked.

"I am, but not in the usual way. I'm drunk with joy."

"Did Vig get you stoned?"

"No, no, no, I have an idea. No, not an idea. The idea. We're going home, Panny boy."

"Really, sire? How can that be?"

Bacchus sat the goat-man on the black leather sofa and recounted the conversation with Vig and the conclusions he'd drawn since.

"I'm essential to the joyful participation in the sorrows of the world. It's not my gifts that are the problem. It's the irresponsible, undisciplined use of them that's the problem. So all I have to do is prove that to the Council, and we're back in the god business, baby."

"And what about Miss Ariana? Have you thought of what will happen to her while you're regaining your glory?"

"Ahh, and that's the best part. The idea includes saving her. Now really, is this not one of my finest moments of genius ever?"

"Seems you've thought of everything, sire."

"Yep, I have."

"So how are you going to reach the Council to tell them your ideas?"

No, how had he missed a detail such as that? He clapped a hand to his forehead. "Strike that. I haven't thought of everything. Oh Titan's dung, must you rain on my parade, old friend?"

"My apologies sire."

Bacchus thought and thought. After fixing himself a Bloody Mary, an idea sprang to mind.

"I've got it. All I have to do is invoke the spirit of the Father."

"And how will you do that? You're no longer connected to the cosmic consciousness, and I don't have access at that level."

"I know, Pan, but I can still contact them the old fashioned way." He dropped to his knees, pulling the satyr with him.

A look of respect lit up his abrupt features. "Brilliant, sire."

"Shh, close your eyes, clasp your hands together, and bow your head. We have to do this right if we want the Father himself to receive it. Okay, how does it go?

"Our Father..." Pan reminded Bacchus.

"Right, right, right. Okay, here we go. Our Father who art in Heaven, hallowed be thy name...."

For the first time in his age-long life, Bacchus lifted his voice in prayer.

# Chapter 9

*Chance for Redemption*

Bacchus sat with Pan in the lobby of the Pantheon Hall. He had forgotten how beautiful the place was. His memories of the hall didn't do justice to the marble columns thousands of feet into the air that disappeared into pearlescent clouds. Urns of flowers stood in each corner. A fountain sprang from the center of the marble floor, babbling with spurts of liquid gold and silver. He had taken all this for granted when he had been a god. True beauty was difficult to find on Earth.

A tiny cherub buzzed past his ear, its wings grazing his cheek as it strummed its harp. A whole choir of cherubim flitted from cloud to cloud.

Pan hummed along with their Muzak version of Procol Harum's, *Whiter Shade of Pale*. His cloven hooves couldn't reach the floor and clattered against the sides of the granite bench.

"Please stop that," Bacchus said between bouts of gnawing on his fingernails. "The humming and the clacking."

"Of course, sire."

An angelic page poked her head out the gilded doors of the main hall. "The Council is ready for you, Bacchus."

Pan hopped down to accompany his master inside, but the page held up a hand. "Just Bacchus, I'm afraid."

"Oh…well, as the humans say, sire, I hope you break a leg."

"We shall see."

As a god, Bacchus had been summoned to the Great Hall only a handful of times. Usually it involved some sort of Bacchanal run amok, and he'd never been formally censured. To be on trial, fighting for his place back amongst his peers, left his mouth dry and his hands damp.

A gulp from his wineskin settled his nerves. He executed an unsteady bow in front of the Father and the Mother.

"Very clever, using prayer to communicate your desire to meet," the Father said.

"Thank you, my lord. I thought so, too."

"Arrogance before the Council will not be tolerated," Discordia snapped.

"Easy, Cordi, Bacchus means no harm." The Father held up a hand. "We're here today to entertain an appeal to the decision that Bacchus no longer belongs to the world of the divine for the greater good of our children. Who's speaking the arguments against the proposal?"

After brushing his wild hair from his fair, Carpenter spoke up. "I am. No hard feelings, Brother Bacchus."

Bacchus shrugged. In the past, Carpenter had supported Bacchus. Discordia must have appealed to the emaciated divinity's infatuation with abstinence and asceticism, but at least Bacchus could trust Carpenter to play fair.

"Our greatest concern is for the purity of our children's souls. Intoxication all too often leads to the debauchery and decadence lining the path to Darkness. Overindulgence leads to fornication and fouls the vessel from which new life should spring, and circumvents the caring and love that should precede reproduction. Rampant fornication leads to disease and death, two of the most powerful sorrows. I'm sorry, my loyal friend, but I feel in every fiber of my being our children are better off without your influence."

Bacchus considered Carpenter's words. "All valid points, my friend. I'm sure I need not remind you that my gift of wine once helped protect them from disease and death by purifying the water essential to their survival." Bacchus made a veiled reference to his role in one of Carpenter's greatest displays of power. "And having lived among them, you and I know better than any here how Darkness can consume them, but they are also capable of such joy, and my gifts are part of that joy. They celebrate happy occasions with champagne. And did you know they even have children who are called 'wine babies'?"

"Wine babies?" the Mother asked.

"Children who are conceived by chance after a night of revelry."

"How charming." The Mother caressed Bacchus's cheek.

Warmth and delight spread through him, and tears sprang into his eyes. So long he'd labored against the icy chill in his heart. He now knew hell was not a fiery pit, but a cold, desolate state of mind that overtook the soul when it was distanced from the love of the Father and the Mother. "And I'm not asking for a blanket invitation back into the fold. But at least give me a chance to prove myself. Let me show my worth to the Council. Let me help the mortals embrace their joyful participation in the sorrows of the world. Was that not my essential purpose, after all? If I can help one soul overcome the sorrows, then may I be reinstated?"

Siddhartha's face lit up with a wider than usual grin. "I think that is a fair proposal."

"Well said." Carpenter nodded.

"Let's put this to a vote," said the Father. "All in favor?"

A chorus of 'yeas' rippled over the majority of Council members.

"All those opposed?" asked the Mother.

A smattering of 'nays' came in hushed tones.

"So shall it be," the Father and the Mother said in unison. "The will of the Council has spoken."

"Who chooses the soul in question?" hissed Discordia.

"Well, I already have someone in mind." Bacchus clasped his hands together. Butterflies flitted around his belly. What if they refused Ariana?

The Council looked into the Oracle and saw Bacchus's dark beauty, still deep in slumber. Bacchus caught a questioning look and nod pass between the Mother and the Father. They murmured something about the *coronae*, the meaning of which Bacchus hadn't a clue. And he was not about to ask.

# Chapter 10

*Divine Intervention*

Bacchus's mind raced as he skipped down the steps of the Pantheon. So many plans to make, so much to do before he returned to his earthly lair. A hiss startled him.

A serpentine lady emerged from the shadows.

Bacchus stopped in his tracks, hands on hips. "What do you want, Discordia?"

"Is that how you greet an old acquaintance who's trying to help you?"

Bacchus yelped. "That'll be the day."

"I know we've had our differences, but surely we can, as they say on Earth, bury the hatchet for a moment. I have some information that may be of help to you in your endeavor."

"Oh really? And why would you be interested in helping me? It's my understanding you were instrumental in getting me tossed."

"What? No, I wasn't a part of this. It's true that I've not been your biggest advocate, but if the Council can defrock you then, who's to say which one of us could be next?"

"I see you've taken a self-serving stance on all this, then."

"Well, if it serves you and serves me at the same time, then that's a win-win situation."

"I suppose it is."

"You, my silly little boy, are charged with the task of becoming this woman's savior, freeing her from her worldly suffering, correct?"

"In a nutshell."

"What the Council failed to tell you is there's a shortcut you can use to help her achieve enlightenment."

Bacchus held up a hand. "Not interested."

"How do you know you're not interested if you won't let me explain?"

"I know the general consensus around here is that I'm not very bright, but even I know enough to be wary of this wooden horse."

"So be it." The snake-like goddess rattled her tail. "Go about it the old-fashioned way. But did you know the Council also failed to tell you humans are pathetically slow creatures when it comes to change? Saving her soul could take a lifetime, three lifetimes, a hundred lifetimes. It would be a pity if you perished before you could move the wretched woman into the light."

Discordia retreated, but not with haste, more with an arrogant slither. Obviously, she knew her new and strange bedfellow would call her back to him.

Bacchus knew it, too. Were he in his immortal form, he'd have all the time in the world to help his lovely Ariana, but as a mortal, his time was limited. A mere blink of a cosmic eye. Bacchus had little experience with hands-on ministrations. He'd need all the help he could get, even from the most unlikely of sources. "Wait, Discordia, please."

"Yes, Bacchus, dear? What can I do for you?"

"Tell me about the shortcut."

"What shortcut?"

"Tell me about the shortcut. Please."

"How can I resist someone who isn't too proud to beg?" She put a conspiratorial arm around him. "The key to wrapping up all of this quickly is your little friend's sorrows box."

"Sorrows box?" He shook his head.

"Please tell me you do know what that is."

Bacchus cleared his throat, hoping to cover his ignorance. "Of course. Should've thought of it myself."

"Well, sounds like you don't need my help, then. Good luck." She patted his chest. "You're going to need it, queenie."

The goddess' expression as she disappeared into a cloud of sparkling black rain disturbed Bacchus. Something told him he would need more than luck, but for now, he'd settle for a little more info about the sorrows box. Time to pay a visit to Vighnesha.

* * * *

Bacchus felt the vibrations of the music before he actually heard it. The raucous strains shook the heavens around him. Swathes of jewel-studded toile hung from every turret, every column, every balustrade of Vig's not-so-humble abode. Scantily clad nymph-like Apsaras materialized around him as he walked up the sapphire path to the main entryway.

"Ladies," he said and nodded at them. Their replies—only flirtatious glances and air-kisses. Tempted to give himself over to the charms of their coconut-scented skin, Bacchus managed to wade through the sea of beauties.

Servants appeared to attend to Bacchus. One to open the massive white marble doors, one to take his cloak, and one to offer him any number of divine concoctions. He chose a flute of vibrant lavender syrup. An Apsara, who was nude save for the gold leaf covering her sex, intertwined her arm with his and escorted him through the opulent receiving hall to the lush oasis out back. As she walked, her bare breasts jiggled.

Liquid-silver waves lapped at the shore of a ruby sand beach. Golden palm trees reached up into the endless blue velvet, diamond-studded sky. Countless merrymakers frolicked in the surf and danced around almost every square inch of open space. Bacchus took a moment to adjust to the grandeur of it all. His mortal senses could barely process so much splendor.

Parting the crowd of bodies, his lovely guide led him into a private tent, set apart from the raging party.

Vighnesha lay in all his glory on a brocade hammock, receiving a saffron oil rub down from the most beautiful of celestial nymphs. Vig's eyes fluttered open. "Bro, you made it up here. How awesome."

"Thanks. I see you're still living large."

"You know it. Pull up a chair. I'll order up some more drinks, get some more nymphs in here."

"You're too gracious, old friend, but I was hoping I could speak to you alone."

Jumping up from the table, Vig didn't bother to cover his nude body. He walked the shapely women to the tent opening. After kissing each of their hands, he said, "Don't go too far now."

They disappeared in twittering laughter.

"It's not the same without you here." Vig put his arm around Bacchus's shoulder, his enormous phallus flopping from right to left. "Oops, just grazed you with my naked bits, didn't I?"

Bacchus chuckled. "Think nothing of it."

They settled into a pile of large of satin pillows.

"So, what's up?" Vig asked.

After taking a long sip from his drink, Bacchus launched into the events that had transpired earlier.

"Discordia is trying to help you? Dude, you are so screwed. Aw, righteous, that rhymed," Vig said.

"I know. But I'm desperate. The fact that I'm even considering advice from that fork-tongued battle-axe should tell you as much." Bacchus flopped face down.

"I hear ya. Well, it's like this. Everybody on Earth's got their own Pandora's box, sorrows box, whatever you call it. But those things are forbidden to leave the palace, man."

Bacchus righted himself, propping on his elbow. "What does the box do?"

"Captures sorrows. But if you really want to know the whole scoop on the boxes, you have to talk to Pandora. She's got loads of box knowledge."

Pandora—now it all made sense. Bacchus's education as a child had been spotty at best. Nymphs made for pretty distractible school marms. He knew the basic story of how Pandora had unleashed suffering upon the world, but how it applied to some type of box assigned to every human soul he didn't have a clue. But if it could help redeem himself and liberate Ariana, then he had to try.

"Do you think Pandora will make an exception and give me Ariana's?"

"Nah, bro. She can't, and don't put her in that position, because she'd get herself in trouble trying to help. She's sweet like that."

"So, I'm screwed."

"Well, there's one god who might be able to help you cuz he don't give a flip what trouble he gets in."

"Oh no, you're not talking about…"

"Yeah—the Green One. He'd probably steal it for you, but you gotta keep your eyes peeled while you're there. Who knows what other crap he'll try to stir up."

"I don't know if I can in my current condition."

"Well, you dudes get caught, don't leave Pandora out to dry. You feeling me?"

"You have my word."

"Cool. I'll send him your way. The Mother and the Father be with you, bro." Vig summoned his entourage.

# Chapter 11

*Pandora's Boxes*

Standing at the base of the steps to the Hall of Earthly Gifts, Bacchus searched for the god he was supposed to meet here. Loki was running late. Not a big surprise. Unable to communicate via thought with the Norse god, Bacchus would have to wait.

He wouldn't be in such a hurry to leave the heavens—in fact under normal circumstances, the longer the stay the better—but Ariana's spirit called to him. True, he'd left her in peaceful slumber, but even in sleep, their consciousness seemed melded together. She couldn't wander in darkness forever. Strange dreams of destiny plagued him as well.

Annoyed, he sat on a marble bench and stared at the grand hall. It appeared to float on clouds, tethered to nothing, rippling and shimmering in the ever-present sunlight. A gilded dome sprouted from the top of the building, a hole in the center where white doves circled and played, swooping in and out of the opening. Flowered vines snaked up the columns and walls. Blossoms of every shade in the rainbow dotted the green foliage. The hall seemed to extend back infinitely into the horizon. No one but Pandora had ever walked the entire perimeter.

Finally, the trickster god, emerald-tinted skin as vibrant as ever, galloped up on his eight-legged horse.

Bacchus shuddered, his arachnophobia flaring. "I will never get used to the look of that thing."

"Home, Sleipnir," Loki addressed the horse. The ungainly beast trotted off without objections. The trickster turned to his fallen peer. "Bacchie, baby, good to see you. You look skinny."

"Why, Loki, does that make you green with envy?"

"Like I've never heard that one before."

"I hear it's not that easy being green."

"Did you have Vig invite me here just to make juvenile jokes at my expense?"

"No, but it's a nice little perk of the situation."

"You want me to help you or not? It makes no difference to me."

"All right, my apologies. So how exactly do you plan to pull this off?"

"Don't you worry. You do your Q and A thing with the spinster Pandora, and I'll do my thing."

The two headed up the hall stairs.

"Why doesn't that make me feel any better?" Bacchus said.

Loki slipped around the side of the hall as Bacchus swung the brass knocker.

The enormous door opened, dwarfing the diminutive goddess who stood in its shadow. "Oh Bacchus, sweetheart, you're back?" She engulfed him in a hug.

"Well, not exactly, but I could use your help."

She ushered him inside the entry salon and pushed the door closed behind them. "Anything for you. What can I help you with?"

Given her history with the topic in question, Bacchus would have to approach it with care. "Well, I have some questions…about um, you know. The box."

Questioning drew together her delicate features. "The box?"

"The box."

"Oh, oh, oh, the box. Right."

She led him straight to the vessel. For all its gilding and ornate carving, it didn't seem an impressive or imposing object. A phrase he'd once heard on Earth, "bigger than a breadbox," popped into Bacchus's head, though if the thing were actually bigger than a breadbox, it wasn't by much.

"Voilá." She presented it to him with a flourish of her hands.

For all of his inspection of the thing, he couldn't find a handle or the lip of a lid, no hinges or fissure in the construction indicating it was anything but a solid object.

"And this is the very box that was opened? You know doom on mankind—screaming, pain, suffering…" His voice trailed off.

"Yes. The very one."

"How exactly does it open?"

Pandora fished a key from her pocket and walked over to the box.

"Whoa, should you do that?" Bacchus asked.

"Oh yes, it's perfectly harmless now."

"Won't hope escape?'

"Hope?"

"You know, the evils escape out of the box, but the lid is closed before hope can escape therefore mankind always has hope."

"Hope isn't a specter. It can't escape, silly boy. Hope is what the box is made of."

The goddess proceeded to release some hidden lock. A keypad of sorts popped up with ancient Greek symbols in bas-relief. Her fingers skipped over the symbols, touching them in a specific sequence. An ethereal voice emanated from the box and asked Pandora, "What walks on four legs in the morning, two legs in the afternoon, and three legs in the evening?"

"Man." Pandora replied.

The box rearranged itself into a golden lotus, its petals splayed out around a gaping, hollow center.

"That looks an awful lot like a—" Bacchus murmured.

Pandora nodded and suppressed a giggle. "It does, doesn't it?"

"Pardon me for asking this, Madame Pandora, but how in Hades did you open this box by accident all those eons ago? It seems well designed against an unintentional breech."

"What? I opened the box? Oh no, I knew better than to open this box."

"Really? It's the only version of the story I've ever heard."

"Well, you are very young as gods go. No, it was not I who opened the box. It was Lucifer. And he didn't open it by accident." Pandora paused to sniff the air. "Do you smell blueberry muffins?"

Bacchus took a half-hearted whiff. "Um, no. I'm afraid I don't."

"I love blueberry muffins. I have some over in the culinary gifts wing. Would you like me to fetch you some with a little tea?"

"No, thank you."

"How silly of me, you don't even drink tea, do you? Would you like some of your own gift to the world? What wine would one serve with a blueberry muffin?"

"Riesling, but thank you, Madame. I'm fine. So, you were saying...?"

"What was I saying? Oh yes, blueberry muffins. Did I tell you about the streusel?"

"Yes, you did, sounds like wonderful stuff." Bacchus fibbed to move the conversation along. "Now, why did Lucifer open the box?"

"He was angry."

"Why was he angry?"

"Some adolescent temper tantrum. The Father had thrown over Lucifer's mother, the angel Lillis, for a human woman—Ellie or Ava or Eve, something like that."

"And how did you get the blame for it?"

"Well, I am the keeper of all earthly gifts, am I not? And hope is an amazing essence. It was the Mother's greatest gift to the mortals. Nothing evil can breech it, so the sorrows were fixed tight until Luci showed up... Honestly, I had no idea he meant to do anything wrong. He was such a beautiful young man, all dimples and blond curls. He asked me to sneak an apple for him... I shouldn't have left him alone here, but how could I have known?" The crinkled edges of her eyes caught the tears threatening to spill over.

Bacchus cupped the aging divinity's face in his hands. A pang of guilt stabbed at him, but he reminded himself the box he intended to steal would be put to good use, not evil. "No, no, my sweet lady, you did nothing wrong. Lucifer tricked you; he used you."

"The Council didn't quite see it that way. I spent two centuries in Purgatory before they let me return to my post here."

"Of the few weaknesses the Father has, his first son is his greatest. He couldn't very well let his Lucifer take the fall for unleashing the sorrows."

"I suppose you're right. But Lucifer wound up falling into Darkness anyway."

"Yes, that he did."

Bacchus reached in his pocket and pulled out a cotton handkerchief. With the gentlest of touches, he dabbed away the goddess' tears. "No more thoughts of unpleasant things now. Hey, why don't you tell me a little more about streusel?"

She clapped her hands together. "Oh my, there's so much to tell I hardly know where to start."

"Could you explain to me the difference between 'streusel' and 'strudel'?"

"My dear boy, they are vastly different things. Streusel is the crumbly topping one would put on a cake or pie or muffin. Strudel is a type of pastry filled with fruit. Or cheese. Or nutmeats. You can, of course, put streusel on a strudel. That's extra lovely. You know who loves a good strudel? Charon. Especially apple. He drops in from time to time for some between ferry runs. Oh, how I love a man in black."

She prattled on for another half hour, discussing the different types of strudels one could make, but Bacchus heard little of her dissertation. Instead, he went through his mental checklist of all the things he needed to know about the boxes and the sorrows. Once she reached a logical moment to pause, having departed to the differences between regular cherries and maraschino cherries, Bacchus patted her hand.

"Love, I'm so sorry to interrupt. I never tire of hearing your stories about fruit fillings, but may I ask you a couple more questions about the sorrows."

"I've always believed the sorrows could be vanquished by strudel."

"Yes, I'm sure. Strudel aside, what else could be used to conquer the sorrows?"

"I'm not sure. They're very much like cockroaches, and they reproduce like rodents."

"What do you mean they reproduce?"

"Well, when the box was opened, the sorrows fractured into infinite pieces and attached themselves to every human who existed and every one that would ever exist for eternity. The Mother planted this garden to contain them, so that when a soul vanquishes a form of suffering, it can be entrapped once again. I have a box for each mortal."

"Oh my, that must be a lot of boxes. Do you keep an inventory of all of them?"

"I do try, but it's tricky because new ones pop open every seven minutes, and once in a while, a soul achieves enlightenment, and a box retires."

"And how's that work?"

"When our children vanquish all their own sorrows, they achieve enlightenment. And the box goes dormant."

"What happens to it then?"

"I really don't know. The Mother comes to collect the dormant ones, but I couldn't tell you what she does with them."

"And what about the boxes that haven't opened yet?"

Pandora took Bacchus by the hand and led him to a stepped, mountainside garden of sorts that stretched as far and wide as either of them could see. "Here's where they lie in wait, ready to attack all those poor newborn babies. When they've opened, I pick them and store them in the Hope Wing of the Hall of Earthly Gifts, and that's where they stay until a soul reaches enlightenment."

"What happens to the souls that die before they reach enlightenment?"

"Souls plagued to death by the sorrows continue through the cycle of birth and death until in one lifetime they are finally able to overcome. Unless they're irredeemable, then, well, you know where they go."

"How horrifying."

"I imagine it is."

She led him in from the terrace and shivered. "I'm sorry to rush you, but I really don't like it out there in the Garden of Evils."

"Don't blame you one bit."

"The moaning of the specters. I hate it."

"May I ask, what exactly is a specter?"

"A specter is pure evil. And what's nasty about the sorrows is they've bonded together into binary specters. Fear is bonded with despair, cowardice with anger, famine with poverty. Envy and greed, cruelty and violence, and, of course, disease with death. Each member of the pair feeds off the success of the other so no matter which one makes the host more miserable, they both win. You get the picture?"

"Indeed I do. And how would a third-party go about capturing another person's sorrows?"

"Why, I've never heard of such a thing. It's up to each man or woman to imprison them."

"Theoretically, though, could it be done?"

"I suppose it's possible. Anything is possible." Pandora smelled the air again. "Are you sure you don't smell blueberries? I'm quite sure I smell muffins—no, wait—maybe not muffins. Blueberry pancakes perhaps? Those are lovely, too."

"Madame Pandora, please focus, love. If a third party wanted to imprison the sorrows for someone else, how would he go about it?"

"Haven't the faintest idea, sweetheart. Maybe if the third party were a god or a demigod, any divine or magical being can see the sorrows attached to a human. How to go about plucking the wee beasties from a host, I couldn't tell you. And once you got them in the box, I don't know if they'd stay. They could pop right out again when you opened the box to put in another."

Out of the corner of his eye, Bacchus thought he caught a glimpse of Loki's verdant skin. If he could perceive the trickster with his feeble human sight, Pandora would surely see the mischievous god skulking about.

"Hey, how about one of those blueberry muffins?"

"Oh, you've decided to try one?" Her eyes lit up. "I'll be right back."

She headed off in a flurry of pink clouds.

Bacchus spoke into the air around him. "Whatever mischief you're up to, wrap it up. I'm not kidding."

"Did you say something, sweetheart?" Pandora reappeared at Bacchus's side with a muffin and glass of Riesling.

"Blessings to you, my dear lady." Bacchus drained the glass of wine then took a bite of muffin. "This is lovely. The streusel really makes it."

"Come by anytime you want one."

"I hope very soon to be able to take you up on that offer, Madame Pandora." He finished his snack. "I'm afraid, though, I must be on my way. You've been such a dear to talk with me about all this."

"As I said, anything for you." She hugged him.

Bacchus loped down the marble steps in front of the Hall of Earthly Gifts. Loki rolled in the meadow off to the side of the path, cackling with amusement.

"What in Hades is wrong with you?" Bacchus snapped.

"Oh." Loki wiped a tear from his eye. "You gotta admit the blueberry muffin scent was genius on my part. What that dingbat has for fruited cupcakes is beyond me."

"There are a great many things that are beyond you."

"But not these."

Loki held up two sorrows boxes.

"What have you done?" Bacchus said through clenched teeth.

"I purloined Ariana's vessel."

"And the other one."

"I'm a genius, a genius. I took one of the boxes that hasn't bloomed yet."

"You pus-for-brains imbecile. You don't even know how dangerous that thing is."

"Bacchie baby, why are you angry? It's just a teeny-weeny cube of evil. And we won't use it unless we have to."

"We won't use it at all. Give me the box."

"No."

"Give it to me."

"No." Loki juggled the two boxes. When Bacchus reached for him, he vanished and reappeared in a different spot, snickering. "You're quite the slowpoke now, aren't you?"

"Nice, make fun of the divinity-impaired."

"I forgot. You really can't catch me." The trickster doubled over in a gale of laughter.

"Fine, you twisted snot-bubble, give me Ariana's box."

"Oh, Hades-Euphrates, I don't know which is which."

"Then you'll have to give me both."

"Or I could give you neither."

"I knew I shouldn't have gotten you involved in this. You louse up everything you touch."

"But you did involve me, so here we are. Nyah, nyah, nyah, nyah."

Bacchus could feel a vein in his forehead throbbing, but he concentrated his awareness on thoughts of Pan. The satyr appeared in a flash of wiry fur, his hand around Loki's throat.

After Bacchus blew the goat hair from his lips, he said, "I may not be able to catch you, but Panny certainly can. You may still have your divinity, Loki, but I have divine friends, and that's something you can't say. No wonder no one likes you."

A scowl darkened Loki's features, and he growled at Pan but handed over the boxes. "Cut the insipid flute music you're piping into my head."

"Once Bacchus is safely on his way." The satyr snarled.

Bacchus clapped Pan on the shoulder. "I am forever in your debt, my friend."

"Think nothing of it, sire."

If Bacchus hurried, he could catch the next lightning bolt to Earth.

# Chapter 12

*Game Plan*

Back home, Bacchus watched Furina study the little ornate box with a powerful magnifying glass. She popped her chewing gum and let out a low whistle.

"This isn't your run of the mill magical object. Where the hell did you get it? On second thought, don't tell me," the Goddess of Thieves said.

"And you're sure this one is Ariana's?" Bacchus asked.

"Yup, her name is engraved in really tiny Greek letters on the bottom. The other one has no name on the bottom, and something inside it is saying the most obscene things. You don't hear that?"

"No. Can you open hers?"

"I won't guarantee I can, but I'll take a crack at it."

She reached into her bag and pulled out a hammer that looked suspiciously like that of a certain Norse god.

"Please don't smash it open. I need to be able to close it and lock it again."

"Ha," Furina barked. "You don't make things easy for a gal."

She continued to chomp at her gum.

"May I offer you a lager? Lambic? Boilermaker?" Bacchus asked.

Furina shook off the question. Drumming her fingers, she tapped out mysterious rhythms as if calculating something. "You said this thing is made of hope?"

"So I'm told."

The brilliance of inspiration sparked in her golden eyes. She pulled a dark orb about the size of a peach from her satchel, slammed it against the wall, then shook it. Pure luminescence bathed the room in a blinding white glow. Furina pushed the orb through the wall of the box and examined it again under the magnifying glass.

"I got you now, you tricky little box," she said.

Bacchus hovered over Furina's shoulder. "What'd you find?"

"You see this pinpoint of light? That's the keyhole." A wistful smile stole over her cupid's bow lips. "I don't suppose you have the freakin' key."

"Would I have called you if I did?"

"True. You have a needle of Athena?"

"No."

"Serpent fang?"

"Nope."

"Phoenix feather?"

"Where would I get a Phoenix feather in South Beach?"

"Okay, how about a satyr hair?"

"That I'm sure I can lay my hands on."

He headed down the hall of the condo, passing the room in which Ariana still slumbered. Bacchus gave into the urge to peek in on her. Though her chest rose and fell with even measure, he couldn't help but be concerned. She was going on day two of this comatose state, but Pan had assured him she was alive and well, just deeply sedated, cradled in the beauty of warm, peaceful dreams. That her spirit still called out to Bacchus caused concern, but he trusted his steward. It was best if she could be spared all these machinations. With any luck, she'd be free of all of life's suffering when Pan administered the antidote to Morpheus's draught.

From the shower drain, Bacchus plucked the makeshift passkey Furina had requested. Once equipped with the hair, she picked the lock with ease. A miniature keyboard, identical to the one he'd seen at the Hall of Earthly Gifts, appeared.

"You gotta be friggin' kidding me." Furina grimaced. "And let me guess, you've no clue as to the combination."

"Your guess is correct," Bacchus said.

Though she affected an annoyed demeanor, a twinkle in her eye told Bacchus the Goddess of Thieves enjoyed the challenge presented by the box.

She pulled a golden snail shell from her supplies and pushed it into her ear. Working methodically, she tapped each one of the keys while she held the box close to her cheek.

"We're in luck. The keys control tumblers. Give me a little while, and I'll crack the combo for you. You have something to write with?" Furina asked.

Bacchus refilled his stein and returned with a notepad and pen for his accomplice.

"So, once I enter the combination, what's the third obstacle?"

"And how did you know there's a third obstacle?" Bacchus asked.

"It's a divine object. Of course the obstacles will come in a group of three. It's not going to explode or shrivel my genitalia or anything like that, will it?"

"No, nothing like that. It'll ask you a riddle, and I think I have the answer, unless the riddle's different from the box I saw opened."

"And if I get the answer wrong?"

"That I can't say. I don't think anything will happen, but maybe we shouldn't assume shriveled genitals are out of the question."

"Thanks for the heads up."

Almost an hour later, Furina uttered a cry of victory. "Sonofabitch, I'm too damn good. Get your ass over here before I put in the last letter of the combo."

Bacchus hurried over to watch her depress the final key.

"The combination spells 'Ariadne,'" she said.

"That's weird."

"It's 'Ariana' in Greek."

"Oh, I guess that does make sense, then."

An ethereal voice came from the small box. "What can consume a man and not have had its fill? What grows larger when you feed it, and when it is starved, larger still? What drives a man to great lengths, but never reaches a destination? What rapids flow, what hurricane blows, what fire rages without cessation? The contented man knows nothing of me. What am I?"

Eyes wide, Furina gave an exaggerated shrug. Bacchus took the pad of paper from her and scribbled down as much of the riddle as he could remember. He read the words over and over again. Something nagged at the back of his mind, but what?

"Please, tell me your first guess," the box said.

For lack of a better answer, Bacchus said, "Jägermeister?"

"Your first guess is incorrect."

Bacchus grabbed his crotch, relieved to find his testicles and cock intact.

"What can consume a man and not have had its fill? What grows larger when you feed it, and when it is starved, larger still? What drives a man to great lengths, but never reaches a destination? What rapids flow, what hurricane blows, what fire rages without cessation? The contented man knows nothing of me. What am I?" the box repeated.

Contented man, contented man, contented... The words rolled around his brain. If one is contented, one doesn't want for anything—Bacchus snapped his fingers. "Desire."

The box sprang open into a smaller scale replica of the golden lotus inside the original box.

Furina snickered. "You know that kinda looks like a—"

"I know, right?"

"Well, my work here is done."

"Thank you so much." Bacchus picked up the flower. "Now, how do I close the infernal thing?"

"I couldn't tell you. I just crack 'em. I don't close 'em." Furina turned to pack up her things.

"How may I repay you?"

The goddess shouldered her bag of tools. "We can settle up once you get yourself back to your rightful place in the Cosmos. Trot your fine ass down to the Underworld and look me up."

She winked at him and laid a hard slap on his buttocks.

"You know I'm more than happy to oblige."

The Goddess of Thieves turned to leave, but stopped, then faced him again. "Oh and I don't recommend opening the other one. There's something really foul inside it."

"Not to worry. The only thing I plan to do with that one is return it to its rightful owner."

"Good deal," she said then disappeared without so much as rustling the drapes.

* * * *

Bacchus's stomach lurched, watching Pan blink in and out of sight, but soon enough the satyr appeared, huffing and puffing.

Pan gulped for air. "They're too quick, sire."

"I thought the specters were supposed to be attached to her."

"That appears to be"—Pan wheezed—"a figure of speech."

"Maybe we're going about this all wrong. I wonder if there is a way to lure them into a trap?"

"If the trap doesn't include running, I'm all for it, sire."

Two hours later, Bacchus threw a half-melted carton of ice cream across the room, painting the far wall with swathes of pink, white, and brown. Perfectly good Neapolitan gone to waste. Nothing he'd tried succeeded in luring the specters away from her for very long. Not gold, not cigarettes, not ice cream, though they'd been mildly interested in the pornographic movie he'd put on in the living room. Pan said they'd peeked around the corner, but the moment the satyr made a move toward them, they scampered back to their host.

Bacchus tried to remember his last visit to Earth, prior to his downfall. For the life of him, he couldn't remember ever having seen a specter. Pan had described the effort to see the sorrows like scanning for a radio station. He'd had to find the right frequency, but once he'd tuned them in, he had a hard time tuning them out.

"I won't even repeat what they said you could do with that ice cream." Pan shook his head. "But they did appreciate the single malt scotch."

"Well, who wouldn't? Always happy to please pure evil."

"Sire, I think it's time to reevaluate our approach."

"I know, you're right. I think we're going to need some back up."

"I took the liberty of inviting a few of your friends over. They'll be here later for brainstorming, refreshments, and gaming."

"Why is it you are always two or three steps ahead of me?" Bacchus shook his head. What would he do without Pan to think of everything?

"Because it's your job to perform in the now. It's my job to make sure you don't have to think about anything but the now."

Bacchus squeezed his steward's shoulder. "Were I given to weepy emotions, I'd be blubbering all over the place right now."

"You should change for the party, sire. I'll take care of the mess here."

Without argument, Bacchus trudged to the master's suite. His thoughts weighed heavy on him, not that he'd expected this task of making himself whole again to be easy. At least they'd made a little progress.

He turned on the shower and climbed in. The billows of steam eased his sore shoulders. This level of stress was new to him. Worry and struggle had once been foreign concepts. Bacchus wondered if—no—when he regained his former glory, would he also be able to regain his former carefree bliss? His head pounded, his muscles ached, and his stomach churned. The promise of freedom from worry was enough to spur on his efforts, and yet, Ariana seldom left his thoughts, either. The fear he'd seen in her eyes, the evil man's bony fingers gripped around her throat, killing the joy and beauty inside her, little by little. But Bacchus wouldn't allow Dezi to crush her, not as long as animus filled his body.

The hot water waned. Had he really been standing there, lost in thought, for so long? He shook off the questions bouncing around his mind. Scrubbing quickly, he hurried to end the shower. Tepid water rinsed away woodsy-scented body wash. A chill gripped him after he exited the stall. On the back of the door, Pan had hung a towel and a robe.

Bacchus rubbed himself dry and threw on the fluffy, terrycloth garment. He inspected the day's worth of stubble darkening his face. Instead of shaving, he opted to keep the shadow of facial hair, but cleaned up the edges. He wondered if he could grow a full beard. As a god, his face had always been flower petal smooth, but he loved how rakish he appeared with stubble.

His favorite blue jeans and black cotton T-shirt waited for him right outside the door. Bacchus took care when buttoning himself into the denim, lest he pinch himself somewhere he didn't wish to be pinched—at least not by a fastening mechanism. Though Pan had purchased Bacchus an array of modern undergarments, other than avoiding the occasional fold of foreskin caught in a button-fly, Bacchus could think of no good reason to wear boxers. They were just one more piece of clothing he'd have to remove before he could sink himself into the fragrant flesh of another. For him, the benefit did not outweigh the hassle.

Once clothed, scented, and stylishly tousled, Bacchus walked out to the living room to greet his guests.

Vig sat at the dining table, shuffling a deck of cards in each of his two pairs of hands. Cúchulainn lazed in a dining chair, his massive thighs spilling over the edge of the upholstered seat, feet propped on the table. Gilgamesh and Heracles circled each other, on the verge of a wrestling match.

"Easy on the tectonic plates, now," Bacchus said, remembering the great quake of 1906 set off by the last throw down between those two.

"Bacchie, how the hell are you?" Heracles clasped his half-brother's hand and squeezed it almost hard enough to break it.

"Agh. Not as sturdy as I once was, I'm afraid."

"Sorry, man."

The immortals gathered around the mahogany and green felt card table. Pan took drink orders—red wine for Gilgamesh, single malt whiskey for Cúchulainn, and ouzo for Heracles. Bacchus requested four fingers of Grey Goose to ease his troubled mind. Vig puffed happily on his hookah, no libation necessary.

"What are we playing tonight, Bacch?" Gilgamesh asked.

"*Tali.*" Bacchus rattled the gold-plated knucklebones. "Ante up, gentleman."

They each threw in a gold piece.

"Pan said you need our help with a situation. What's up?" Heracles said.

With a heavy sigh, Bacchus recounted his plan to recapture his former glory, leaving out certain finer points, namely the theft of two of Pandora's boxes. He told them about the confrontation with Ariana's boyfriend and the sweetness that still existed in the woman's heart, despite all the hardships she'd known.

Vig blew out a cloud of violet smoke. "Lemme see if I got this. You need a plan to rid your lovely lady of all human suffering."

"Yep." Bacchus coughed. "That's it in a nutshell."

"You don't make it easy on yourself, do you, bro?"

"Apparently not. But we're immortals, heroes, legends, and gods. There's got to be a way to save Ariana from fear…cruelty…um, envy. Pan, how are they paired off again?"

The satyr appeared with the tray of drinks. "Fear and despair. Cowardice and anger. Famine and poverty. Envy and greed. Cruelty and violence. Disease and death."

"Thank you, my friend." Bacchus took his glass of vodka and swallowed it in one gulp. "Another, please."

Heracles took the first toss and rolled a combination known as Midas.

"Let's take each suffering one at a time," Gilgamesh suggested.

"Excellent suggestion, Gilly." Bacchus nodded. "Your turn to throw, Cúchulainn. What do you wager you can beat Heracles's Midas?"

"Fifty." The demigod threw in a gilded chip.

"See your fifty," Vig said.

Pan asked, "A silly question, I'm sure, but how can we propose a solution to suffering when we don't understand it? We don't experience it."

"Just because we don't suffer, doesn't mean we can't comprehend the state of being. Siddhartha says humans exist in ten worlds," Vig went on.

"I've read about them." Pan nodded. "They're Imprisonment, Desire, Savagery, Rage, Stoicism, Ecstasy, Observation, Internalization, Compassion, and True Balance."

"Pan-man, you got it. Righteous," Vig said.

Bacchus waved. "Wait, wait, wait. What, by Hades, does all that mean?"

After an hour and half of Vig's best efforts to explain the ten worlds to Bacchus, Vighnesha closed his eyes in deep thought. The tinkling sound of bamboo wind chimes filled the room, and a crimson shower of sequins rained down on the party guests. Kannon, the bodhisattva, appeared—

both male and female spirits curled around each other. He—and she—started to speak.

A voice, both melodic and strong, captured the attention of all at the table. "The Ten Worlds are human states of being. All of the worlds serve a positive purpose in their earthly lives, but nine can lead to suffering when a being spends too much time in those worlds. Entrapment leads to fear and despair, desire brings greed, envy, cruelty, violence, even disease. Savagery and rage... All the worlds herald the same evils, except True Balance. With True Balance, one can find indestructible happiness and freedom from suffering. No matter what life brings."

"So, True Balance is like a permanent four-beer buzz?" Bacchus asked.

Kannon stroked Bacchus's hair and neck. "In a manner of speaking, yes, my child."

Bacchus soaked up the love and warmth pouring from the bodhisattva's aura. "My eternal gratitude, Kannon."

"Namaste," she and he said, bowing to the room of deities, then disappeared in an incense-scented fog.

Bacchus clapped his hands. "Whose roll is it?"

"Gilgamesh. But aren't we going to pin down a game plan for the lovely Ariana?" Vig asked.

"Oh, I know what I need to do for her."

"What's that, brother man?"

"At the root of this woman's suffering—the fear, the anger, the entrapment, the despair, all of it—is one Mr. Alonso Desiderio. We eliminate Dezi from her life, we eliminate her suffering"—Bacchus snapped his fingers—"just that easy."

"Well, what do ya know." Heracles laughed.

"What?" Bacchus asked.

Still snickering, Heracles said, "Desire is the root of all Ariana's suffering—*Desiderio*. It's Latin for 'longing.' Get it?"

With groans, the motley crew pelted Bacchus's half-brother with a shower of cheese puffs.

# Chapter 13

*Fear and Despair*

Bacchus checked the clock again. It was already noon. Pan had said the antidote could take a couple hours to work, but almost four hours had gone by. It was bad enough he had to rouse her without freeing her from all earthly suffering as he'd originally planned, but now he feared his meddling had put her into a permanent comatose state. He poured himself a glass of wine to calm his nerves then heard a rustling behind him.

"Good morning," Ariana said. "I'm so sorry, Bach. I feel like I've been asleep for a year."

"Oh, no, not a year. Four days. Good morning, I'm so very glad you're awake."

She started. "Four days? What are you talking about?"

"It's Wednesday, love."

"Wednesday? How the hell can it be Wednesday? How did I sleep for four days?"

"Well, there's something we need to talk about," Bacchus said after a sip of Merlot.

"My God, I'm so sorry. Don't worry. I'll clear out of your place tonight. I can't believe I slept for four days. You must think—"

"No, no. I'm not worried about that. In fact, it's my fault you slept for so long."

"What do you mean?"

"Okay, hear me out. Pan and I gave you a sleeping potion—"

"You rufied me?" She edged away from him.

"No, no, no. Nothing like that at all. Look, we're trying to help you."

"By drugging me?"

"Not drugged so much as enchanted. Well, we were hoping to have everything worked out by the time we woke you up."

Ariana grabbed a knife from the bar. "Don't come any closer to me."

"No, Ariana, honey. You misunderstand. I'm trying to help you."

"Sure, whatever." She skittered toward the door, but Pan appeared in his true form and blocked her path.

"Miss Ariana, please calm down." The satyr reached for her.

She screamed and slashed a wild arc around her, then froze, the knife clattering to the floor.

"Do you have a hold of her?" Bacchus asked.

"I'm sorry to use mind control on her, sire. I didn't know what else to do." The goat-man threw his hands in the air.

"You didn't have a choice."

Pan walked her over to the sofa and settled her into a seat.

Bacchus sat next to her and stroked her hand. "Ariana, please don't be afraid. I don't think I'm going about this the right way. I don't have a lot of experience with hands on miracles, but really, I am trying to help you." He turned to his steward. "Pan, can you do that knowledge transfer thing you do so she can see what's at stake here?"

"Of course, sire."

Her body stayed perfectly still, except her eyelids jumped wide open. In under a minute, Pan announced he was finished with the mind connection.

"Okay, Pan, go ahead and release her." Bacchus cringed away from the woman, in case she flipped out again.

When the spark of free will returned to her expression, she glanced from Pan to Bacchus several times. A squeak escaped her lips, and her eyes rolled back as she crumpled into a heap on the floor.

Bacchus knelt down, supporting Ariana's head. Her eyes fluttered open, and she emitted murmurs of nonsense.

"Pan, did you fry her brain?" Bacchus pressed a hand to her forehead.

"No, I did not, Sire," Pan said, his tone as close to insubordination as Bacchus had ever heard it.

"I had the strangest dream," Ariana said.

"It wasn't a dream, love." Bacchus stroked her hair.

"There really were mushrooms dancing around the living room?" she asked.

"Okay, that was a dream. Do you remember anything else?"

"Pan said you were a god, and he's your steward, and you were kicked out of heaven, and you need to save me."

"Oh good, you did get most of it."

The satyr stepped into full view, and Ariana gasped.

"Please don't be afraid, madam," Pan said.

"But you can't—this can't be real." She shook her head, face blanching again.

Bacchus helped her upright and held out his right hand to her. "It's all true. My real name is Bacchus. I once was the god of intoxication and ecstasy. I'd like to be again. And I'd like to help you get yourself free."

She hesitated for a second then took his hand and shook it. "Free from what?"

"The sorrows that plague your life. Namely Dezi."

"I need a drink," she said.

"Ah, you're in luck." He jumped to his feet and strode to the wet bar. He moved a large panel, to revel four shelves of wine and liquor. "Pick your poison."

"I don't want anything to drink."

"But you said…"

"I know what I said." She massaged her temples. "This is a lot to process. You gotta give me a minute."

"Of course." Bacchus folded his arms then looked to Pan.

The satyr shrugged.

"I'm losing my mind, right? None of this is really happening. I've lost my mind," Ariana said to no one in particular.

Bacchus leaned against the bar. "I assure you this is all very real."

"On second thought, I think I will take that drink now. Rum and coke please."

"A woman after my own heart. *Una Cuba libre*, coming right up." He sliced open a lime.

\* \* \* \*

Four o'clock in the afternoon rolled around, and Bacchus had to go to the club. Unwilling to leave Ariana alone in her fragile state, he brought her with him. The staff had already decanted his first bottle of wine.

After taking a sip of an excellent 1982 Bordeaux, Bacchus rang the kitchen. He requested another bottle and a roast beef sandwich. For two.

"I'm not hungry." Ariana pushed a jet-black lock from her cheek.

"Nonsense. You need to eat."

The muted rhythm of the club's sound system hammered beyond the office walls, a hit pop-song-turned-house-music by some aspiring DJ. But the melody gave him no joy tonight. That Ariana's face was taut with weariness excluded all other sources of happiness. Never before had the emotional state of another being directly impacted him. The phenomenon alarmed him. What if she stayed miserable forever? Would he never be happy again, either?

He rose from the spot where he leaned against the robin's egg blue wall near his desk. His bare feet sank into the creamy Persian rug, which covered the center of the wooden floor. Inlaid parquet floor to be precise, Bacchus had spared no expense revitalizing Eliseo so that it more closely resembled the bit of heaven for which it was named.

A hand against her cheek, he said, "I know it's a lot to process, but I promise, this will all work out in the end."

"I don't even understand what 'this' is. I have no choice but to believe that you are who you say you are…who Pan showed me you are, but it's all so unbelievable. I'll be honest; I always thought you were the stuff of mythology, but here you are telling me that not only you exist, but so does every other god and goddess ever worshiped. And you're all one big happy family."

Bacchus sat next to her on the white leather sofa. "Well, I wouldn't go that far, but yes, we all to work together for the betterment of mankind. It's the only thing that unites us."

"So God, Jesus, the mother Mary…?"

"All very real."

"Yahweh, Allah, Krishna? Venus?"

"Yes, they exist, but some are the same deity, known around the world by a different name. Or the personification of aspects of the same god."

"And the Devil?"

Dipping his head to the side, Bacchus nodded. "Unfortunately, yes. He exists, too."

"And some gods are more powerful than others?"

He nodded.

Twisting a curl around her finger, she seemed to struggle with what she wanted to say. "What—what happens when we die?"

"It depends on what you believe as to your final destination, but if you achieve enlightenment, or perform major selfless and heroic acts, or are very innocent, then you are sent to a pleasurable afterlife. Most souls are reincarnated for another chance to achieve enlightenment, which can take some time, so they are held in Limbo. Some souls are so marred they cannot be given another chance and are punished for eternity as described by their religious beliefs."

Her face grew ashen, and some unseen force compelled her to her feet. She wrapped her arms around herself and began to pace slowly. Her usually red lips had turned a dusty, sickly tan.

"Ariana? Are you okay?" asked Bacchus.

Her hands trembled, and she looked like she was about to cry, but no tears fell. "Why do you want to help me?"

"I told you, to rid you of your earthly suffering and therefore, regain my dominion." He shrugged. "It works out well for both of us, don't you think?"

She dropped into the couch again and sank her face into her hands. Her voice suddenly so small, she asked, "And what if I don't deserve your help?"

The statement made no sense. Why wouldn't she be worthy? "What do you mean, love?"

At this, she let out a gasp of a sob. Olympus help him, why did she keep doing that? Unsure of what to do, he stared at her. Words of comfort rose in the back of his throat, but none seemed up to task. Especially since he didn't know what his exact task was. Was she upset with him? Did he say the wrong thing? By the gods, what did she need from him?

"I—I don't understand," he said.

Her eyes turned to stone and she shouted, "Don't you get it? What if I'm one of those 'marred souls' you were talking about?"

"No." He stayed rooted to his spot, still unsure if he should offer comfort, or instead, retreat. "No. That's not true, Ariana."

She turned away from him, shoulders shaking. "You don't know the awful things I've done. Th-that I was forced to do."

Bacchus held out a tremulous hand, but she didn't take it. The darkness that usually cast a mere shadow over her sunny disposition rolled in as a full thunderstorm, punctuated with lightning strikes.

"I don't know how to explain this, but I see you. Not just your outward appearance, but what's inside, and please, trust me when I say you are not irredeemable. Quite the contrary. There's so much beauty in you, but it's hindered from fully blossoming by your lot in life. I can change all that."

"But you—" She fiddled with the edge of her t-shirt. "You presided over intoxication and ecstasy. How can you say what's in store for a Catholic soul?"

"I might be less worshiped than the Prophet or the Carpenter, but I've been known to pull off a miracle or two in my day. There was this one time King Pentheus's henchmen had kidnapped me and were going to sell me to sexual slavery in Egypt. Bastet and I got the biggest laugh out of that, as if sexual slavery would be any sort of punishment for me. Anyway, the captain of the ship stood up and refused to doom me to what he thought would be a cruel and torturous situation. His men turned on

*Cindy Jacks*

him. Finally, I knew I had to act. I bound the ship and its entire crew in ivy so no harm might come to the brave man. In gratitude, he set me free."

"What happened to the captain?" asked Ariana.

"Pentheus captured him and sentenced him to death."

"And this story is supposed to make me feel better how?"

Bacchus waved. "Of course, I went back for him, silly. I ferried him to Olympus. Acetes still lives there today, working a sea of endless fish, piloting a gilded schooner with a crew of paradise's fairest mermaids. Not too shabby, ey?"

Ariana shook her head. "But you're no longer a god. I don't mean to be rude, but there's no one in this world who can stop Dezi. He's an animal. A machine. He will kill you and me both, then step out for a night on the town with no more guilt than if he'd squashed a couple of bugs."

"I may not be in top form, but I have an endless supply of powerful beings willing to help. One of the perks of having been the party god. Everyone loves me."

"Then why were you cast out?"

He stuck his tongue out at her. "Quiet, you. That was a philosophical issue, not an act of aggression."

Discordia's snake-like visage popped into his head. Still, if it resulted in the salvation of one of their children, no god in heaven would oppose his mission. He could but hope the Prince of Darkness wouldn't throw his hat in the ring. Lucifer had a habit of fighting for each and every soul he could add to his minions.

Perhaps Bacchus should mention the perils of their undertaking to Ariana, but then again, no. No sense bogging down the dear woman with facts immaterial to the case. Vig, Pan, and the demigods would keep their undertaking off the Devil's radar. It was, after all, only one teensy, little soul.

Nor had he bothered to mention the sorrows box or the fact he literally held her future in his hands. She had enough to deal with, or at least, this was how Bacchus soothed his nagging conscience.

"You really can do all you say you can?"

"That and more." Bacchus dotted her nose with his forefinger.

Rubbing her temples, she gave a soft groan. "My head is killing me."

"That's because you're exhausted and hungry." He placed a hand on her arm. "Come now, no more talk of being irredeemable."

A knock at the door interrupted their discussion. A handsome young waiter set up the bottle of wine and towering, double-decker sandwich. Bacchus caught himself admiring the youth's broad shoulders and narrow waist. Golden brown curls framed an angelic face. Ah-ah-ah. No time for distractions. Handing the waiter a fifty, he dismissed the boy.

"Is that not the most divine sandwich you've ever seen?" he asked, circling the plate under her nose. "Hmm?"

Ariana shrugged. "I guess so. Okay. Fine. I'll have a bit to eat, but only because you twisted my arm."

"Bite your tongue. I'm not fond of coercion, love. Seduction, however, is another matter altogether."

He handed her a goblet of Bordeaux, pleased a bit of twinkle had returned to her eyes.

\* \* \* \*

At closing time, Pan appeared to escort Ariana to the condo. Bacchus had some after-hours business to attend to, another favor to request from a goddess to whom he was already indebted. No matter, it would all come out in the wash.

"Sire," Pan whispered in his master's ear, "the specters of fear and despair have been absorbed into the box. Miss Ariana is free of them."

"Now, that is good news." He clapped his hands. Finally, some proof the plan had a hope in Hades of succeeding.

# Chapter 14

*Cowardice and Anger*

Bacchus sunk lower into the sofa cushions. He'd laid out his plan for Ariana, but instead of the praise he'd expected, she folded her arms across her chest and shook her head. "I should do this myself."

"But Ariana, please, it's an unnecessary risk. Why not let the pro handle it?"

"Because they're my things Dezi's holding hostage. My personal effects, not Purina's or Furita, or whatever her name is."

"Furina and she is the patron goddess of thieves. This is what she does best so why not let her do it? I'm not even going."

"I'm going, or we don't take back my stuff at all."

"Obstinacy, thy name is woman." Bacchus poured himself a glass of Pinot Grigio, then another. Ariana herself had complained last night at Eliseo she had none of her things, none of the pictures of her family, none of her clothes. No toiletries, no purse, no identification, not a cent to her name. *Nada.* And no hope to get any of it back because Dezi would have the condo staked out. Not to mention she didn't have a key to her own place. Part of Dezi's master plan to control her every move.

Now, here was Bacchus offering her a brilliant solution to the problem, and the woman had the gall to refuse. Sinking into a chair, he ran a hand through his hair. For several minutes, they sat in silence.

Finally, Ariana heaved a sigh. "It's not the things. And it's not that I doubt your friend's abilities, or that I'm ungrateful you've set this all up. It's just I want—I need to face this. I need to take back what's mine."

Hand to brow, Bacchus steeled himself for the conversation with Furina. The goddess would not be pleased.

\* \* \* \*

"Sure, no problem," the Goddess of Thieves said between pops of chewing gum.

Bacchus threw up his hands. Once, he had believed he understood the female psyche, but clearly, he could no more make this claim. As of late, they zigged when he thought they'd zag and zagged when he expected them to stand still. "Can you guarantee her safety?"

"Oh, yeah. That's no problem. I have Perseus's invisibility cloak around here somewhere. We'll be in and out before anyone knows we were there. I've been casing the place with the Oracle at Delphi. There are two goons parked out front and two in the alley. Dezi's usually out from noon until the wee hours of the morning. There's a shift change with the thugs around six, and they usually sit and bullshit for a while. I think that's the best time for us to slip in. She's got some premium clothes and jewels, electronics. It'll be a nice haul."

"How are we going to move all of it, just the three of us? I'm not as strong as I used to be, you know."

"Don't worry your pretty little head about it. I've got a bottomless bag, makes everything light as a feather. We could haul away the fridge in it if we wanted to. Do we want to? It's a nice ass fridge."

"I don't think so. Ariana only wants what's hers."

"That's all well and good, but I still get my cut. *Capisce*?"

"Understood and agreed." Bacchus nodded. "Thank you for doing this."

"No worries. It's like asking Midas to turn something to gold, you know?"

They concluded their meeting with a firm handshake and a smile. Tomorrow evening, Ariana would have her chance to face down the evil that plagued her.

* * * *

Furina materialized with Bacchus and his lady friend in the middle of Ariana's apartment dressed in fluorescent pink. Contrary to popular belief, the goddess had no need for black or camouflage; her considerable will alone hid her presence from prying eyes. With all the usual precautions in place—a distraction charm on the goons outside, protection spell on domicile—it was time to get to work.

"Where do we start, sugar lips?" the goddess asked Ariana.

"In the bedroom, most of what I want is in there, though I've got some photo albums in the living room and some cookware in the kitchen. I'll need to sort through some of it."

"You're kidding me. This would be so much easier if you'd let me whisk everything into my bag in one swoop. You can sort it out somewhere else."

"No." Ariana was insistent. "Dezi bought most of this, and I don't want it."

Bacchus gave his colleague an apologetic look. It seemed his therapeutic exercise was turning out to be more complex than he'd anticipated. With the flick of her wrist, Furina could clean out the joint, but he intended to make Ari feel empowered, so he begged the goddess for a little latitude.

"It's your party." Furina shrugged, though she did swipe the considerable DVD collection into her magic sack when Ariana was busy in the bedroom.

Bacchus watched the goddess work her way through an entire package of Bubbalicious—strawberry, judging from the scent—and Ariana had yet to emerge from behind closed doors.

He poked his head in and asked, "You all right, love?"

But he saw from her tear-stained face, she was far from all right. He crossed the room and enveloped her in hug.

"What's wrong?"

"It's gone," she croaked.

"What's gone?"

"My mother's wedding ring. It's gone. I can't find it anywhere."

Bacchus had a theory about what had happened to the ring, but he kept quiet. There was no point upsetting her further. "We'll find it. I promise. But we have to clear out of here soon."

"No, we have to clear out of here, now." Furina's gruff voice in the doorway drew the couple's attention. "One of the ape squad is in the living room. I froze time before he saw me, but we have to go. The Council gets really bitchy when you stop time for too long, so let's vamoose."

"But—" The objection melted on the woman's lips. In a flash as bright as lightening, they popped from Ariana's apartment to Bacchus's living room, and all the contents of her apartment had come with them.

Bacchus's mouth ran dry as he surveyed the wall-to-wall garage sale that had once been his spacious domicile. Surround-sound system equipment stacked on top of his wet bar, another sofa stacked on top of his. A king-size bed clogged the pathway to his kitchen, not to mention all the tchotchkes littering every available surface. The woman must have had a thousand glass figurines of angels—and every one had landed in his living room. Some of her delicates spun slowly from the blade of the ceiling fan. "Furina, what happened?"

The goddess shrugged. "We had to get out, so I transported all the stuff here. We didn't have time to be choosy."

Ariana's gaze roamed over her surroundings. "But I didn't want all of this. Not the furniture, not the electronics. Definitely not the appliances."

Furina snapped, and all but the woman's personal effects and clothes disappeared.

"Did you put the stuff back?" asked Ariana.

"Of course I did." The goddess rolled her eyes. "Not."

Sensing an argument between the two females, Bacchus stepped in and put his arm around his colleague. "Furi, thank you so much. Your help has been invaluable."

"No trouble, sweet cheeks." A grin twisted her petite red lips. "But next time, we'll leave the flesh bunny at home."

Bacchus wanted to point out to Furina that he, too, was now a "flesh bunny," but thought better of it. Instead, he kissed her hand and wished her a fond farewell.

"That's all I get?" Furina bristled. "What about that one-on-one time you promised me?"

Bacchus glanced nervously at Ariana. Furina gave a smirk of dissatisfaction, but without a sound, the goddess evaporated.

Ariana busied herself collecting her bras and panties. "I don't think she likes me very much."

"Gods and goddesses don't like anyone very much. We're—they're not the same emotionally as humans."

"What does that say about you?" She stopped cleaning to face him.

"Me? Oh, I love everybody. It's in my nature."

"Should I be worried?"

Bacchus made his way around the minefield that littered the floor—more angel figurines. He put his arms around her. The softness of her skin and the vanilla scent of her hair filled him with warmth. "Not a bit, love. Not a bit."

Turning her face, she gave an exaggerated exhalation. "We're never going to get all this cleaned up."

He picked up a porcelain depiction of the archangel Michael. The naive image amused him. Michael, all ivory skin and blond curls. In reality, he was fire incarnate.

"Michael looks nothing like this," said Bacchus.

She took the small statue from him. "The angel collection was my mother's, too."

"Well, don't worry. Pan will find a safe place for everything."

In a burst of fur, the satyr appeared. Ariana gave a muffled shriek.

"My apologies, madam. Didn't mean to startle you." He turned to Bacchus. "You need me, sire?"

"Yes, Pan." Bacchus motioned to the mess around the house. "Could you get all this into Ariana's room? Oh, and see if her mother's wedding ring is somewhere in this chaos?"

In less than a second, all of Ariana's things vanished, and Pan grimaced. "No ring, sire."

"Thank you, Pan. That's all for tonight."

"You are very welcome, sire." Pan vanished in an explosive cloud of fur.

Bacchus dusted himself off and held out a hand to Ariana. "Shall we?" He nodded to the couch.

"I'm too keyed up to sit. I know Dezi has my mother's ring."

He picked up a bottle of Cabernet Sauvignon and steered her to his sofa. "I'll give you a massage and help you relax. And I promise, we shall find your mother's ring. Don't you worry your beautiful little head."

"All right. I put myself in your hands."

After settling her onto her stomach across the couch cushions, he rubbed his hands together to warm them. A master of Shiatsu, Swedish, and every other discipline of massage, he knelt on the floor beside her and began to knead her neck muscles. As his mind wandered, he let out a soft chuckle.

"What's so funny?" she murmured.

"I was thinking. Can you imagine that meat puppet's face when he entered an apartment full of stuff, and then a second later he found himself surrounded by nothing?" Bacchus mimed a shocked expression.

Ariana turned to look at him and gave a halfhearted giggle. "Yeah, well, Dezi's reaction won't be so amusing."

"Love, it's either laugh or cry." Bacchus waved away her concern and went back to work on her lumbar region in silence. "I choose laughter."

The snicker started small, but grew in intensity until a belly laugh shook the tiny woman. She rolled onto her back, still laughing. "You're right. I'd give anything to have seen that guy's face."

Bacchus joined her in a fit of raucous laughter.

# Chapter 15

*Survival*

Images flashed across the panel, threatening to swallow the wall across from Bacchus's sofa. Television—Ariana had suggested they watch a bit to take her mind off her troubles. After a quick visit from Hephaestus, the appliance flared to life.

Bacchus had heard so many bad things about TV, but as puerile as the programming might be, he couldn't tear his attention away from the infernal contraption, unless, of course, he had to refill his wine glass.

Ariana sat next to him, nibbling popcorn. All evening she'd explained to him the plot lines of the dubious morality plays performed on this display of light and magic.

"What you're telling me," he said, "is that these folks are abandoned in a treacherous climate to survive as ancient people once did."

"Yes, that's why it's called *Survivor*. I mean the show's crew is there if there's an emergency or something."

"And the contestants have to form tribes, and every week someone is eliminated from said tribes?"

She nodded.

"Do they execute the cast out member?"

"No." She laughed. "No. The player that's voted off goes home until the season finale."

Bacchus wrinkled his nose and furrowed his brow. "Then, what exactly have they 'survived'? A few weeks of a bland diet and no shower? The world has gotten awfully soft. Gladiators of old fought until the death."

Ariana cast a look around Bacchus's home. "You're one to talk, Mr. I-can't-survive-in-this-hell-you-call-Earth."

"That's different."

"Uh-huh."

"It is. I was a god, Ari. A god. Now, I'm a mortal, not even a human. I'm some sort of undefined, in-between creature. Imagine not only how you live changes, but your fundamental make up. All things considered, I think I've handled the disgrace admirably."

"What disgrace?"

Bacchus rubbed his forehead. "Didn't Pan show you?"

"He did. I know you were thrown out, but I don't know why."

A knot formed in the pit of his stomach. He doused it with a few gulps of Cabernet. *In vino veritas.* Bacchus liked to think he had no idea why he'd been cast aside. Were he honest with himself, he did know the reason, but how to express it?

"I think my decline was centuries in the making. It's hard to assign blame to one action or lack thereof."

"But what was the final straw? They had to give you some explanation."

"They did, not that I fully understand it. The Father said my gifts caused more misery than joy."

Ariana put a warm hand against his arm. "In my experience, that's true."

Her candor slashed at his core. Staring into the flickering candle on the cocktail table, a metaphor occurred to him. He ran his fingertips over the coolest part of the flame.

"It's like fire. Harnessed properly, fire is an indispensable tool. It provides warmth, lights darkness, cooks food. Left unconstrained, it can be an agent of devastation and destruction, but I don't see Prometheus sharing my fate. Oh sure, he had his liver eaten out daily by an enormous eagle for thousands of years, but once he and dear old Dad patched things up, it's all sunshine and lollipops for him.

"Anyway, the responsibility to use Prometheus's gift wisely lies with the user. My gifts are no different."

"Fine. But how is intoxication a useful tool?"

"Ah, the lamentable Puritanism running rampant these days. Not to mention the—as you said—'creature comforts' available to some modern humans. It was not always so, my dear. And isn't so for millions of your brethren today."

She fidgeted with the ends of her hair. "You don't have to tell me. I've heard the stories about Cuba from Papa."

"Then you have part of the picture. But imagine Cuba without as much modern convenience as it has."

At the height of Bacchus's power, when the Earth was still golden and green and smoke belched only from Pele's volcanoes, the life of a human was a harsh cruel thing.

Pain, disease, the daily struggle for survival, made every second of every day at best hard labor and at worst excruciating pain. With no corner drugstore to turn to, the liquid produced by fermented grains and fruits provided respite from physical and emotional agony. But more than that, it could be used alone or in conjunction with herbal concoctions to connect with alternate states of consciousness. The divine.

Different cultures used different words to describe the state—rapture, ecstasy, bliss, grace. From tribal shamans to St. Teresa de Avila, when the human mind is freed from its boundaries, it has the ability to achieve great spiritual revelations. Bacchus's gifts were at the core of the revelations. Which was not to say alcohol was the only intoxicant he championed. The scent of a lover's hair, the curve of full lips, the feel of one body against another, orgasmic pleasure, all served to bring human beings closer to understanding themselves and their place in the higher order.

"I don't think so," Ariana said. "The main purpose of sex is reproduction."

"Is it? If that were true, why was the act blessed with such pleasurable side effects?"

"I don't know. I'm not a biologist. I'm sure the physical pleasure serves a purpose."

"Look at the vast majority of species in this world. They reproduce either asexually or through copulation that is no more than a physiological imperative. Not so with humans. There is seduction, free will, and ecstasy. Sweet tremulous orgasms that rock the body and spirit."

Color rushed to Ariana's cheeks. "Well, when you put it that way… But drugs and alcohol lead to more trouble than they're worth."

"Tell me this. When you have a headache, what do you do?"

"Take a couple aspirin, but that's different."

"Is it? Without my gifts, how would humans know they could alter their body chemistry with other chemical compounds? A substance like aspirin would never have been discovered."

"You're taking credit for aspirin?"

"Not directly, but alcohol was one of the first medicinal substances known to man. I paved the road, so to speak, and I'm tired of being seen as disposable. Expendable. I care about humans as much as the next god. Not to mention, everyone's gifts have their dark side, and some are created only of darkness. Take war for example. What good does war serve? But I don't see Ares out on his leather-clad fanny."

"Okay." She stroked his arm. "Okay, I see your point. Did you argue your case this passionately with the Council?"

He shifted, folding his arms across his chest, the knot in his stomach churning harder. "Uh, no. I was blindsided by the dismissal."

"You had no clue this was coming down?"

Bacchus ran his hands through his silky curls. Were he honest with himself, he'd have to admit his tenure as a god had been in steady decline since the fall of the Roman Empire. And that lunatic, Carrie A. Nation, didn't help much. Prohibition. Bacchus shuddered at the thought. Point of fact, he'd been a minor deity for centuries, and he told Ariana as much.

She stroked his arm. "Sorry if this sounds harsh, but it seems to me you weren't demoted because your gifts aren't useful. It's because you didn't make sure they were used in a responsible way. You let things happen instead of making them happen."

In no mood for any more introspection, Bacchus pressed his lips together and focused on the TV screen.

Ariana tried to make more conversation, but he shushed her, pretending he wanted to hear the show. The tribal council was about to vote out a castaway. After a barrage of commercials, the council's decision was revealed. A strong, charismatic player found himself the victim of an alliance's machinations. When the young man extinguished his torch, Bacchus's heart went out to him.

His throat felt as though a vice tightened around it; his skin felt hot and cold at the same time. Ariana's point hit home. Perhaps the castaway didn't deserve to be put out, but he had been all the same because he'd thought he was untouchable. By Hades, if that infernal woman hadn't hit the nail on the head and gotten under his skin. Unaccustomed to feeling anything akin to humiliation, Bacchus excused himself with the intention of retiring to the master's suite.

"Did I upset you?" Ariana asked.

"Not at all, love. Not at all." He rushed from the room.

Hands shaking, he splashed cold water on his face. How unpleasant to be accosted by guilt, shame, embarrassment, and sadness all at once. He'd never experienced such complex emotions as a god and couldn't bear the sensation. If he'd been given to violence against himself, he would've dug his heart out of his chest and, as his last action in this realm, cast it off the balcony to be flattened by a passing car. Or better, a Mack truck. But how could he compound the tragedy that had become his life by desecrating the exquisite form he admired in the mirror? Somehow, he had to pull it together.

A faint knock interrupted his bout of self-pity. When he didn't answer, Ariana peeked around the bedroom door, eyes closed. "Are you dressed?"

"Yes." He blew out a sigh. His ears burned, and a knot twisted in his already roiling stomach. Was she here to point out more inadequacies Bacchus was loath to face?

She opened her eyes and gave him a searching look, but if she expected him to break the silence, she was sorely mistaken.

He crossed the room, poured himself a glass of scotch, and downed it in one gulp.

"I—I think I've upset you. I know you say I didn't, but well, it's kind of obvious." She picked at one fingernail.

"You haven't upset me, love. My general lack of usefulness has upset me." He poured himself another drink. What he wanted to say—what he'd meant to say—was when faced with her selflessness and restraint, he felt small and spoiled, a self-indulgent child in the presence of a saint. It mattered to him what she thought of him. It mattered to him that she see him in a positive light. He said none of those things. Instead, he tossed back the amber liquor and growled at the fire racing down his throat.

She sat gingerly on the edge of his bed. "Would you like some company?"

"No, thank you." He poured another drink.

"I don't think I should leave you alone in this state."

Bacchus waved. "I think this is the perfect time for you to leave me alone."

Cheeks splotched with red, she hopped to her feet.

He caught her hand. "I'm sorry. My stupid words are exactly why I think you should abandon me tonight. I don't mean to vex you."

She offered a hollow chuckle. "Yes, we wouldn't want you to vex me."

Bacchus ran a fingertip down her cheek and neared her lips, but stopped short. He couldn't bring himself to touch their velvet softness. "You see? Stupid words."

She nodded and bade him good night.

Only after she'd left the room, he whispered, "Sleep with the cherubim and seraphim, sweet lady."

\* \* \* \*

Once he was sure Ariana had retired to her bedroom, Bacchus settled onto the sofa with his scotch, unable to sleep with the lead weight in his chest. By the time he'd dulled his senses enough to pass out—which required nearly the entire bottle—Pan appeared in a flurry of goat hair.

*Thhhbt. Thhhbt.* The cast-out deity tried to blow the fuzz from his lips and cackled. "What up, player?" The colloquialism sounded strange, even to himself.

"Oh, sire. You're in bad shape."

"I beg to differ. For the first time tonight I feel fantastic."

"I see. I stopped by to let you know cowardice and anger have disappeared."

Bacchus stumbled to his feet and hooked an arm around his friend. "Have I told you lately that I love you?"

"Perhaps not in those words, but yes. And thank you." Pan struggled against Bacchus's grip around his neck. "May I help you to bed, sire?"

A half-hiccup, half-wet burp worked its way up Bacchus's throat. "That might be wise."

The moment he hit the mattress, Bacchus began to lose consciousness. The last thing he remembered was another shower of goat fur from Pan's exit.

# Chapter 16

*Truth and Consequences*

A jangling screech—which turned out to be the ringing in his ears—tore Bacchus from his slumber. Light blasted around the edges of his blackout drapes. His pillow wet from a round of cold sweats, he felt as though he'd been eaten by Cerberus and shat out.

"By Hades." He sat up. A wave of nausea hit him. Ariana's words from the night before tumbled around his brain. One would think the condition known as a hangover would be incentive enough for humans to regulate their visits to the realm of intoxication. Thank the Father and Mother for ibuprofen. He staggered into the kitchen.

Ariana was gathering supplies for breakfast.

"Please, water and Advil. Lots and lots of Advil." His voice sounded as though he'd gargled with kitty litter. The taste of his breath made him wonder if indeed he had.

She handed him the items along with a cup of strong coffee. "Rough night?"

"Yeah."

"Did you go out after I went to bed?"

"Nope."

Studying the cup of coffee on the counter before her, she chewed at her thumbnail. "I didn't mean to upset you last night."

"You didn't. You were right. I've never taken responsibility for my position in the Cosmos. My life has been one, long adolescent party."

"Well, you are the god of those kinds of things."

"Was. Was the god of such things." He rubbed his temples and closed his eyes in an attempt to block out the sunlight assailing him. "Time to grow up at bit, perhaps."

"Like not downing a bottle of scotch because you're upset?"

Bacchus squinted at her, heat creeping up his neck and ears.

"Come with me," she said, leading him to the sofa. After tucking him in with a pillow and blanket in front of the TV, she headed to the kitchen and started to cook. The most divine scent of chicken, tomato, and herbs permeated the condo. It even broke through his intense queasiness and stimulated his appetite.

About ninety minutes later, she clicked off the television, interrupting his first viewing of a game show that entailed guessing the monetary value of household products.

"But I was watching that. It's fascinating."

"Leave the TV off." She balanced a tray on his lap and headed into the kitchen. When she returned, she brought with her a bowl full of fragrant soup. After placing the bowl on the tray, she flipped open a napkin and tucked it into his collar. He leaned forward and took in a deep breath, inhaling the delicious aroma.

"What is this heavenly concoction?" he asked.

"*Sopa de pollo*—chicken soup."

"No, no, no. I've had chicken soup. Soggy noodles that slither out of a can with what can only be described as 'flakes' of chicken to accompany them. This is not chicken soup." He inhaled again and stirred the rich, golden broth with a spoon. A riot of color swirled around the bowl— vegetables presumably, though Bacchus wasn't very familiar with said food group. Chunks of chicken marinated in a bath of herbs and spices. He slurped a mouthful and patted his lips with the napkin. The broth left behind a silky feel on his lips. Complex flavors heightened the simple ingredients.

"By the gods, woman. You are a sorceress in the kitchen," he muttered, cheeks still stuffed with sofrito and meat.

Ariana gave a soft chuckle under her breath as she retrieved a cup for herself. "I'm glad you think so."

After she sank into the sofa cushion next to him, they ate in relative silence. He longed to think of something to say, but nothing came to mind. When he'd finished his soup, she took the bowl from him and walked to the sink.

"Feel better?" she asked.

"I do, very much so. That is a miraculous preparation, Ariana. Thank you."

"You're welcome." She pursed her lips. "Papa always needed a bowl or two after a bad night."

He reached for the remote control but caught a look of Ari's consternation. "What's wrong, love?"

She walked over to him and snatched the remote from him. "Didn't we just have this discussion last night?"

"I'm sorry?" Bacchus bit the inside of his cheek. What in the Cosmos was she talking about?

"Seriously?" She shook her head. "Last night, you're all remorseful because you let your position as a god slip away, and you drown your sorrows in a vat of alcohol. And today, you're content to watch *The Price Is Right* all day?"

"Do you think it's still on?" Excitement bloomed in his chest. He'd found the pageantry of the show quite engaging.

She growled at him. "Do you even have a plan to get back your rightful place?"

"You know I do. We eliminate the root of all suffering from your life—Dezi, and then I get my domain back. Easy peasy."

"And how are you going to go about eliminating Dezi from my life? Stealing my things back is one thing, convincing him to leave me alone is another."

Bacchus opened his mouth, but no words came. She was right. He hadn't thought anything through yet.

She shook her head. "Your silence makes me feel so much better... Seems to me you have some things to think about."

Bacchus stared, mind reeling and gridlocked all at once. He knew she was right. He knew he had started something he had no idea how to finish. Any move would be better than sitting there useless and idle, but he couldn't force himself to rise...Ariana pulled him to his feet. Shoving him toward the shower in the master bath, she collected a pair of charcoal Versace slacks and a black dress shirt.

"Shower, shave, and then put these on."

He shrugged and did as instructed. When he emerged from his room, she stood in the living room, arms crossed, gaze fixed out the picture window somewhere far away. She did not turn to acknowledge him, but spoke in an even tone.

"My mother used to tell me, 'a dream is a wish without a plan.' Are you wishing or planning, Bacchus? Because it's not fair to get my hopes up if you're not serious."

His throat constricted. Damn these mortal emotions. He'd hurt less if she'd stabbed him in the chest. Instead of spilling hot blood over his skin, she'd given him another kind of wound. One that turned his blood to ice.

After crossing the floor in a few strides, he stopped behind her and studied her reflection in the glass. Her face, her eyes, her lips, all remained still. No twinkle of thought or downturn of her mouth to give him any indication what he should do next. He'd have to rely on the scant instincts he'd developed during his time on Earth.

Bacchus placed his hands on her shoulders with the lightest of touches. "I promise you, love, I am serious."

She nodded, as if to say she'd heard the words, but had yet to believe them.

Though Bacchus had never before been called upon to prove his worth, he swore to himself that this time he would not fail or become distracted. This time, he would see something—one thing—through to its conclusion.

He turned and left the condo. It was time to get to work.

* * * *

A timid knock at his office door broke Bacchus's concentration. It was hard enough for him to focus on the task at hand without this intrusion.

"What is it?"

"Sorry, Mr. Sabazios, but there's a problem. Some…some thugs, for lack of a better word, are at the back door, and they won't leave until you come out," the head bartender, Fede said.

Bacchus didn't have time for this silliness this morning. Summoning Pan, he marched to the back of the club. Dezi and his goon squad waited there, and Pan strolled up behind them.

"Mr. Desiderio, so kind of you to drop by this afternoon," Bacchus said.

"Fuck you, *puto*. You know why I'm here." Droplets of spittle flew from Dezi's lips. His hands shook, clenched in fists at his side.

"Oh my, Panny. I think he's a little upset with me. I can't imagine why." Bacchus turned to Fede. "Perhaps a round of drinks for everyone. I'll take a Bloody Mary. Dezi?"

In reply, Dezi ground his teeth.

"Nothing, then? You're sure?" asked Bacchus.

"Stop fucking around. You have twenty-four hours to give me back my possessions—including that bitch—or else."

"Or else what?"

Dezi reached for his holster.

"There will be no need for that." Pan took a hold of the man's mind, and those of his crew, and stripped them of their weapons. When he let go, the thugs stumbled backward.

Taking several panted breaths, Dezi shook his head. "I don't know what the fuck is going on, but I promise you, *maricon*, if I don't have my shit by tomorrow, you're a dead man. I don't give a fuck what Santos says."

"Wait, wait. I saw an inscription the other day on the back of a car that's perfect for this situation. Now how did it go? Oh, yes. 'Your lips keep moving, but all I hear is blah, blah, blah.'"

The gang started their retreat, but Dezi turned to face Bacchus one last time. "Twenty four hours. I ain't fucking around."

Pan tossed the guns and knives in the dumpster. "That went well."

"Better than expected." Bacchus nodded. "Well, it's back to the grindstone."

His servant looked up with a quizzical look. "You're working on something?"

"Yes. I'm fleshing out the plan to help Ariana. And why are you looking at me like I'm giving birth to Zeus through my left nostril?"

"Well, sire, it's just that you don't—What I mean is, I've never seen you, you know, undertake something—anything like this, all by yourself."

Bacchus chewed on his lip and tried to think of a retort, but realized Pan was right. He clapped the satyr on the back. "You're right, old friend. Isn't it about time I do?"

"Well said, sire, so I shall leave you to it."

A flash of fur and then Pan was gone.

Once he'd returned to his office, Bacchus reviewed the papers he'd written. He'd mapped out the binary pairs of the sufferings. Fear and despair. Cowardice and anger. They'd been taken care of. That left Famine and poverty, envy and greed, cruelty and violence, and disease and death. The latter two pairs were easy to dissipate once Dezi was cast out of Ariana's life, either by cunning or by force. Famine and poverty, they were a different story.

First of all, Ariana was neither starving nor destitute. However, without Dezi's support, or the source of income Santos forced on her, she'd have only her job as a cocktail waitress. She might be able to support herself, but not exactly a stable career choice. From what Bacchus could tell, she had no advanced degrees, no trade training. He'd have to discuss with her a way to make her financially independent.

Bacchus could, of course, bestow upon her a large trust, but somehow, he knew the idea didn't have wings. She probably wouldn't accept the gift, and even if she did, the action wouldn't be a permanent solution to the threat of financial collapse. Give a man a bottle of wine, he drinks for a day. Teach the man to make wine, he drinks for a lifetime. Using this philosophy, they'd have to figure out a career that suited Ariana and could sustain her for all her days.

Envy and greed proved more confusing to Bacchus. Ariana didn't seem to covet anything. She longed only for freedom. How these specters applied to her life, he had yet to figure out. He wrote the words over and over, but couldn't figure out what Ariana was greedy for or envious about.

Anyone else, Bacchus could've pinned down their desires no problem. These things came through in their aura loud and clear. But Ariana's aura was all sunshine and buttercups, except for the dark cloud Dezi's polluted soul cast over her. Since she'd been free of that evil man, even that darkness had lifted.

Dezi. The source of all her darkness. The man was made of nothing but sin, envy, and greed. Maybe that was it. Perhaps the specters had inflicted envy and greed on her through him. He desired her. No, not her. Control over her. He tried to possess her with his jealousy. And violence.

If his theory were true about envy and greed, then the same could be said for cruelty and violence. Even disease and death. No doubt, Dezi would've killed her one day in a murderous rage.

The demigods had hit the nail on the head. Eliminating Dezi from her life in some permanent way would be a good place to start. And Bacchus had come up with a way to do exactly that. Operation Pentheus. Oh, how very clever.

But her healing had to go deeper. She had to understand the beauty inside her and of the world around her. Only then would she be free. And that's where Bacchus intended to start, with Ariana's sense of self. If he could hold up a mirror and help her sees herself, the way he did, she'd have to see her inner worth. Simple as that. Simple, but not easy.

# Chapter 17

*Famine and Poverty*

The question Bacchus had posed to Ariana had been straightforward enough. What did she want to do with the rest of her life? But for some reason, the woman seemed unable to answer it. "So, what you're saying is, you have no idea, no inkling of what you have a passion for?"

"How to make you understand this?" She leaned against the kitchen counter and rubbed a palm across her forehead. "Humans are not born with a map or instructions. Most people spend their entire lives struggling to find themselves. All I've ever done is take care of my father. And try not to piss off Dezi while performing at Santos's beck and call."

Bacchus worked on opening a bottle of Chateaux La Tour de Rothschilde. "Perhaps you should be a tightrope walker."

She barked out a sarcastic laugh. "Yeah, maybe you're right."

He set aside the decanter. "We'll let that breathe. Shall we adjourn to the sofa?"

Shoulders humped and head hung low, she allowed him to steer her to the couch. She tucked her legs beneath her as she sat down. Bacchus took the seat next to her.

The woman's lips went from slack and expressionless to a hard, thin line. Her eyes glittered with tears.

"Ariana, what's wrong?"

She wiped underneath her eyelashes and cast her gaze toward the ceiling. "Everything, Bacchus. Everything."

"Take a breath." He rubbed her back, his own chest tightening. It was as if all the time they'd spent with each other since the night on the yacht had left him no better aware of her needs. At least as far as emotions were concerned.

Luckily, she through him a lifeline and asked, "What was it like?"

"What, love?"

She waved in an all-encompassing gesture. "You know, being sure from the day you were born what your life would be all about."

Bacchus stroked his chin. He remembered being taken from his mother's womb. He remembered being sewn into Zeus's thigh, the sound of thunder that coursed through his father's body and into his. It was by this force Bacchus burst forth when it was time to join the world.

And in some ways, his existence had been just as Ariana had said. He'd known as long as he'd existed that he held the power of life at his fingertips. And death. But Bacchus had chosen the majority of his tenure as a god to focus on life. Life sprang forth at the touch of his feet on the earth. He could coax open flower petals with a kiss. He never once had to question anything or think beyond the here and now. Gods didn't die. They didn't retire—unless forced to do so. Little about their existence changed.

"It was...comfortable. And easy."

"I bet it was." She nodded. "What about when you lost it all? What was that like?"

Bacchus studied his cuticles. "Hard to say. It's been one big jumble of feelings I can't put a name to—which in and of itself seems cruel and unusual punishment."

"I guess it would."

His fingers grazed her length of her arm. "But getting to know you feels like I'm being rewarded. Everything that was once so simple had become complex and unnavigable. But now, with you again, things appear quite simple again, like when I was a child."

Touching her palm to his fingers, she held his hand against her upper arm. "I wish things were simple for me."

"Maybe they are." The contact with her skin warmed him from head to toe. "What did you dream about being when you were a child?"

She chuffed. "A princess. I had a tiara and everything."

Princess. Princesses. What were princesses known for? Something she'd said earlier when they'd talked about Dezi...gifts he'd given her. A glimmer of an idea lit up the dark space of Bacchus's mind. "I think I know what we should do."

"Oh yeah? What's that?"

He rubbed her hand, the tightness in his chest and abdomen giving way. "Let's get you unpacked."

\* \* \* \*

Across Bacchus's dining table lay several sets of sparkling jewels. Whatever could be said about Dezi, he certainly liked to spend money. A little on the gaudy side, but each necklace, bracelet, and set of earrings would impress even Hades—the god of the Underworld and riches.

Ariana chewed on her bottom lip and hissed out a heavy exhalation. "I don't know if I feel good about this."

"I know you don't, but it's a brilliant idea." He leaned against the table, looking up at her, and tried to catch her gaze.

Her brows drew together, but she offered no response.

"You don't have to decide today," he said.

She nodded, and he studied her face. To the uninitiated outsider, her expression might appear placid, but Bacchus knew better. It was a mask, one she wore whenever she felt confused or frightened or overwhelmed. It appeared for all the world that she was under control, and if he didn't have the ability to see the storm beneath, he might've bought the act. So much conflict, so much pain. She needed guidance, and though Bacchus was not known for his sage advice, he would give it his best shot.

He took her by the hand and led her to the sofa, away from the dazzling manifestation of Dezi's warped sense of love.

Bacchus put his arm around her and rubbed her shoulder. He offered her a drink from his glass of wine, and she accepted.

After Bacchus took a sip himself, he said, "I know you don't want to profit from your relationship with that man, but dear, the proceeds from these gifts could set you up for a long time. Turn the missteps of the past into a brighter future."

The idea was this—take the considerable jewelry Dezi had purchased for Ariana and throw an auction at Eliseo, all the profits to go toward setting her up in her own place and pay for a few semesters of school, though she hadn't a clue what she wanted to study. But if Bacchus had learned anything here on Earth, it was the power of riches. True, money couldn't buy happiness, but it sure as Hades could purchase freedom and give one choices. Both of which Ariana desperately needed.

"I'll think about it, okay?" she said and took another long drink of wine. As she handed the glass back to him, a bead of red streaked from her upper lip to the edge of the bottom one. It beckoned to him, and he longed to dab at it with the tip of his tongue. Instead, he cupped her face and wiped the drop with his thumb.

Her mouth opened, but her words caught in her throat. Her gaze flickered upward, met his then darted away. He moved his fingers across her lips. Her breath heated his palm, and he fought with himself. Every fiber of his being needed to kiss her, but he wasn't at all sure if he should.

While Bacchus struggled with a rare bout of indecision, she swept away his doubts by closing her eyes and sliding her cheek against his hand. Her head rested there, her exhalations picking up speed.

He saw her spirit, a spotted fawn nestled in the grass. Vulnerable and a little scared, she welcomed the contact because she needed to be comforted. This was no time to make a play for seduction despite the erection pressing at the fly of his pants. He grappled for control of his arousal, their lips so close a mere dip of his head would close the gap. How sweet it would be to taste her, to inhale the wine on her breath. Were her lips as soft and smooth as he imagined? Would she tremble as he caressed the expanse of caramel colored skin that ran from her throat to the swell of her breasts? He longed to bury his face between her thighs and draw in the musky scent of her sex. But he would do no such thing.

Closing his eyes and swallowing hard, he put his arms around her and held her. Merely held her.

Her face buried in his neck sent set off goosebumps along his chest and arms.

"I don't know what to do," she murmured.

Though he felt the same, he tried to project an air of confidence—and prevent his hard cock from poking into her hipbone.

"Everything will be all right. You'll see."

She looked up at him, her eyes studying his bare neck and arms. Her fingertips grazed the dots of his pebbled flesh. "Are you cold?"

He shook his head, dropping her gaze.

"I thought you were going to kiss me." She breathed the words more than spoke them.

Throat tight and words strangling him, he pushed out a reply. "I was going to."

"Then, why didn't you? I wanted you to."

He parted his lips to answer, but his tongue stuck to the roof of his mouth. By the time he had peeled it off and tried to offer her an explanation, she had pulled away and put a finger to his lips.

"It's okay. I know. You don't have to say it, 'It's not you...'" the thought wilted on her lips. She made her way to her bedroom and closed the door.

He blew out a sigh and finished the sentence. "It's me."

\* \* \* \*

Two days later, the printer's proofs of the invitation had arrived via e-mail. Ariana took a bite of eggs and turned her laptop toward Bacchus.

"Which do you like?" she asked.

He washed down a bite of strawberry with a gulp of mimosa. "The more ornate one, with the gold scroll work."

She checked the appropriate box and sent a reply to the printer. Grinning sideways at him, she said, "This is coming together, isn't it?"

Indeed, it was. Though Bacchus had helped to get the word out by enlisting the aid of Hermes, the messenger god—Ariana had organized the entire thing. From the music to the models to the catering menu, the woman was a dynamo with details. She'd researched how to pull off an auction like this, made the plan, and then executed it without a hitch. That she'd decided to use Bacchanal as the theme for the party brought a tear to his eye.

The last few details remained, such as save-the-date cards for the patrons on Eliseo's mailing list, but with those ordered, she and Bacchus were rounding the home stretch. Who knew party planning could entail so much work? Back at Olympus, all he'd ever had to do to whip up a soiree was contemplate the desire to engage in one.

"What's your plan for the day?" she asked and speared a strip of ham.

"I was thinking I'd lounge around here until I have to leave for work."

"So, business as usual," she said in a teasing tone.

"Well, yeah. What's on your considerable agenda today, love?"

"The Bacardi rep is coming at noon to let me sample some limited edition aged rum. I want to pick something special for the Bacchanal. Would you like to come with me or should I swipe your credit card from your wallet and leave you to your lounging."

"You had me at 'aged rum.'"

She laughed, put her hand on his thigh, and kissed his cheek. She'd become more and more comfortable sharing moments of physical intimacy with him—a fact that both emboldened and distressed him. His breath caught in his throat.

"I know, I know. A baby deer in the grass and all that." She half-grimaced at him, but he could tell she wasn't really put out.

He exhaled. After the near miss in the kitchen, he had explained why he wanted to take things slowly. Of course, this reticence to throw her down and make mad, passionate love to her was all new to him. By the gods, it wasn't that he didn't want to sink himself into her perfumed flesh. The growing tension inside his blue jeans gave testimony to that fact. Speaking of which, he tried to make a subtle adjustment to keep from injuring himself against the zipper.

"I'm sorry. It's just every time I look at you, that's what I see," he said.

"Don't be sorry." She kissed his cheek. "It's sweet. Weird, but sweet."

She picked up his hand and pressed it against her much smaller one. "Do you think you'll ever see me differently?"

"This current display of your diminutive size isn't helping." He nodded at the comparison of their palms. "But yes, the images you cast out keep evolving. I think this is just a phase."

"Let's hope so." She interlaced her fingers with his and used her free hand to stroke the back of his neck, toying with locks of his hair.

He chewed at his lip. "Evil temptress."

She stuck out her tongue and flitted off to change as if unaware of the feelings she stirred in him. And she was unaware of the immense restraint required to keep himself from acting on those feelings. It was a restraint Bacchus had no idea he possessed until now.

Since his first lover, the satyr Ampelos, who became the grapevine from which Bacchus made the first wine, to the incomparable Aphrodite, a parade of consorts attended to Bacchus's every sexual desire. His travels to explore other realms of spirituality brought him a wealth of willing partners from exotic goddesses to frenzied women who made up the bulk of his followers. Whenever the urge struck the god, a willing body—or three—awaited his passion. He'd never once thought to delay gratification. The notion still seemed absurd, and yet, a strange enjoyment came from resisting temptation, tamping down the lust he felt for Ariana. The more she tempted him, the greater the enjoyment he derived from holding out for the right moment.

Bacchus licked his lips and savored the ghost of the feeling that her fingers still tickled the back of his neck though she'd left him here to stew in his desire. He imagined sinking himself inside her and feeling her breath across his ear. She would kiss and nibble and lick at the junction of his jawline and throat. His hands roaming over her golden skin, a mouthful of her large breast. By the gods, his shaft ached for her.

She disrupted his flight of fantasy, high-heeled shoes clacking against the hard wood floor. "You ready to go?"

"In a second." He shifted his shirttails, attempting to conceal his arousal.

Resplendent in a peach colored silk shirt and cream linen slacks, she fiddled with the clasp on a pair of small gold hoop earrings, still oblivious. Still beautiful.

Evil temptress, indeed.

# Chapter 18

*Bacchanalia*

Bacchus pulsed to the Mambo beat shaking Eliseo's dance floor. All of Ariana's meticulous planning came to fruition. Spinning disco balls and lights, bejeweled the sea of slick flesh. The party swung with an energy all its own, as any good Bacchanal should. The crowd pulsated with heat and sexuality.

Through the middle of the throng ran a long, black catwalk. Models marched by, displaying Ariana's considerable jewelry collection for partygoers in a circuit of poses. For the right bids, several wealthy patrons would leave the soiree with these stunning pieces.

Not even at the height of his power and adoration could the god have put together a more raucous bash. Okay, he could have, but it would have been purely by accident. That she seemed to have a skill for organizing a gala further cemented the fact she was his perfect match.

An energizing fervor seeped into his pores, coursed through his veins. His chest swelled with excitement and arousal. Jiggling mounds of flesh, curvaceous forms everywhere. Pouts, simpers, and youth as fresh as morning dew surrounded him, but his attention drew to the center of the swirling frivolity—Ariana.

Clad in a simple white dress, her sparkling eyes and smile outshone every beauty in the room, no matter how lavishly adorned. Understated in his own couture—black tailored slacks and a black silk shirt—he reached for Ariana's hand.

"You have outdone all the gods of Olympus, love," he said.

She hugged his arm in response.

A waitress fluttered by, dropping two ice buckets with champagne for Bacchus. He thanked her and popped open the first one. Pouring a glass for each of them, he watched shades of delight and joy pass across Ariana's face.

When relaxed, her mouth resembled two rose petals on the gilded surface of her butterscotch complexion. When angry, it pulled together in the most tempting pucker, but when she laughed—like she had many times this evening—that same mouth became the gateway to heaven. Bacchus lost his himself in every euphonious note. Really, his heart had been hers for the taking since first they met.

"I can't believe we pulled this off," she said.

"You pulled this off. It's awe-inspiring."

"All right, let's not go overboard."

"I mean it. You've humbled me. And I'm supposed to be the master reveler. I mean the style of party is named after me. It's called a Bacchanal for a reason."

She looked up at him, her expression more serious than he would have expected. "Thank you. For everything."

Her gaze dropped and long, black lashes grazed her cheek. He took in her scent, springtime and fields of flowers. Heat and tension blossomed in the pit of his stomach as he realized the baby deer was long gone. He was losing his grip on his self-control, a silken rope slipping through his fingers.

Feeling out the moment, Bacchus slid a hand along her neck and cradled her face, brushing his thumb along her jawline. Cheek turning into the caress, she sighed. A thousand times before, he had made this same gesture with countless lovers, but never resulting in the singular warmth spreading through his core.

Sweetness.

Depth.

Reduced to one-word thoughts, he struggled to name what he felt. His considerable vocabulary came up short. Aware that actions spoke louder than words, he dipped his head, bringing his lips closer then paused. Would she come to him? Would she bridge the distance?

Joy spread through him as she leaned into the kiss. Their mouths grazed one another. Bacchus inhaled, the scent of her perfume reminding him of a fresh rainfall in the valley where he grew up. Home. Could true love be as simple as finding someone whose presence provided shelter after a long and pointless journey? Simple, yet at the same time, grand.

Deepening the kiss, Bacchus licked her tongue, tasted the champagne on her breath. She threaded her fingers in his hair, pulling him closer. He knew the music still blared, and a crush of humanity danced below, but heard nothing and saw nothing. His senses blocked out everything but Ariana. The most complete intoxication he'd ever known.

Bacchus traced her jawline with the back of his hand. The caress had just started to meander down her neck, but a rustle at the velvet curtain separating the balcony loge from the rest of the world drew his attention. Without hesitation, he stood, placing himself between Ariana and the unknown intruder.

"Sire, I'm sorry to interrupt," Pan said, "but we have a bit of a situation."

Bacchus took Ariana's hand and kissed it. "I'll be right back, love."

She gave an uncertain nod.

Following Pan through the curtain opening, Bacchus moved closer to the upstairs bar and farther from the speakers so he and Pan could talk without shouting.

"What's going on, Panny?"

"He's here, sire," the satyr said.

"Who?"

Pan picked at the skin around his thumbnail. "Dezi."

"What do you mean he's here? I thought you were going to put a protection charm on the club."

"Well, I did, but it's not so cut-and-dried." Pan fidgeted with his goatee. "If I used an Invitation-Only charm like I did with the condo, then guests you didn't invite to the club couldn't enter. That wouldn't be very good for business. And I tried an Evil-Out charm, but apparently, he's not pure evil, because he was able to enter."

"He's as close to pure evil as I've ever seen in a mortal." Bacchus shook his head. "Toss him out on his ass and make it clear if he shows up again, he'll be in several worlds' worth of hurt."

Pan accepted his orders and was about to take off down the stairwell, but Dezi had beaten them to the punch. He raced up the steps, a wolfish snarl on his face.

"Go to Ariana," Bacchus instructed his steward. The satyr flew toward the balcony loge. Bacchus folded his arms across his chest and hardened his expression. "Mr. Desiderio, what an unpleasant surprise."

Dezi narrowed his eyes but didn't respond in kind. Instead, he asked. "Where's Ariana?"

Bacchus studied his manicure. "That's none of your business anymore."

Shoving his hands in his pants pockets, Dezi set his jaw. "Look, *puto*, I'm not here to start any trouble with you."

"Your very presence here is starting trouble with me."

"Where's Ariana?"

"Last time I'm going to ask nicely." Bacchus pulled himself to his full height, a head taller than the man, and glared down at him. "Please, leave."

Dezi opened his mouth to reply, but Ariana's voice behind them caught both their attention.

Bacchus turned to see her striding at a clip down the hall, and Pan skittering after her.

"*Que carajo quieres*, Dezi?" Eyes narrow, lips pinched, she thrust her hands out to the side.

The man smirked and said to Bacchus, "You let her kiss you with that mouth?"

She marched up and planted her feet. "What do you want? Why are you here?"

Dezi drew up his shoulders. "It's a free country, isn't it? I mean, it's my shit you're selling off tonight. Don't I get to see how much you profit from the presents I gave you?"

Her eyes watered, but she tightened her face, as if she would not allow the tears to fall. "I might as well get something from the hell you put me through."

Good one. Bacchus moved closer.

Dezi turned around, ran a hand through his hair, and turned back to her. "Look, *mi'ja*, I didn't come here to fight."

She licked her lips. "Well, then?"

"I came to tell you I won't be bothering you or your little *maricon* boyfriend any more. Have a nice life, okay?"

Still towering over Dezi, Bacchus said, "That's very big of you."

Splotches of red colored the man's face, but he said nothing.

Ariana swiped her forehead with a shaking hand, but kept her voice even. "Thank you. Is that all you have to say?"

Dezi dipped his head to one side.

Bacchus clapped his hands together. "As much as we love having you here, Mr. Desiderio, please feel free to leave. Now."

Pan put a hand on the man's shoulder, but Dezi shook it off. He said, "I'm going. I'm going."

He turned to navigate the packed stairway, but Ariana shouted after him, "And I want my mother's wedding ring back."

Dezi looked over his shoulder, nodded, and proceeded down. Pan followed close behind.

Bacchus faced Ariana whose whole body trembled. He put his arms around her. "You did magnificently, love."

Burying her face in his chest, she hiccupped a strangled sob. "You think so?"

He wiped away a stray tear. "I know so."

"Thanks." Her grip on him tightened, and he stroked her hair, keeping an eye out lest any more surprises lurk in the dark corners.

A deep breath helped her regain her composure. She stepped back and wiped beneath her eyes again. She excused herself to the VIP ladies' room to fix her makeup.

He watched her walk away, the sway of her hips and the swish of her dress tempering his ire. He wondered what in Hades could've fueled Dezi's strange admission of defeat. It was too out-of-character. Too neat. Bacchus had no idea what had motivated the soulless one to make such an odd move, but now, Bacchus was really worried.

\* \* \* \*

The night's success mellowed into glowing exhaustion. The party and auction had pulled in high five figures, not that either of them cared right now. Not even Dezi's dramatics tainted their good mood.

Ariana's head in his lap, he reclined against one sofa arm, legs stretched out on an ottoman, and fed her fat, luscious grapes, one at a time.

She munched and swallowed. "Shouldn't you peel these for me?"

The suggestion tickled him. "I wouldn't even know how to go about it."

"So back in the day, you had people to do those things?"

He chewed his bottom lip. Had he had a grape peeler? Not that he could recall. "I don't think I had a servant specifically for that, but yes, there were beings tasked with my every need."

Chuckling, she shook her head. "I was kidding."

"Oh."

She turned on her side, propping up her head on one elbow, and met his gaze. "Has it been very hard for you?"

"What? Doing without all that?"

She nodded.

Bacchus popped a grape into his mouth and chewed. When he'd first landed among the mortals as one of them, he'd felt more despair than he could comprehend. Especially since he didn't understand the nature of emotion itself. But once he came to terms with his new existence, he'd sailed along without much thought given to his former life. Now with Ariana to brighten his days, he thought it might not be so bad to stay here on the earthly plane. Not that he wanted to stay here. The thought of losing her to the hands of death terrified him more than anything he'd ever faced. If he could take her to his former home, then he would truly have the best of both worlds.

Folding his arms around her, he took in the spicy scent of her skin. "It's not so bad. Not bad at all."

He leaned down to kiss her forehead, but she tilted her mouth upward and captured his lips. A slow burn worked its way from his chest to his groin.

"Still seeing visions of Bambi whenever you look at me?" she asked in the middle of the kiss.

"Who?" The only Bambi he'd ever known was a stripper from New Orleans.

"Bambi." She nipped at his mouth. "Cute little deer."

The realization took him by surprise. "No, not at all. That vision hasn't popped up all night."

"Good."

Pressing her lips to his, she scrambled to sit up and straddle his lap without breaking contact with his mouth. Heat seared him to the core, and he grasped her curvaceous hips. The last of his self-control disappeared, the last grains of sand slipping through the aperture of an hourglass.

He broke free, struggling to catch his breath. "You're sure?"

"Shut up."

He did as told.

It was as if someone had lifted a blindfold from his eyes—though the mental image gave him pause. A blindfold? No, no. Not the time for games. Maybe later.

The warmth of her cheek pressed to his thrilled him like the sun on his face after a long, rainy weekend. His hands shook, but they managed to skim the outside of her dress, tracing the silhouette of her body.

Since the day they'd met, he'd fallen asleep dreaming of her bare form against his. He'd imagined in meticulous detail how he would touch her, kiss her, slide himself inside of her. But now, faced with the reality of it, he was unable to do anything more than respond. She'd taken the lead, and he didn't mind giving way to her control.

She worked open each button on his shirt and unzipped his pants. Hand slipping inside, she stroked his hardening shaft. A shudder racked him as she teased the sensitive skin around the head of his cock.

Pure need claimed him. Breaking free of his trepidations, he pushed up her dress and took it over her head, then dropped it to the floor. Taking a moment to drink in the curves of her glorious form, he longed to kiss every inch of her silky skin.

He caressed the slope of her buttocks. A few thin strings made up the back of her thong underwear. They broke apart with a gentle tug.

Ariana chuckled. "I loved those panties."

"Mmm...sorry, I'll buy you a new pair."

"It's okay." She pushed him back on the couch, covering his mouth with hers.

Mounds of flesh spilled over the top of her bra and grazed his chest. He cupped one breast and drew it to his mouth. The sweet bud grew taut between his teeth. She moaned as his tongue teased one dusky, plum-colored nipple.

Working his belt and zipper, she used her hands and feet to push his pants down his legs. He'd barely wriggled out of them when searing heat enveloped his shaft. Pleasure claimed his entire body. By the gods, she felt divine. He sucked in a breath through clenched teeth and sank his fingers into the soft flesh forming the swell of her hips.

One palm on his chest, she rocked forward and back, rubbing against him as much as riding him. He arched into each thrust, pushing his full length inside her. He shook, aching for release, but he had to hold on. Suddenly, the meaning of, "Think about baseball," made perfect sense. So that's why human men advocated the practice during sex. To prolong the moment. Now if Bacchus could only remember what the game entailed. Oh to Hades with it. He abandoned the effort.

Ariana's body tightened, and he relished each and every moan. Yes, she was close to taking her pleasure. There was no more beautiful sight than a woman in the throes of ecstasy, and to see Ariana come—shivers racked him at the very thought. Leaning forward, she licked and kissed his lips. The warmth surrounding his erection turned molten hot, liquid smooth.

He delved into her again. Her thighs quivered, and her head lolled back, exposing her throat. Sitting up, he wrapped his arms around her as though he could contain her quaking orgasm. He drank in every ripple of her muscles, every quiver, every whimper. A more glorious sight he had never seen. His chest swelled with elation.

Ariana stammered his name and begged him not to stop. He had no intention of doing so. His arms folded around her, he pushed forward, and she bore down on his shaft. The tension in his lower abdomen built to the point of bursting.

Waves of ecstasy crashed over him. Yes. She was perfect. Yes. And beautiful. Yes. And his. Yesss. He held her flush against him as he came.

She wilted, head against his shoulder. Spasms jerked his limbs, forcing him to hold her tighter. He clung to her until his body quieted.

A tear dripped down her cheek, and Bacchus kissed it way. Were he given to weeping, he might have joined her in this release. He stroked her hair and cradled her, their bodies still united.

# Chapter 19

*Envy and Greed*

The morning—well, afternoon—started with Bacchus's arms around his beautiful Ariana.

She yawned and snuggled against his chest.

He strummed her shoulder, made slow, lazy circles then tripped down her arm. He gave her a long kiss. "Good morning."

She smiled and nuzzled his chin. "Good morning."

"It was a good night, too."

She agreed, and he brushed his lips against hers. He stroked her hip and between her legs.

Tensing and giggling, she said, "No, no, no. I don't have the energy. I need food."

Bacchus affected a pout. "Fine. If you insist. Then, I get to have my way with you.

"Agreed."

The couple ousted themselves from bed. Ariana put on Bacchus's dress shirt from the night before. Her hourglass shape transformed the garment. It clung to her in all the right places, and he nearly abandoned his promise to engage in breakfast prior to ravaging her again.

Naked, Bacchus followed her to the kitchen.

She looked at him and laughed. "That's a good way to singe something important." She gestured to his genitalia.

"But modern clothing is so restrictive."

Ariana shrugged. "It's your *paloma*, but don't blame me if the bacon pops you."

Good point. Bacchus scurried into the bedroom and fashioned a sheet into a makeshift toga. He returned to the kitchen triumphant. "Ta da."

She chuckled. "You're so crazy."

Wrapping his arms around her, he brushed his lips against hers. His tongue darted, seeking hers. "That's a good thing, right?"

"Uh huh." She leaned in for another kiss. One kiss bled into another, and then another. Her hands came to rest on his shoulders, and she gave him a gentle nudge. "Food, remember?"

"If you insist." Bacchus dragged himself from the bed.

Bacchus made his way over to the fridge and pulled out bacon, eggs, a tomato, and Monterey Jack. He helped her prepare omelets and delighted in the cheesy goodness of the finished product. He drained his glass. What was this awful, sour concoction?

Oh, right, Ariana had convinced him to leave the orange juice virgin this morning.

"Blech." He smacked his lips and rubbed his tongue against the roof of his mouth.

"*Pobrecito*," she teased.

"Poor thing is right. This stuff is terrible straight."

Ariana got up and started clearing the table. "You're the biggest baby, you know that?"

Bacchus pulled her onto his lap and kissed her. Without breaking away from her, he took the dishes from her hands and put them back on the table. He'd held out as long as he could, but now that they'd eaten breakfast, he had to have her.

Easing off the chair and onto the floor, Bacchus laid her out beneath him. She pulled the sheet from his body and cast it aside. His fingers worked the buttons on his shirt, desperate to take it off her.

Just as Bacchus had settled between her legs, a familiar whoosh and a burst of goat fur interrupted the couple.

"Sire, it's time to—oh! Oh my." Pan's face turned bright red and spun around.

In an attempt to protect what was left of her modesty, Bacchus covered Ariana with the sheet and threw her over his shoulder. He carried her into the bedroom, and she squealed and laughed the whole way.

After he flopped her on the bed, she covered her face with her hands.

"Do you think he saw?" she asked.

"No, I don't think he saw." He patted her thigh. At least not everything. After slipping on a pair of pants, he joined Pan in the living room.

The satyr paced back and forth. He jumped at the sight of his master. "My sincerest apologies sire. I had no idea. I...I...I..."

"Calm yourself." Bacchus put a hand on his steward's arm. "It's no big deal. I'd lost track of time and forgot you'd come to remind me about work."

"Yes, sire. Exactly. I didn't mean to…"

"I know, Panny. I know." Bacchus escorted the flustered satyr to the door. "I tell you what. You can do me a favor. Watch over the club this evening. Let me take the night off, and we'll call it even. All right?"

"Yes, sire. Of course, sire. I can do that. No problem."

Bacchus bid Pan a hasty goodbye. After the satyr had gone, Bacchus ran back to the bedroom and shimmied out of his jeans. He jumped in bed beside Ariana.

"I have a surprise for you." He nuzzled her neck. "I'm taking the day off from work, and tonight, I'm going to wine and dine you, love."

"But it's not even night, yet. What are we going to do until then?"

He pulled the sheet off her and covered her body with his, kissing his way across her collarbones. "I have a few ideas."

\* \* \* \*

The ocean air stirred locks of Ariana's dark hair. They fluttered around her neck, flirting with her bosom. The South Beach area had started to awaken, about ten at night as usual. Past their patio table paraded extravagantly dressed women and muscular young men, less garishly dressed, though no less impressive. Bacchus's gaze roamed over every nubile form, but Ariana focused on her lap.

He tilted her chin up to look at him. "What's wrong, my love?"

"*Nada*. Why?"

"Why do you study your napkin when there's so much else to feast the eyes upon."

"Enjoy." She smiled and took a sip of water.

"That's not how this game is played. It's no fun if you don't leer along with me."

"Oh no. I couldn't."

"What's the harm?" Bacchus pointed out a shirtless Adonis. "What's not to like about that young man over there?"

She shrugged off the question. A waiter showed up, discouraging any further probing. Bacchus ordered lobster bisque and roasted quail. Ariana chose a salad of spring greens and poached salmon. They'd decide upon dessert later. The waiter confiscated the menus and scurried inside the restaurant.

Dark clouds rolled in over Ariana's mood.

"Hey…" Bacchus took her hand. "I didn't mean to upset you. It was just a game."

"I know."

He shifted in his seat, suddenly aware of its hard, cool surface. "I've done the wrong thing, haven't I?"

"No." She sighed. "You didn't. It's me."

Bacchus's throat constricted. Why did he turn into a bumbling idiot around this woman? Seamless seduction, that'd always been his *modus operandi*. Not even in his first few days as a mortal had he felt so inept.

Ariana cleared her throat, staring out into space. "Dezi would… He would smack me around if he even thought I was looking at another man."

A noose tightened around Bacchus's neck, and a fire brewed in the pit of his stomach. "I promise you. He will never lay a finger on you again."

She wrung her hands, a half-smile tugging at her lips.

"Jealousy is the sign of a weak mind." He placed a hand over hers. Her fidgeting ceased. "And you don't have to worry about that from me. Not ever."

She nodded. "I know."

"I'm glad."

"Me too." She sucked in a breath, and her gaze shifted to the tablecloth, though the expression on her face made it seem as though she saw through the tabletop, through the surface of the Earth's crust and beyond. "Because I'm falling…falling in love. With you."

The words pushed a rush of air into his lungs. "With me? I think… I mean I know—as much as I know about love…because I don't know a lot." He paused and sucked in a deep breath. "I love you, too, Ariana."

She covered his hand with hers, and he leaned in, brushing his mouth against hers. Since his mouth had run dry, his lip stuck a little.

"Sorry." He took a sip of wine. "I'm in very unfamiliar territory here."

"Why do you always say that? For someone who claims he doesn't know about love and emotion, you're the most caring, giving man."

Bacchus swallowed hard. "It must be you bringing out these qualities in me. All my life, the way it used to be, it was never about connections or caring or nurturing anything."

"Not even when you were a child?"

"No. Not even then…especially not then."

"Why do you say that?"

Closing his eyes, he breathed in the salt air on the warm breeze. Poseidon caressing the night. Oh yes, Uncle Poseidon. And Uncle Hades. Auntie Demeter. One big happy family. Or not. A god shouldn't require the same kind of nurturing as a human child. Perhaps it was Bacchus's human side that could feel pain. And he couldn't put a name to that ache until now.

"You don't know the story?" Bacchus opened his eyes.

Ariana's cheeks turned pink, and her eyebrows drew together. "I'm sorry, I don't. Why don't you tell it to me?"

He licked his lips and took another sip of wine. Where to begin? Well, at the beginning, of course. Starting with Zeus's seduction of Semele and Hera's treachery, the story had been chronicled in any number of histories and tomes.

His father Zeus had seduced the fair Semele, a Phoenician princess. Once Hera, Zeus's wife, found out about the liaison and the subsequent pregnancy, she'd tricked Zeus into appearing before Semele in his divine form. Unable to withstand the sight of the god in his full glory, Semele dissolved into ashes. Zeus rescued the unborn Bacchus and sewed the baby into his own thigh.

Once born, for the second time, Bacchus was by no means safe. Hera tried any means of assassination, prompting Zeus to place the child on Earth with the wood nymphs. Though indulged and spoiled, Bacchus grew up with an affinity for nature, which turned into power over it.

When the Olympians reincarnated Bacchus's first lover as a grapevine, the young god was struck with inspiration and turned the juice of Ampelos's fruit into the first wine. A miraculous creation the world had never seen the likes of before.

"And once I'd come of age, I set out to gather my flock. Bacchantes, my worshipers are called. Were called." He shook his head. Still so hard to think of his reign as a god as over and done. "They used to gorge themselves on wine and lust, and then rip men apart with their bare hands."

"Really?"

Noting the sudden disappearance of her smile, and the widening of her eyes, Bacchus hurried to explain. "But not anymore. I haven't condoned that ritual in hundreds of years. And of course, the point is moot now anyway."

Ariana smoothed over wrinkles in the tablecloth. "You're angry with your father, aren't you?"

"I suppose I am."

"I can see how you would be." She tilted her head to the side but didn't meet his gaze. "Why don't you rescue your mother from the Underworld yourself?"

Bacchus chewed his lip. How to help her understand this? "Well, in this mortal form, I don't think I'd last a day in the Underworld. Even when I was a god, I couldn't waltz up to Hades and demand my mother. I mean, first of all, it's totally forbidden to mess around in another god's domain. But also, she's human, and human souls aren't that durable. If I'd sent a hero down there to save her, and she didn't survive the cross over to Olympus, she'd be lost in Chaos—the void of nothingness. And there's nothing worse than Chaos." A chill tightened Bacchus's chest. "At least as it is now, she's safe."

She gave him a gentle smile. "And I thought my childhood was screwed up."

"I'm sorry." He took a gulp of wine. "We're supposed to be celebrating. Enjoying each other's company. Not hashing out mommy and daddy issues."

"It's okay. You can talk to me about anything. I mean it."

"Thank you, love." He leaned in and kissed her, savoring the sweetness of her lip-gloss and the wine on her breath.

The waiter returned with their food. Bacchus settled against the back of his chair and watched Ariana. Though the parade of flesh continued around them, she was the only woman Bacchus could see.

\* \* \* \*

The street lamps on the way home glowed brighter than they had earlier that night. Or any other night for that matter. The breeze fresher, flowers more fragrant. Bacchus's senses had somehow become enhanced. Was this the rush of love he'd heard of so often in epic poetry and songs? He was sure it was. The experience deserved every word written about it and more. No wonder humans were so enamored of falling in love.

All the conquests, all the grand passions, the seductions, the ecstasy that had come before this moment paled in comparison to this magnificent creature who'd given herself to him with honesty, trust…and love. Yes, therein lay the difference. For all he had experienced, he had never tasted true love. It felt inexplicably unique. No other emotion compared.

Hera had seen to it that no mother's affection had ever shone upon him. The nymphs who raised him with their considerable charms, lavished him with attention, but how easily that attention strayed at the appearance of a handsome sprite or fetching lad.

Even the goddess of love knew little of the human incarnation of the emotion she presided over. Love, an all-consuming fire here on Earth, Bacchus gladly offered himself to be devoured by Ariana.

Now, in his bedroom, in her arms. There was nowhere in the Cosmos he'd rather be.

Declarations of adoration dripped from her tongue. Bacchus shivered, combing his fingers through her hair. Wild passion and lust were one thing, this slow burn aching in his chest and loins was something else.

"I—I don't know how to do this," he whispered.

"What do you mean?"

Her gentle touch against his brow sent his pulse skyrocketing. Words died on his lips, his body trembling. How to manage this.

Finally, he managed to say, "This is a first for me... I mean like this."

"Like how?"

He pressed his palm to hers and splayed their fingers apart. "Making love." The phrase had never made sense to him, as if love was something that could be made.

Ariana shushed him. Her lips met his. Softly. Gentle at first, but then with the hunger he wanted so much to understand. A fog clouded his head, and he closed his eyes.

Warm hands slid up Bacchus's body and stripped off his t-shirt. Cooled by the draft of air-conditioning, his skin contracted into pebbles of gooseflesh. Her fingers traveled over his body, down to the button of his blue jeans. After freeing him, she discarded the garment. Pulling a single knot from the back of her halter dress, it too fluttered to the floor.

An expanse of smooth, caramel skin ran from her hairline to the tips of her toes, marred only by a small, jagged scar near her ribs. His hand strayed to the mark, but she brushed it away. He understood the gesture. They'd spent enough time tonight on scars, physical or otherwise.

She nudged him toward the bed, pushing with her mouth as much has her body. Tongues toyed with one another. The taste of his beloved filled his senses.

Bacchus scooped her into his arms and fell to the mattress. Hunger turned into pure heat, searing his heart and settling between his legs. Want turned into need, an ache stronger than he could bear.

Tucking Ariana beneath him, sheltering her body with his, he parted her legs. She opened her body to him. His flesh sank inside hers, and her sheath enveloped in silken heat. Though he'd been inside her last night, this time she felt different. Not that he could stop to contemplate the mysteries of his dark beauty. A tide of passion swept him along, banishing coherent thought.

She wrapped a leg around his backside and pulled him deeper. Her lips sought out his, her tongue skimmed along his.

He struggled to keep his rhythm steady. Her inner walls gripped his shaft from tip to base as he made love to her with long, languid strokes. Abdomens pressed flush together, he felt her every movement, every involuntary shudder. Perspiration dripped down his torso, but Bacchus didn't slow or falter. He felt the quaking between her legs and exquisite pressure building in his core.

Her tremors built in intensity, and her fingernails dug into his back, but he didn't object. The little bit of pain only served to heighten the pleasure coursing through his veins. Thrusting into her and keeping himself buried there, he pulsed his pelvis against her clit and covered her mouth with his. They're bodies remained joined as the couple came together.

The intensity of sensation began to recede, and Bacchus nestled his cheek against her neck. Gulping in air, he tried to catch his breath. A storm of emotion dragged him under and strangled him. Sex had never been like this. Not like this. Not ever.

Finally, Bacchus knew love could indeed be made.

\* \* \* \*

Ariana's chest rose and fell with the automated rhythm of slumber. Bacchus couldn't sleep, though he wanted nothing more than to curl himself around her delicate form. Frenetic thoughts swirled around his brain. He imagined himself reinstated, transporting his beautiful Ariana to his golden palace. She deserved all the glorious things he could give her…well, he once could've given her. His star would rise again. He'd see to that much.

Tormented, Bacchus stood and walked to the living room, not bothering to cover himself. A snifter of brandy might help clear his mind. Couldn't hurt anyway. Pan appeared without making a sound. A shudder passed through Bacchus, and he struggled to keep hold of the snifter.

"By Hades, you nearly made me drop my drink. We both know what a travesty that would've been," Bacchus said.

"My apologies sire. I wanted to report two more nasties have appeared inside the box. Envy and Greed are trapped."

Bacchus turned to watch the twinkling city lights, a sip of fine liquor warming his throat. "She's free from the petty jealousy, the selfishness that imprisoned her. That man's evil hand no longer clutches at her throat. Or her mind."

"Well said, sire. Good night, my lord. Sleep well." Pan excused himself and vanished as quickly as he'd come.

Bacchus sipped brandy, but his chest warmed for a different reason. One step closer to the desires that consumed his every thought, his dominion and Ariana to share it with.

# Chapter 20

*Cruelty and Violence*

Sunlight. Morning. A good morning with Ariana snuggled against him. He secured his arms around her and inhaled the scent of her hair.

"Are you sniffing me?" she asked, voice heavy with sleep.

"Sorry, love, but you smell so good. Didn't mean to wake you." Cradling her chin, he gave her a kiss. "Good morning."

Glancing over her shoulder at the clock, she corrected him. "Good afternoon, you mean. Seriously, we have to start getting up before one PM."

"Why?"

"Because…Well, I don't know why, but we just have to."

"Okay, love." He brushed his lips over hers, stroking her warm, nude abdomen.

"This might be the reason we're both so tired, you know."

"Fair enough." He chuckled. "It's my fault. I can't stop touching you."

"Not that I want you to stop touching me."

Rolling her onto her back, he planted whisper-soft kisses down the length of her torso. She sighed and relaxed beneath him.

"I'll make you a deal." He kissed his way up to her neck. "You stay here and rest up while I go to work. I'll stop by for a couple hours, do only what I absolutely have to do, and I'll come home to ravage you then."

"Deal." She hugged him with her legs.

"Now that's not helping," he chided.

She laughed and released him. Loath to do so, he pulled himself from the warmth of the bed and her body. This responsible, upstanding citizen routine had better be worth it in the long run.

In a hot shower, he let his mind roam. With most of Ariana's suffering vanquished, it wouldn't be long before he could take his love to his home.

Show her his full glory and power. And this time, he'd rule his domain with restraint and a sense of responsibility. No more orgies for the sake of orgies. Excess only when excess was required, if that made sense. And it did make sense to him now. It was all right to lose oneself for a little while, as long as one foot remained firmly on the ground. Intoxication could be spiritual if shared with another for the right reasons. If another's body were taken with a sincere depth of feeling, there was no limit to the power making love could bring. Clarity. Joy. Passion. Confidence. And no more pain. What a powerful drug was love.

He turned off the spigot and toweled himself dry. A song in his heart and on his lips, Bacchus dressed for work and kissed his beautiful Ariana goodbye.

\* \* \* \*

Bacchus drank in the silence of the now empty club. In a few hours, patrons would fill the building to capacity, but for now, he welcomed the blessed peace. His plan was humming along like greased lightning. He'd have his love and his rightful place in the Universe back in no time.

With a snifter of brandy and a plate of strawberries, he retired to his office. So chipper was his mood, Bacchus didn't even mind going over receipts and purchase order manifests with the accountant. The few hours spent on the most dull, mind-numbing work imaginable seemed to fly by. Love did indeed cause the spirit to soar. And all this time Bacchus had thought only Red Bull and vodka could give you wings.

He reclined in his leather office chair and sipped from his lead crystal glass.

A burst of fur showered Bacchus. He wiped his face and dusted off his shirt. Pan stood in the center of his master's office, wringing his hands.

"Sire, she's gone."

"What?" Bacchus jumped up and walked around his desk, heart pounding its way into his throat.

"Miss Ariana should've been at the condo where she'd be safe, but I found this when I got there this afternoon." Pan handed a note to his lord.

> *Bacch,*
> *I went to the store. We're out of OJ and TP.*
> *XOXO,*
> *Ari*

Next, Pan gave Bacchus a DVD. "I found this on your doormat. It's— it's pretty hard to watch, sire. I can tell you about it instead."

Bacchus's stomach flip-flopped, but he had to watch it himself.

Pan set the video up on Bacchus's computer. Within seconds, the images that flicked to life confirmed his worst fears. Ice water ran through his veins.

Ariana was bound and gagged, her shirt bloodied, her head hung slack.

Dezi strolled into view and tilted the woman's head up to face the camera.

Though he'd known the contents of the video, nothing in the Cosmos could have prepared him for the sight of his beloved battered and bruised. Tamping down the urge to vomit, Bacchus bit the inside of his cheek to the point of pain. The metallic taste of blood coated his tongue.

The despicable man grinned. "I told you there'd be hell to pay if I didn't get back what was rightfully mine. Meet me at pier thirty-seven, warehouse F at seven tonight, or she dies. And no cops or she dies. Don't be late."

"Turn it off." Bile rose in Bacchus's throat.

Pan did as instructed and laid a hand on Bacchus's shoulder. "I've scoured the area he indicated for her aura, and I couldn't find her. I feel her in a neighborhood on the outskirts of town. That's where he's holding her, sire."

The bastard must've been watching her, waiting for her to make just such a mistake. His apology and concession of defeat had lulled her into a false sense of security. Why didn't she wait for him or Pan? What if it was too late and Dezi had—no—Bacchus couldn't afford to think horrible thoughts. "Transport me to where she is, Pan, and summon the boys. Please."

Bacchus braced himself, but trans-ether-portation still made him nauseous. He cursed his mortal form as he struggled to steady himself.

Heracles, Cúchulainn, and Vighnesha popped into the earthly plane in colorful flashes of smoke and lightning before Pan flashed forth.

They approached a two, maybe three bedroom house, the roof of which sagged as if it had no pride in itself or its owner. The rusted wrought iron fixtures agreed with the roof as did the peeling paint and cracked walkway. A house used for peddling drugs or some other nefarious purpose.

"Do you want me to secure Dezi's men, sire?" asked Pan.

Bacchus ground his teeth in an effort to keep his wits about him. "No, my friend. It's divine vengeance time. Let them have a sporting chance to run away from their inevitable death."

The other deities roared in agreement.

He nodded at Heracles who ripped the front door off its hinges. Cúchulainn rushed in first, sword drawn. Vig and Bacchus followed in time to hear a chorus of, "*Que carajo?*" from Dezi's men.

In wife beaters and creased slacks, the guards sat around a table, drinking and playing dominoes. Six of them all sported large caliber guns.

Cúchulainn beheaded two of them before any could draw their weapons. Heracles crushed one with his bare hands, gore splattering the walls. He picked up another, but Bacchus didn't hang around to watch.

He stormed the back rooms and kicked in each locked door, searching frantically for Ariana. In the smallest bedroom, she lay unconscious on a dirty twin-size mattress. Her hands were bound behind her back, and her ankles were secured to a slipknot around her neck. Face black and blue, she lay in a pool of vomit.

Bacchus fell to his knees. Bile seared his throat. "Ariana, love. By the gods, what has he done to you?"

She opened her eyes but couldn't focus. Her swollen and split lips pushed out one groaned word, "Bacchus?"

"Yes, love. I'm here. I'm here and I'm going to get you out of here." He worked the knots around her limbs, but his hands shaking couldn't free them. "Pan," he called.

The satyr appeared in the doorway and flinched.

"Get her out of here. You get those vile ropes off her. You get her to a hospital. Do it now, Pan." Bacchus rose, unsure his trembling legs could bear his full weight. "Get the ropes off her, Pan."

The satyr snapped out of his daze and whisked Ariana away.

Enraged, Bacchus marched to the front of the house where Cúchulainn held the last guard at sword point. Picking the man up, Bacchus spun him around then slammed him against a wall. "Tell me where he is."

The man's stink filled the room. The thug had soiled himself but refused to speak.

Bacchus loosened his grip and wiped sweat from his adversary's forehead. "If you tell me where he is, I'll let you live."

The man opened his mouth, his voice high and thin. "His condo."

"The place Ariana used to live?"

The man nodded. Bacchus tossed him aside. "Take me there, Vig." He turned to Cúchulainn and Heracles. "We'll meet you at the club."

The blue-skinned god nodded. As Bacchus and Vig faded into the ether, Bacchus relished the sound of the man's screams. After all, Bacchus had promised he would let the man live. The demigods were not as forgiving.

\* \* \* \*

Bacchus struggled to steady his breath, doubling over lest he lose his lunch.

"You all right?" Vig asked.

"Yes, thank you."

"But man, you are twelve shades of green."

"Not helping."

"Sorry. So, what's the plan?"

After one more deep breath, Bacchus swallowed hard, nodding. He knew just what to do. "Pentheus."

"Yeah? No shit? Ha ha. So righteous."

"We'll need your brother-sister's help. You think Shivakali will mind lending a hand?"

"I'm sure he-she will be down for it."

"I thought so." Bacchus straightened up and shook his head. "I'm ready. Let's go get the son of a whore."

"Right on." Vig skipped through the wall and unlocked the door for Bacchus.

Dezi stood in the kitchen, making a sandwich.

Vig snatched him into the ether—and like space—there was no one to hear Dezi scream.

# Chapter 21

*Vengeful Gods*

The nurse had told him Ariana hadn't been raped. Cold comfort, but some comfort nonetheless. Bacchus's ribcage felt two sizes too small. He choked on guilt and regret. He'd looked away for a second. Just a second. And she'd slipped through his fingers. Now, here she lay, broken and beaten. But she was still here. Still with him.

Bacchus took Ariana's bruised hand, careful to avoid the needles and tubes connected to her. "Oh, my love." He wept silently. He'd broken his promise to her. He'd sworn Dezi would never touch her again, but the man had.

In doing so, Dezi had signed his own death warrant. Of that much, Bacchus was certain.

She hadn't regained consciousness. The evil bastard had beaten her, pumped her full of heroin, and left her for dead. Doctors had stopped the internal bleeding and stitched up the split over her left eyebrow. She'd been given medication to make her comfortable and to heal her body, but what irreparable damage had Dezi done to her spirit? Only time could answer that question.

He grasped her hand a little tighter, bowing his head. For the second time in his long, long life, Bacchus raised his voice in prayer.

* * * *

Bacchus strode through the club to the backroom where Pan and the demigods awaited him, their special guest already bound.

"How's Ariana?" Vig asked.

At the sight of Dezi, acid rose in Bacchus's throat. "She's resting. The doctors will know more in the morning."

Vig clapped Bacchus on the shoulder. "It'll be good news, man. I know it."

No time for pleasantries, only vengeance. Oh and vengeance he would have. King Pentheus had suffered a far more appealing fate than the one Alonso Desiderio was about to endure. "Let's do this."

Heracles held the struggling gangster still.

With a pair of tongs, Bacchus pried open Dezi's mouth. "Beer bong."

Vig handed off the ingenious human device. "Beer bong."

"Vodka."

"Vodka." Vig passed him a pint of Aristocrat.

"Ew, really?" A shiver racked Bacchus. "Where did you even get this abomination? Not in my club."

"You really want to waste good liquor on this fuckwad?"

"We may be vengeful gods, but we are not needlessly cruel. Hand me the Kettle One."

Vig gave it to Bacchus.

"Tab of acid," Bacchus said.

"LSD of the gods." Vig snickered into Dezi's face. "This shit is going to fuck you up, man."

Vig, Bacchus, and the others exited the room, leaving the potent combo to churn in the gangster's stomach. Once Dezi had begun to prance around the room, catching imaginary butterflies with a nonexistent net, the conspirators agreed it was time to unleash their secret weapon. But first, a costume change for Mr. Desiderio, which Pan volunteered to take care of.

Skin the color of a creamy latte, oiled with sandalwood and lavender, a ravishing siren slinked into Bacchus's office. Her full breasts bounced behind a thin veil of fiery organza. A purr filled the void between her inhalations. Every being in the club longed to touch her, to give over to the seduction incarnate that was Shivakali, even though most of them knew nothing of the deity's existence. Her emerald cat's eyes peered into Bacchus's soul. "And here I was, hoping you'd summoned me so I might sample your delectable flesh."

"At any other time in my life, I would have been happy to oblige."

"And who's our vic—ah, I mean, the lucky fellow? Who gets to take a ride on the merry-go-round?"

"That piece of dung in there." Bacchus pointed out the man prancing in a merry widow and thigh-high boots. "But, Kali, take it easy with him. I want him alive to suffer the aftermath."

"Don't worry. He'll feel no pain." The goddess slipped into the room with the gangster.

Whether from morbid curiosity or a desire for all to go right with his plan, Bacchus watched the show from the doorway, careful not to upset the video camera on its tripod.

Kali fell to her knees and took Dezi's hard cock into her mouth. Posing for the camera, she made a show of tasting his shaft and testicles. After only a few teasing licks, the man came in several white, sticky bursts. The goddess wiped her mouth and gave him a wicked grin.

"Naughty, naughty boy." Wrenching his arm behind his back, Kali shoved him to his knees. "Now you will be punished."

She kicked him forward with her boot and paddled his ass. Dezi let loose with maniacal laughter and moans. The camera, however, captured a very different image. Bacchus set his jaw, a tingle in the pit of his stomach. Oh yes, Dezi would suffer all he deserved.

* * * *

Hours later, Dezi groaned as he broke through the shroud of unconsciousness.

"Why good morning." Bacchus slapped the man's cheek. "Time to wake up."

The gangster came to with a start. "Where the fuck am I?"

With exaggerated turns of his head, Bacchus pretended to survey the dark leather upholstery surrounding them. "I believe it's called a limo. It's the only way we could all fit in one car."

"Yeah, you sure know how to punish a guy." Dezi smirked.

"Been enjoying my hospitality, have you?"

"Lemme see, you get me drunk and high, set me up with the finest bitch I've ever seen, and drive me home in a limo. I'll have to piss you off more often."

"Oh good. I firmly believe a man's final hours should be spent living well."

Dezi clucked his tongue. "My final hours, huh?"

"Yep."

Bacchus picked up the device Hephaestus had sent with Heracles. He flipped through a few screens on the iPad.

"Ah, here we go. The camera loves you. Just loves you."

He handed the tablet to the gangster who blanched at the video on the screen. "What the fuck? Turn this shit off." Dezi trembled. "This—this isn't what happened. She was gorgeous, all woman. I don't know how you faked this."

"That's the wonderful thing about Shivakali. She-he can choose to project her masculine side for those watching. So even though you enjoyed the attentions of the most seductive female in the Cosmos, it appears you're making out with a guy. A very well endowed guy at that. But don't worry, you're a superstar now. The video is racking up huge hits online. Something called YouTube. Oh, and Pan was thoughtful enough to forward a copy to all your work associates. They can't wait to have a little chat with you. I think you have much larger problems to worry your pretty, little head about, *entiendes*?"

"I will kill you if it's the last thing I do."

Bacchus laughed. "I very much doubt that. I believe the last thing you'll do is soil yourself while your associates use you for target practice."

The limo halted outside a dilapidated warehouse. Dezi's eyes widened, and he white-knuckled the car door handle. His ashen lips hardly moved as he said, "You can't take me in there."

"Of course we can. I'm sure your friends are dying to see you. You can tell them all about your wild night."

"You know what they'll do to me. *Hijo de tu puta madre que te pario*, you set this up."

"You really shouldn't talk about my mother that way. Sensitive topic." Bacchus turned to Cúchulainn and Heracles. "Let's get him inside, boys."

The demigods dragged the man from the car. He twisted and bucked. Heracles accidentally tore Dezi's left arm out of the socket. The man screamed, his useless arm limp at his side.

"Quit squirming so much or you'll be limbless by the time we meet up with your co-workers." Donning a pair of black Ray Bans sunglasses, Bacchus followed his men.

Two of Dezi's former colleagues emerged from the building.

Sr. Santos walked two steps behind them. "Mr. Sabazios, nice to see you again." Santos extended a hand.

Bacchus shook the old man's hand. "Always a pleasure."

Dezi's head hung low. Santos grabbed the man's face and gave it a vicious shake. "I told you to let go of the obsession you had with that *puta sucia*—"

"Please don't refer to the woman I love in such a foul manner," Bacchus said.

"My apologies." Santos held up a hand and Bacchus nodded. The old gangster went on. "I warned you, Dezi. I said Sabazios is more dangerous than you think. I know about these things. I told you. But no, you kept saying, 'I'm not afraid of *eso maricon*.' But look who turned out to be the faggot?"

Dezi jerked against the demigod's grip. "It ain't true, Sr. Santos. You know I like girls. I love *chocha*. You guys know that." His voice cracked.

"It's not about the truth. It's about the fact that you've embarrassed me." Santos backhanded Dezi. "Do you have any idea how many of our associates saw that video? I warned you, but you made a fool of me, and for that, you will pay."

Bacchus's crew passed the man over to Santos's thugs. They threw him to the ground, duct taped his feet and hands like a hog ready for slaughter, and dragged him to the warehouse. His screams and pleas for mercy earned him a piece of tape over his mouth.

"Again, I apologize, Mr. Sabazios. Dezi won't bother you again."

Bacchus nodded and left without another word. Problem solved.

The limo dropped Bacchus by the hospital. Before he disembarked, the demigods asked if he needed them for anything else. He told them no and sent them on their merry way. The poor limo driver was in for a long night.

# Chapter 22

*Disease and Death*

Bacchus wasn't sure anything in the hospital vending machine was edible, but his rumbling stomach insisted he choose something. He selected a pale orange for himself and cup of green Jello for Ariana. She was still on a liquid diet.

His mind wandered to her tearful apology earlier. Once she'd left the condo, Dezi intercepted her near the bodega. He'd asked her to get a cup of coffee and talk, and then he'd return her mother's wedding ring. When she refused, he'd forced her into the car, drugged her, and beaten her. The rest, she'd said, was a blur. That she felt she had anything to apologize for broke Bacchus's heart.

When he returned to her room, Ariana was sitting up. A syndicated crime drama flickered on the TV screen, but she flipped it off as soon as he came in. Dark circles smudged the delicate skin under each eye.

He sank onto the bed next to her, cupping her face, and ran a finger over the apples of her cheeks. "You should rest, love."

She burrowed against his chest.

He needed no more invitation to scoop her into an embrace, her scent reminding him of springtime. Oceans of yellow flowers stretched out in his mind's eye, but dark clouds still blotted out the sun. "What's wrong?"

She let out a long exhalation. Her hot breath traveled through his thin shirt and across his chest. Goosebumps rose on his arms. "Ariana, what is it?" He stroked her hair.

"The doctor was here…" Her voice sounded so small it pierced his heart. "He—he said there's something wrong with me."

"What? What do you mean?"

Her hand strayed to the crown of her head. "They can't operate. It's too big."

"Operate on what?"

She didn't answer.

He let her down onto the pillow and grabbed her copy of the diagnosis. Skimming the medical mumbo jumbo, he found the dreadful word— aneurysm. The doctors had discovered a brain aneurysm during scans to assess her other injuries. The same disorder had killed her mother. By the gods, if it couldn't be corrected, this was a death sentence. The room spun and all the air left Bacchus's lungs. "This can't be."

She cried. Not sobs of disbelief or outrage, but the quiet river of tears that came along with acceptance. Head hung low, she nodded. "It's true, Bacchus."

"No. Someone made a mistake. The plan was perfect." He tossed the papers to the floor. "This is a mix up. A mistake. On those shows, on television, doctors make mistakes all the time."

"It's not a mistake—"

He held up a finger. "It could be. Doctors make mistakes." Turning on his heel, he clenched his fists, then stalked from her room.

At the nurse's station, he found the attending on duty and cornered the man. A good foot shorter and much grayer than Bacchus, the doctor cowered in Bacchus's shadow. Nonetheless, Dr. Robeson insisted the exam results were accurate.

A vice gripped Bacchus's throat, his whole body shaking. "If this is about money, I have plenty. You fix this thing. I don't care what it costs."

"It's not about money, Mr. Sabazios. I assure you I examined all the options with our neurosurgery team. We simply can't find a way to work on the aneurysm without leaving her with brain damage. And that's the best case scenario."

A chill settled in his chest. Bacchus knew all too well what the *worst case scenario* entailed.

"I'm very sorry," the physician said.

Unbelievable. Did the healer expect Bacchus to care about apologies? Stalking down the hall, Bacchus clenched and unclenched his hands. This would not stand. There might be nothing the doctor could do, but Bacchus would be damned if he'd lose Ariana.

\* \* \* \*

A rolling, pea-soup fog filled Bacchus's condo. As it cleared, Brigid, the Celtic goddess of healing, materialized. "Bacchus, darling, so good to see you again. You look well, considering the circumstances." She patted his shoulder.

"Thank you, Brig."

She meandered over to the dining table and ran her fingers over Ariana's records, but didn't pick them up to study them. "Very tragic."

"Then, you know why Pan invited you here."

She offered a wistful smile. "I'm not the first deity with healing powers you've summoned for this task."

"No offense intended."

"None taken. I'm just pointing out word gets around."

"You're not going to look at her file?"

Brigid shook her head. "How long have you known me, Bacchus?"

He shrugged, in no mood for meaningful questions or life lessons. "A very long time."

"And though I hate to admit it, you and I are too much alike. Stubborn and only interested in the here and now." A smile lit up her face. "Remember our trip to Mexico with Quetzalcoatl?"

Bacchus closed his eyes, trying to block out the memories to no avail. "Yeah. What of it?"

"We had a grand time but caused a lot of trouble. That poor chicken farmer never was the same again. And the Mexican wrestling federation…" She clapped her hands and laughed, but as quickly as the mirthful expression overtook her features, it vanished. "Well, this time. You've got to think about the bigger picture."

He sank into a chair. "So you're not going to help?"

"I think you know I cannot." She traced his brow.

Bacchus dropped his head into his hands. "Thank you for coming in person. Most others sent messengers."

She sat next to him. "I came because I want you to understand. The healers can't help, because her destiny isn't ours to change."

A fire lit in his chest. His hands shook. How could she speak of destiny? Why was the entire Cosmos against him and Ariana?

"Do you understand?" she asked.

Unable to answer, Bacchus tried to swallow the lump in his throat. He understood nothing.

She stroked the back of his neck and whispered in his ear. "I'm sorry it has to be this way."

Another cloud of fog, and she was gone.

\* \* \* \*

On the way back to the hospital, Bacchus ran through the meager options left. He'd find a specialist or a better hospital. Humans performed their own miracles every day.

After he'd parked his Alpha Romeo in the garage, he took the elevator to Ariana's floor. He trotted into her room. Why in Hades was she stuffing toiletries into her duffel bag?

"Why are you packing?" he asked.

"I'm going home today." She didn't look at him.

"But—but how can they send you home if you aren't better?"

She raised her eyebrows. "I'm as better as I'm going to get."

He put a hand on hers to stop her packing. "You can't give up. I mean, I'll figure out a way to fix this. Maybe I can make another deal with the Council. If I can become a god again, I can make this right."

She laced her fingers with his. "It's okay, Bacchus. You can't take care of everything for me, and it's okay."

He pulled her to him and wrapped her in his arms. "Don't say that. I need to fix this. For you. I promise I'll find a way."

She hooked her arms around his shoulders. "You said—" She took an unsteady breath. "You said Jesus and Santa Maria, they're real."

Knives pierced his chest. She couldn't be saying what he thought she was.

"And there's an afterlife…right?"

"Well, yes, but—"

"Then, it'll be okay. I can see my mother and father again, and I'll wait for you."

"No." He pushed her to arm's length and searched her eyes. "You don't understand. It's not that simple. Even when I was a god, it wasn't that easy." How many times had he searched for his mother? None ever came to fruition. If Ariana were lost to him as well, he couldn't bear the thought.

Ariana's eyes glittered with tears. "This is hard enough to deal with, Bacchus. Please. I'm so tired."

He wiped her eyes. "Okay, love. Okay."

They could talk about this later when she was better rested and could think clearly.

"Let's get you home." He took the satchel from her. "Allow me to finish this. You sit."

She flashed a weak grin and took a seat on the bed.

He finished packing her few things and shouldered the bag.

A nurse wheeled Ariana to the elevator, and they rode to ground floor. Bacchus met them with the car at the main entrance.

He helped buckle Ariana into the passenger's seat.

"Bacchus. I'm not this fragile. I'm not going to die today. And maybe not for a long time."

He fastened his seatbelt and gripped the steering wheel. And maybe not ever, if he had anything to say about it.

* * * *

For days, a parade of divine beings had marched through Bacchus's condo. Confucius, Athena, Kannon, the finest minds in the Cosmos had examined the facts. Considering the portentous dreams, their fateful meeting, and the agreement with the Council, one thing seemed clear. Destiny had charged Bacchus with Ariana's fate. No way around it.

Now if only the Council would listen, but thus far, they'd left his prayers unanswered. Bacchus knew a cold shoulder when he saw one.

Exasperated, he snatched a pint of gin from the wet bar. He didn't bother with vermouth or olives, but belted it straight from the bottle. Fact was he'd spent very little time sober since Ariana's release from the hospital.

All the friends, all the divine counsel, even Pan—they'd all gone. He sat alone, an awful ache gnawing at his insides. The heat of the alcohol did little to dull the pain. He sank onto the couch.

"Did everyone leave?" She sounded far away, though she stood in the doorway of her room.

"They did, my love." He took another gulp.

Her footsteps tapped behind him. Her fingers lit on his forearm. "And you're drinking again. It didn't go well, did it?"

"Nope."

She moved around the sofa and snuggled next to him. She twirled rosary beads. "You did your best. It's in God's hands now."

The Father, whatever. "Yeah, well, a fat lot of good that'll do you." He gulped gin until she wrested the bottle from him.

"This isn't going to do any good, either."

Bacchus pried it from her hands. "But it's not gonna hurt."

"It hurts me to see you like this."

He bit his bottom lip, shaking his head. Why couldn't she understand how painful this was for him? "Oh, Ariana. It must be hell for you to watch me fail." He patted her arm. "But you should try living it some time. And you're right. I did my best. I did my best, and it didn't matter. I had it in my grasp to regain what I lost, but I failed. Perhaps the Council was right to defrock me and cast me down here. I appear to be rather worthless."

Ariana pulled her knees to her chest. "What is it that's bothering you?"

"You know the answer. You have a bubble of blood in your brain, and it could burst any day now. Or maybe you'll die of old age. Who knows?

"When I had the power to take this from you, we never crossed paths. Now that I'm pathetic, weak, and helpless, I get a front row seat to watch you die. The only love—true love—I've ever known, and you're slipping through my fingers." He banged his fist on the coffee table. Pain shot through his hand and wrist.

Ariana stood up, wrapping her arms around her body. "You know what I keep hearing from you? The words, 'I, me, myself.' *Coño*, and here I was thinking I'm the one with the life-threatening condition. How is this somehow all about you?"

He slid to the edge of the sofa. "If I were a god again—"

"*Basta*." She held up a hand. "I've heard enough about who you used to be and who you wish you could be." She pointed to her head. "It is what it is. And you are who you are. Right now. Get over it, Bacchus."

Wounded and at a loss for words, he took another drink.

"You know, I'm okay with the fact that one day I will die. It's part of being human."

"I wanted to give you so much more."

"Listen to yourself."

"I did this all for you."

She stared at him, mouth agape. "Don't kid yourself. You didn't do all this for me simply out of the goodness of your heart. You did it so you could become a god again. What happens to me when you get what you desire most? Have you thought of that?"

"Yes, I have. You'll come with me. I want to give you everything you deserve. My palace, my kingdom, it's more beautiful than you can imagine, and it's yours. It's all yours, but I have to be divine again to give it to you."

"And you decided all this without ever consulting me. You decided to alter the course of my life without even asking me if I wanted you to."

"But you're free of Dezi. I helped you get free. Isn't that what's important?"

She hung her head, her mouth pinched, nostrils flared.

"I never asked you for anything. And I'm grateful for your help, though I think if you're honest with yourself, I was simply convenient. You needed someone to save, and there I was, in need of saving. But you know what's sad?" she asked, shaking her head. "I've done it again. You may be kinder than Dezi, and you may treat me with more respect, but I'm still in a position in which I'm totally dependent on you for protection, for solutions…hell, now for salvation. If only you were a god, little Ariana wouldn't have to face the fact that she has a time bomb in her head. Don't kid yourself, Bacchus." She spat his name. "You haven't changed my life. You've only changed who's running it… And you know what's so sad, is that I've let you do it. I haven't done a damn thing for myself."

He remained silent. What could he say? And he couldn't bear the way she was glaring at him.

She let out a long sigh. "I can't keep repeating this pattern. And that's exactly what I'm doing with you."

"But…" he began, realizing before he spoke them, his words of protest had no merit. Ariana was right. He'd taken away her control, just as Dezi had. Instead of finishing his thought aloud, he took another swallow of Bombay Sapphire.

She snatched the gin and threw it to the floor. "And put the goddamn bottle down."

His gaze cast downward, he watched with his peripheral vision as she picked up her purse and headed for the door. Rubbing his head, he stared at the wooden floorboards and broken bottle. "I may be a flawed and stupid soul, but please, never doubt I love you."

His words were met with only teardrops and sniffles. She closed the door. A hole gnawing itself through his sternum, he forced himself to stay put. She'd be back once she'd come to her senses.

# Chapter 23

*Hell to Pay*

Ariana was gone. No way around it.

She.

Was.

Gone.

He had failed, and she was gone. The thoughts played in an endless circuit, swimming around his brain like sharks circling wounded prey.

Ariana had come by the condo at a time Bacchus should've been at the club. He hadn't been to work since the night he and his friends had set up Dezi.

"Sorry, I'll come back," she'd said.

He'd begged her to come in and talk, but she pushed him away, stating she'd only come for a few things.

"I love you, Ariana," Bacchus said.

"I know you think you do." She rubbed her arms, though not to warm herself. "Maybe you really do, but I can't, you know? I can't."

"I don't know. Please, help me understand."

She shook her head and turned to leave.

"Wait." He caught her arm. Though his grip was gentle, she gasped and flinched.

"No, love. No. I would never…" A chill stopped him in his tracks. He released her arm and held up his hands. "Listen, you stay. I'll leave. Most of the things here are yours, anyway."

She didn't reply. And she didn't ask him to stay.

Bacchus had shuffled out in silence, pulling the door shut behind him.

In the couple days that followed, he'd tried to call her, which was no small feat since he had never used a telephone before. But after a couple wrong numbers and a lengthy conversation with a widow named Margaret

Horrowitz in Boca Raton, he'd managed to get the transaction right. But each time he tried, a recording of Ariana's voice came on, telling him to wait for some beep. Why did he have to wait for a beep? The whole thing confused Bacchus to no end, but one thing seemed abundantly clear— Arianna didn't want to talk to him.

And he'd gotten as much response from The Council. He prayed, and he prayed, and he prayed to no avail. Even though he knew better, he could understand why so many humans saw only an empty sky when they turned an eye toward the heavens.

Now he sat on a bar stool somewhere in Key West, forsaken and forlorn, unsure of how he got there. Not that it mattered. No doubt, he could find something in this town to dull the pain.

* * * *

Bacchus roused to the sound of a base beat thumping through the wall next to the bed where he slept. He thought, at first, the pounding came from inside his head. It ached in an all too familiar way. Too much wine. Barrels and barrels of wine had passed through his system in the last week. And a drink right now would be just what the doctor ordered. Hair of the dog as the humans liked to say.

But when he opened the door that led to the great room of the Key West bungalow, he realized the rhythm came from music. Music blaring from the sound system in the living room. Scantily clad women danced with each other or even more scantily clad young men.

"Good morning, sleeping beauty." A woman in a bikini handed him a Bloody Mary. The smell of the drink turned his stomach, but Bacchus sipped it anyway. Anything to alleviate the hangover ravaging his system.

He noted his fully clothed body. He hadn't partaken of any of these beautiful people. His abstinence was further evidenced by a total lack of desire for any of them. Not one roused his loins. In fact, the entire party grated on his nerves.

Storms brewing in his mind, he marched to the entertainment center, angled it away from the wall, and yanked the plug from the outlet. The cacophonous music cut off. The two dozen partygoers gasped, looking around.

"My sincerest apologies, ladies and gentlemen, but the party is over. I'd appreciate it, if you clear out post haste. You don't have to go home, but you can't stay here."

He abandoned the mixed drink on a side table and picked up a stray bottle of vodka. Why bother with the tomato juice and horseradish? He longed to fall back into dreamless sleep. With any luck, he might not wake up at all.

"You have five minutes to clear out." He stalked into the cool darkness of the bedroom and slammed the door behind him.

\* \* \* \*

"Wake up, useless." A familiar voice broke through his semi-conscious stupor. Bacchus let out an alcohol-laced belch.

"Oh, very nice," the voice went on.

Bacchus cracked open an eyelid, struggling to focus on the verdant face in front of him. "Loki?" His voice sounded hoarse and strange. "What in Hades…?"

"You are a right, pretty mess, Bacchie. By Thor, you smell like that foul fermented shark dish they eat in Iceland."

"Leave me alone." Bacchus rolled over. Where was he, anyway? Palm trees waved outside the tinted bedroom window. Still in Key West.

"I came here in an attempt to clean you up, but even a god has his limits, you know?"

"Piss off, Loki. No one wants you here."

"Perhaps not, but you need me here."

"Only if you're here to tend bar. Otherwise, piss off." The words hissed through Bacchus's clenched teeth.

"Okie dokie… But I know how you can get to see the Council again." The trickster moved closer to Bacchus's ear. "I know how you can save her."

Loki jumped up and danced around singing, "Save her. Save her."

Bacchus hurled an empty liquor bottle at him, but the emerald-skinned god darted aside. The bottle shattered against the far wall. "Get out, you overgrown Brussels sprout. I'm not interested in your help, and I'm too hung over to listen to your cavernous mouth."

The trickster furrowed his brow and touched his palm to Bacchus's head. "What's a Brussels sprout?"

In an instant, the throbbing headache, churning stomach, and cold sweats dissipated. He felt physically better than he had—well, since he'd left Miami. No booze coursing through his veins to scramble his thoughts. But with a clear head came the emotional pain. It crushed him without a wall of alcohol to hold it at bay. All the anguish he'd been trying to escape, it writhed in his chest and abdomen. If he couldn't drink it away, he yearned to gouge or scour or cut it out. Any means necessary. A sob gurgled in his throat.

"What? W-why are your eyes leaking?" Loki recoiled.

"Please, Loki. If you have anything resembling compassion in you, end me. End me now. Send me to Hades, because this—" He thumped his chest. "This is a special kind of hell. And I can't do it. I can't do it anymore."

Loki sidestepped Bacchus's outstretched hands, the green god's eyes wide, and lips curled in disgust. "No can do, my friend."

"Why? You aren't my friend. You never liked me, even when we were equals. Here's your chance to squash me underfoot. I'm begging you to do it. Please. You win. Just finish me. Or at least take this mental anguish from me as you did my physical pain…please."

"No." The trickster dotted the fallen god's nose with his forefinger. "Because where you're headed, you'll need that pain to keep going."

* * * *

Loki's idea was simple enough. Simple and insane.

First things first, Bacchus had to figure out a way past Cerberus. If he got around the three-headed beast, then there was the river Styx. In the event that Bacchus could swim—which he couldn't—the black water would dissolve the flesh from his bones in a matter of seconds, but it wouldn't kill. He'd be left an animated skeleton, eternally starving with no way to sate his hunger.

Charon, the ferryman, wouldn't take a live mortal across the river, and there was no other entrance to the Underworld from the earthly plane.

"How is this helping me?" Bacchus gritted his teeth. "This stupid idea of yours."

"Is the idea stupid or the person who's going to execute it?" Loki scoffed.

"I swear by all that is sacred, if you're screwing with me, I will find a way to bind you to the foulest demon in Hell and stuff the two of you in the deepest, darkest hole for eternity."

"As terrified as I am, Bacchie, I assure you I'm not leading you astray. Since the Council won't listen to you, it's the only way to get an audience, force them to hear you."

Bacchus rubbed his eyes with his thumb and forefinger. This didn't make sense. Loki didn't assist anyone. Loki didn't do anything unless it amused or benefited him. If Bacchus had to guess, it would be that the trickster thought it would be great fun to watch Bacchus fail and wind up imprisoned. But the last laugh belonged to Bacchus, because he was already in prison.

"Are you listening to me?" asked Loki.

Bacchus nodded.

"Good, because if you don't, there will be Hell to pay…literally."
True to his word, he took to heart everything Loki had to say.

# Chapter 24

*Abandoning Hope*

Bacchus had double and triple checked his supplies for the journey. Pan had done well to prepare his lord. All packed, Bacchus bade his steward—and friend—farewell.

"Not farewell, sire, but until I see you again, and take care." The satyr bent at the waist in as graceful a bow as he could muster.

Fighting back an ache he knew all too well, Bacchus pulled Pan to his chest and clapped him on the back. "You do the same, old friend."

When they released each other, Pan sniffled and cleared his throat. "Are you sure you don't want me to transport you to your destination?"

"I'm sure. I don't need to start this adventure with a round of vomiting." He patted the satyr's arm. "And I get the feeling, somehow, I'm supposed to do this by myself."

In the taxi on the way to the airport, Bacchus thought about how alone he would be on this quest. Once he'd descended into the Underworld. No—not the Underworld, into Hell. They were two very different planes. The Underworld, ruled by Hades, could run the gambit from a land of riches, milk, and honey for fallen heroes to the Fields of Punishment. But Hell, it was a palace of evil that existed only to recruit new souls to the dark side.

During his tenure as a god, darkness had never held any special allure. He wondered if, as a mortal, his selfishness and malice would be easier to illicit and harder to fight. He gripped his pack tighter and hoped he'd brought the things he'd need to get through the trials. He blew out a sigh. No time for self-doubt now.

Once settled into his first-class seat on the plane, he ordered a glass of Merlot. He pulled the copy of Euripides's *Bacchae* from his backpack. The account of his time in Thebes should keep him focused on the straight and narrow. Bacchus snickered to himself at the memory of King Pentheus dressed in drag. And more recently, the video of Dezi, but Bacchus pushed that thought from his mind. Thoughts of Dezi only led to thoughts of her and thoughts of her... They led only to pain and longing. To desire. Another mirthless chuckle parted his lips.

Indeed the Council had been correct. The root of all suffering was desire. The desire to touch her, to hold her again, to grant her everlasting life. His hand trembled as he reached for the plastic cup in front of him. He downed the ruby liquid in one gulp and hailed the flight attendant to order another. It was going to be a long flight to California all alone with his musings.

* * * *

The bronze structure stretched up toward the darkened night sky. Demons and beasts of all varieties emerged from the metal's rich patinated surface, one of Rodin's most famous creations. Though the original of this sculpture resided in Paris, and replicas populated museums all over the world, this one here in Stanford, California was the only one that stood outdoors with twenty-four hour access. Breaking and entering had never been Bacchus's forte, especially not in his mortal form.

He touched the gate—Rodin's *Gates of Hell*—and murmured the words Loki had given him, "Abandon hope, all ye who enter here."

Nothing changed. The cold metal remained motionless beneath his fingers. He cleared the catch in his throat and repeated louder, "Abandon hope, all ye who enter here."

Nothing. Bacchus set his jaw. Perhaps only wayward Christians could perform this incantation with success. But really? Who knew more about sin than the former deity whose name was synonymous with orgies? He banged his fist against the hollow sculpture and yelled, "Abandon hope, all ye who enter here."

The heavy doors creaked to life and began to swing back. Perhaps Lucifer's minions were hearing impaired and required a forceful plea for entry.

Bacchus had expected searing heat and blinding flame, given the traditional depictions of this plane of existence, but the gate yawned wide, offering only a portal to frigid darkness.

Now or never. He stepped over the threshold into the black void. A preternatural chill racked his body. Though he'd packed a jacket with his supplies, there was no coat heavy enough to repel this cold. It seeped into his pores and cooled his blood.

The gates began to swing closed behind him. He hurried to light the electronic torch known as a Maglite. The bluish LED bulb sprang to life as the doors sealed behind him. Puffs of white breath swirled in front of his face. So much for fire and brimstone.

According to Loki, Bacchus could encounter the three-headed dog, Cerberus, at any time along this corridor. He extracted the countermeasure he'd packed for said canine and crept forward. Despite the bright light thrown from the flashlight, he could see only a couple feet in front of him. It was as though the complete and perfect darkness swallowed up all but the most immediate rays of light.

He slid along, testing the surface in front of him with each step. Smooth underfoot, the ground resembled water-beaten stone, and he had no clue as to the scope of the rest of his surroundings. There was no smell, other than soil tinged with moldy dampness.

Hitting a patch of moss, he slipped, but caught himself before he tumbled to all fours. The gift he held for Cerberus let out a shrill squeak at the pressure of his hand. The sound echoed around the cavernous space. The reverberations seemed to go on for miles. If the powers-that-be hadn't known someone entered the gate, they did now.

His breath picked up speed. He slowed his already snail-like pace and tried to calm his nerves. A drink from his wineskin in any other situation would've helped, but here, it didn't even spread warmth in his chest. Still, the flavor of his favorite fermented grapes reminded him of home, steeling Bacchus to carry on.

Then, he heard the footsteps.

They were not the two-legged gait of a man or upright deity, but the slapping of great paws as some creature loped along. And a low growl accompanied its approach. Cerberus would be upon him soon. Bacchus set his feet in a wide stance and backed up slowly. He fogged up the air around him, and no amount of relaxation techniques would calm his agitation.

Finally, his hands met with a hard surface. He pressed his back against it and sneaked along until he came face to faces with the great beast. The cave walls bore a rough texture, like scrubby pine needles or cropped fescue grass.

The beast's growls shook the cavern walls. Cerberus was close now. Bacchus could smell the animal's fetid breath. He stopped and swung the flashlight around, but the light barely illuminated a foot around him. Resuming his creeping pace, he held the light out in front of him.

Little by little, he stretched out his arm to extend the light's reach. Noticing an opening in the cave ahead of him, he felt the archway. The same scratchy texture, and now the stone seemed to undulate. It looked as though it was breathing—oh no...not stone. Not wall. And it was breathing. Bacchus had managed to walk the length of the treacherous dog, all the while stroking its coat. And what he'd thought was an archway was the beginning of a neck attached to one gruesome head.

A fang the length of Bacchus's thigh hung at eye level, a strand of drool dripping from one snarled lip. If he stood on tiptoe, he would've been shoulder height to the beast.

All three heads had turned toward the intruder, and tufts of hot breath blew from all six nostrils. Resembling a cross between a Rottweiler and saber-toothed tiger, the stocky creature could've gulped down Bacchus in one bite. But the mouths weren't the worst of the beast. Its eyes—terrible eyes glowed, not with light or flame, but something else. An unnatural phosphorescence that was still visible through veined eyelids, even when the dog blinked. The center head gave Bacchus a deep sniff.

"Good, doggie. Good, gigantic, horrific, terrifying doggie," Bacchus said in a soft, singsong tone. The object he held looked ridiculous. No way it would be enough distraction, but it was his only hope.

Closing his left hand around the giant latex hamburger, Bacchus started at the shrill squeak. Thank the gods Loki had convinced Bacchus to go with the extra-extra-large chew toy.

In unison, the three heads snapped to attention. Six ears pricked up, and the dog let out a chorus of deafening barks. It bounded back and forth as Bacchus had seen dogs do on Earth.

"You're just an overgrown puppy, aren't you?" Bacchus gave the toy a few more squeezes. "Here goes nothing."

With all his might, he chucked the hamburger at the gate and tried to move aside to let the animal pass. "Fetch!"

It leaped after its quarry, barreling through Bacchus. Tumbling like a leaf on the wind, Bacchus rolled aside and smacked into the real wall of the cave. The flashlight skittered across the floor and came to rest, illuminating the hound.

Once the darkness ceased to spin, Bacchus picked himself up. He edged close to Cerberus to retrieve the Maglite. The dog pounced on the squeaky toy and jumped back each time the hamburger squealed. One head dipped to smell it and another snapped at it. The last head nipped at the other two. Very soon, a civil war would break out over the plaything, and Bacchus didn't intend to be there when it did. He snatched up the flashlight and took off in the opposite direction. The River Styx couldn't be far.

Though he hustled to put as much distance between himself and the giant dog as he could, the escalating squabble amongst the heads rang loud and clear throughout the cavern. Bacchus kept up a fast jog until his lungs could no longer bear the pace. As he stopped to catch his breath, he saw a glow in the distance to the left. Those had to be the torch markers to the river's edge. Once he'd regained his wind, he headed toward the light.

Over several miles, the terrain changed from smooth rock to gravel. Surely, by the time he shuffled along a pebbled surface, he should've been close to the light source, but he was no closer to it than when he'd started walking. Fatigue weighed down his limbs. Frustrated and sweating, despite the frigid air, he stopped, threw down his pack, and sat.

Water.

If he could get away from the water's lapping noise and think for a moment, he might figure a next move. Crashing waves mocked him, followed him. Closing his eyes, he listened to the shushing. It sounded too even, probably an auditory illusion.

A red glow behind his eyelids surprised him. He opened his eyes, and a sprite floated in front of him. Its gray skin emitted a luminescent mucus. It gnashed its needle-sharp teeth and cackled. That explained the unreachable light. Bacchus sighed and waved away the grotesque creature.

It flew to the ceiling, and all at once, a thousand sprites, hanging from the ceiling wrapped in leathery, bat-like wings, blazed to life. The same fluorescent slime oozed from their skin. After his eyes adjusted to the brightness, Bacchus found himself on an island in the center of the very river he'd been looking for. The "pebbles" crunching underfoot were tiny sprite skeletons. So many, they'd formed a bridge of bones leading from the mouth of the river to the center, but now the water was rising. High tide. Black waters covered the bones, leaving him stranded on a rapidly shrinking island. The sprites howled, dripping green-glowing spots on his shirt and pants.

After scrambling to his feet, he shouldered his pack and climbed to the center of the bone heap. The move would buy some time, but soon, the caustic water would be upon him. Stupid, stupid, stupid. Bacchus should've known better than to follow an alluring light. Nothing in the Underworld, or Hell, was as it seemed. Loki's warning flashed through Bacchus's mind:

"If something seems too easy down there"—the green god drummed his fingertips together—"then it's probably a set up. I helped design some of the security systems." He bared his teeth in what perhaps was a smile, but didn't resemble one.

Bacchus swore under his breath. He looked down at the shrinking six-foot circle of dry land he had left. And to add insult to injury, he wore his Kenneth Cole boots. What a travesty they'd be dissolved right along with him.

A rush of wind drew his attention, followed by a roaring hum growing steadily louder. A thick fog rolled in and cloaked the river's surface. A burst of blue flame and a figure appeared. It seemed to float across the surface of the water without conveyance. Charon. And not a minute too soon.

Bacchus heaved a sigh, wiping a palm across his forehead. With luck, the ferryman would save both Bacchus's hide and his beautiful boots.

As Charon drew closer, Bacchus saw no face occupying the dark hood. In fact, the entire black cloak was suspended mid-air with no substance beneath it. But then the figure reached up and pulled back his hood. Bacchus marveled at the sight of Charon's face. Handsome as any man he'd ever seen, high cheekbones swept up to an arched brow from a strong jaw. Black curls caressed the ferryman's forehead and cheeks. Plump red lips parted in a half-smile. And his eyes—purple with flecks of green. Fire danced in those unusual eyes, and Bacchus couldn't turn away. Heat thawed the air around them, and Bacchus basked in Charon's warmth.

A few beads of sweat dotted the ferryman's unlined brow, but then, the beads turned to a trickle. The first drop that streamed down Charon's face didn't seem out of the ordinary, but the ones that followed...was his flesh melting?

The ferryman's head burst into onyx flame, taking the robe with it and revealing a skeleton beneath. He screamed and writhed as his eyeballs sizzled and popped, splattering Bacchus with gore. From his ribcage, a greasy brown serpent oozed out his mouth.

Bacchus reeled backward, stumbling into the black water. A final shriek rang through the cave, and Bacchus couldn't tell if it came from him or the charred ferryman.

# Chapter 25

*Fire and Ice*

Charon doubled over with laughter, wiping a tear from his now restored face.

Dripping wet and sullen, Bacchus pushed away the ferryman's extended hand.

"Come on. Don't be like that." Charon took a few deep breaths. "Seriously, that joke never gets old."

"Yes. Ha ha. Very funny." Bacchus furrowed his brow. "And how was I supposed to know the water isn't really acid like everyone says?"

Charon motioned upstream. "Oh, it is. Farther up, but here, the sprite snot evens out the pH balance."

"You ruined my boots."

"Sorry, bub, but you shouldn't be here anyhow." Charon eyed Bacchus up and down. "Hey, do I know you?"

Bacchus studied his soggy boots. Ruined, just ruined. "I doubt it."

"Nah, I'm sure. I know you." The ferryman closed one eyed. "Hmph. It'll come to me. Anyway, what's a living person like you doing here? You lost or something?"

"Not exactly. I need passage to the Fields of Fire."

Charon took a toothpick out of his cloak and dug at the spaces between his pearly white teeth. "No can do, buddy. No living thing is allowed in these parts. You go back where you came from before you get both of us in trouble."

The ferryman turned to leave, but Bacchus remembered the offering in his pack. Thank the gods Furina's bag was waterproof. He opened the drawstring pouch and pulled out the Entenmann's box. The apple strudel had gotten a bit jostled along the way, but wasn't too much worse for the wear.

"Well, that's too bad. I guess I'll have a snack while I wait for low tide. No sense getting any wetter than I already am." Bacchus shrugged.

The black hood swiveled around, and Charon craned his neck to see what Bacchus held. "What you got there?"

"This?" Bacchus opened the box, hunching over it. "It's a little thing I brought from Earth. It's an apple strudel. I'm sure you wouldn't like it. Very sweet. And sticky."

Charon jumped ashore. "Now, let's not be too hasty. Is it topped with streusel?"

"Of course." Bacchus broke off a chunk and shoved it in his mouth. It was, in truth, quite tasty.

"I'll make you a deal." The ferryman licked his lips. "You hand over the apple strudel, and I'll take you anywhere you wanna go. But this is just between us, *capisce?*"

A look Bacchus knew all too well shadowed Charon's handsome face. It was nothing short of pure, unadulterated desire. Pandora had been right on the money about Charon's love of apple strudel—with streusel, of course.

"Well…" Bacchus pretended to deliberate. "I wouldn't want to get you in any trouble."

He took another piece and let it melt in his mouth, groaning in enjoyment.

"Look, bub. You wanna get to the Fields of Fire or not?"

Bacchus looked up at the beasties on the ceiling. "I do need to get there, and I don't really want to stay here." He screwed up his face in exaggerated thought. "Okay. Here you are."

Charon snatched the pastry from Bacchus's hand and gobbled a large chunk. "Fuck me, that's good."

He stepped aside to allow Bacchus to board a sleek, black cigarette motorboat. "What happened to the gondola one sees in pictures?"

Licking his fingers, the ferryman shot Bacchus an annoyed look. "I'm five thousand years old. I should irritate my carpel tunnel syndrome pushing that stick around?"

"Sorry. Just asking." Bacchus settled into a black leather seat.

Charon turned the key, and the boat's engine roared to life. "Next stop, Fields of Fire."

The powerboat tore through the water and sped along at a fast clip. Once they'd cleared the sprites' lair, pitch-blackness closed in on them. Charon flipped on halogen lights and further opened the throttle.

"So, what's a topsider want in the Fields of Fire?" asked the ferryman.

Bacchus shrugged. "The usual. What does anyone want in the Fields of Fire?"

"Nothing. That's why I'm asking. I never seen anyone, alive or dead, go there voluntarily."

Studying the wave crests on the dark water, Bacchus shook his head. "It's something I have to do. I have to get to the palace gates."

Charon barked out a laugh. "And you picked this as your route. You must be one crazy human."

Ahead, the waterway forked. A sign indicated Yomi, Tuonela, and Hades to the right, the route to Naraka, Jigoku, and Hell lay in the opposite direction. Charon steered the boat to the left.

"I can't very well waltz through the front door. Dying in glorious battle isn't as easy these days as it once was."

"You're telling me? And suicide would bring you here to me, too. Yeah, you got a point. Might as well keep your flesh and bone in tact if the result's all the same. And you got something—or someone to go back for, doncha?"

"I hope so."

"Ha. I like you. You got balls, buddy. So what route you going to take to get to the gates?"

"A friend told me to follow the river Phlegethon through the Fields of Fire, across Demon Gorge and work my way through the Hall of Souls."

Charon nodded. "Yeah, that'll get you there, but don't follow the Phlegethon."

"But I'll get lost otherwise."

"Nah, nah, nah. You stick to the banks of the Phlegethon, and you'll tack another whole day onto your journey, and I get the feeling you're in a hurry. Am I right?"

Bacchus nodded. True, he was in a hurry.

"Okay, then," said Charon. "What you wanna do is cut through the back brush. Keep an eye out for the burning bushes. They're stadion markers. Start counting when you run into the first one, and once you get to a hundred and one stadia, take a right. You'll be at the narrowest part of Demons Gorge. It'll save you a day, easy."

Easy? The word set off bells and whistles in Bacchus's mind. He thanked Charon for the directions, but doubted he would heed them.

Switching off the motor, Charon coasted up to the shore of the Fields of Fire. A misnomer indeed. A barren stretch of tundra replete with ice, snow, and lichen comprised the Fields.

"Is this the right stop?" Bacchus asked.

"What? You insult me, my friend. What? I don't know the Fields of Fire? I only been running this route five millennia, but what do I know, huh?"

"I'm sorry. I didn't mean to offend. I thought from the name there would be...you know, more heat, flames. That kind of thing."

Charon flicked Bacchus's temple. "Well, that's what you get for thinking, buddy. It's called the Fields of Fire because it's so friggin' cold it burns."

Great. "Will the temperature kill me?"

"Nope. You ain't that lucky." Charon growled a laugh. "Have fun, quest-boy. And watch that first step. You fall in this time, and you won't have to worry about saving your skin anymore."

Bacchus thanked his guide and leaped to dry land.

"Hey, and thanks for the strudel. Good stuff, man," Charon called ashore, cranking the boat's engine.

Bacchus waved and turned into the howling wind. Frost formed in his hair, and though he knew it to be pointless, he dug his overcoat and a pair of gloves out of the pack. Hopefully, he wouldn't freeze off anything important.

\* \* \* \*

Every inch of Bacchus's skin stung, even the unexposed parts. His toes and fingers had gone numb. His lips, dried and cracked, stuck together. He should've listened to the ferryman. Checking the watch he'd purchased for just this occasion, he shook his head. As it was, he'd already spent twelve hours trudging along the riverbanks, and there seemed to be no end in sight. And some "river of fire" this had turned out to be. The "flames" were actually ice stalagmites that formed on top of the frozen river formed by centuries of droplets splashing down from the cave's ceiling. The ice's mineral content formed the various red, yellow, and orange hues streaking up the sides of each formation. At first glance, the river did appear to be made of fire. That was until the chill wind blew.

Not only had the physical discomfort become unbearable, but with each passing minute, his heart grew emptier. Loki had warned him about this side effect of the Fields of Fire. The area existed to suck the hope of enlightenment and redemption from the souls of the damned.

"You'll need something to keep you inspired," Loki had said.

Bacchus had brought along several full wineskins, but no matter how hard he tried—or how much he drank—he couldn't focus on his goal. He yearned to curl up in a ball and let the snowdrifts cover him. Tossing down his pack, he sank to his knees. As his fished out his wineskin, his fingers grazed the picture of Ariana he'd brought. He plucked it from the bag and took a long look at her.

"I have failed you, my love." He wiped his thumb across the frost building up on the picture's surface. A long drink of Cabernet Sauvignon did little to rouse his spirits. He should've listened to the ferryman. He'd be out of here by now if he'd only heeded Charon's advice. The mistake gnawed at him.

"Failure," a voice hissed in his ear. It tempted him to rest. "Put your head down and go no farther. Give up."

Bacchus lay down and tucked his knees to his chest. Yes, it would be all right if he slept for a little while. He'd sleep an hour, no more. An hour of rest and he'd be good as new. And did he care if he wasn't?

* * * *

"Where's the crown?" A deep voice rumbled across his dreamscape. At least, he hoped Bacchus was dreaming, because otherwise, Heracles was very, very lost.

"What crown?" Bacchus asked.

Heracles pointed to the sky. The Underworld ceiling split open and the Milky Way stretched above Bacchus. The stars sparkled before his eyes. Heracles broke apart into the celestial bodies that made up his constellation. A swirling vortex appeared to the right of the collection of stars ready to devour the Universe.

The disembodied voice of his demigod brother rang in Bacchus's ears. "Where's the crown?"

The black hole began to suck in Heracles's stars, and he screamed, "Where's the crown?"

A cold sweat broke out on Bacchus's brow. "What crown? I don't understand. What crown?"

The black hole turned into a beast with great swirling arms, consuming all the light in its path. Immense gravity ripped Bacchus apart. Agony tore at his muscles and joints.

The priestess of the Oracle appeared and clapped her hands. "Find the crown."

Bacchus snapped awake. A blanket of snow had covered him, but Heracles's voice echoed in his head. He had to get up. He had to press on. Bacchus would find the crown. Whatever that meant.

# Chapter 26

*Sex, Lies, and Oedipal Complex*

A few hours later, the snowstorm started to abate, and another hour later, the precipitation disappeared altogether. The ground beneath Bacchus's feet grew spongy and wet. He could hope the worst of the cold was behind. He'd made it through the Fields of Fire. Hope. Miraculous, bright, and shiny hope.

He crested a ridge leading to the edge of a canyon. The permafrost was gone. In its place, a gorge across which heat rippled. It stretched on as far as the eye could see. Baked rock, weakened by fissures due to the scorching temperatures, led straight down several hundred feet to a bottom of cracked, dried mud. He'd made it to Demon Gorge. At least he'd have some company along this journey.

"Believe nothing of what they say," Loki warned. "Demons are notorious liars who will say or do anything to break your free will. Turn a deaf ear to them."

Bacchus stripped off his coat and shirt and tucked both items into Furina's bag. He took out climbing gear, a set of ear buds, and a device that played music. Pan had loaded flute and lyre solos onto the tiny machine. He stepped into the harness, pulled on a set of gloves, and secured the safety gear. With the pack strapped to his shoulders, Bacchus set the anchors in the rock walls and dropped over the side, ready to rappel down.

Without a descender, the ropes whizzed through his gloved hands. The iPod had gotten tangled in the ropes, and it fell onto the jagged rocks below. So much for his musical distraction.

Bacchus continued to rappel and did his best to regulate the speed, but he'd only done this one other time in his long existence. And that time, he had been drunk, scaling the sandstone wall that housed Xerxes' harem.

Oh what a week that had been. He doubted this endeavor would be as pleasurable.

When Bacchus was half way down the cliff, the first demon struck. A female demon, luscious curves and blonde curls. Her giggles tinkled in his ear. She hovered in the air around him.

"Hey there, big boy." She simpered.

Bacchus reminded himself to ignore her, but the temptress made the feat close to impossible. Her breasts jiggled in his face; she stroked between his legs as he continued his decent.

"Come with me." She ran a razor sharp fingernail over one of his lips, nicking it, and drawing blood. Her tongue laved the droplets, but he kept moving.

She moaned and shimmied against him. The robes she wore evaporated, and he could smell the musk of her cunt. Against his will, he felt his loins stir. She was as ripe as a Merlot grape, swelling in the August sun.

"Ignore her," he chanted under his breath.

"Look at me," she sang. "Look at me."

Bacchus kept his eyes trained on the ground below.

"Look at me," she said more forcefully. Though he knew better than to stare, Bacchus couldn't help but sneak glances at the demon. Her supple skin turned a withered shade of gray, and her face aged ninety years in a split second.

"Look at me," she rasped.

Blood poured from her eye sockets and a river of flies rushed from her wide-open mouth. She screamed, "Look at me."

Unable to get what she wanted, the screeching form broke into globs of tarry slime and then evaporated entirely. The sulfur stench she left behind gagged Bacchus, but he managed to finish his descent.

At the bottom of the gorge, he saw nothing. Only a vast, barren wasteland, but he knew better than to think he was actually alone. The gorge spanned a distance that would take a few hours to cross. If he could continue to pretend he was the only being here, he'd be fine.

He started the crossing at a jog, but soon slowed to a walk, and even resorted to the water he'd brought with him. The heated air seared his lungs, and sweat dripped down his bare torso. Then, the whispers started. The voice sounded like Ariana's, but he knew it wasn't.

"Bacchus," she murmured.

He kept his eyes trained on the gorge wall on the other side.

A spirit appeared in front of him in Ariana's form. She laughed. "Bacchus, what's the rush?"

He remained silent.

She fell in step beside him. "I'm so glad you're doing this, but it's such a long walk. Why don't we take a rest?"

Again, Bacchus gave no reaction. The false Ariana tried to take his hand. He refused to let her.

"*Mi amor*, I'm tired. Take a rest with me."

The demon nuzzled his cheek. Bacchus had to give them credit. They'd gotten her scent right and the feel of her skin. For the briefest of seconds, he wondered, had they perhaps dragged his beloved to Hell? No. He shook the thought away.

Don't let them get to you, he reminded himself.

Suddenly, she dropped to the ground in front of him. She cried, "Bacchus."

He tried to move around her, but he couldn't. She grabbed onto his feet, and he tumbled to the ground. She proved too strong to wrestle with—unnaturally strong. He grappled with her to regain his footing, but she pinned him to the ground with her knees. Laughing she bent down to kiss him. He froze.

Reminding himself over and over again this was not Ariana, he drew all his strength and cast off the demon. His feet slid against the dried dirt as he tried to stand. A few stumbled steps forward and he drew himself upright.

"Bacchus." The demon in Ariana's clothing sobbed. "Help me."

His reflexes spun him around before he could catch himself. He saw Ariana on the ground, blood pouring from her nose, her eyes rolling around in her head.

"Help me, Bacchus. Help me," she cried.

The sight pushed his heart into his throat, and tears prickled at the corner of each eye, but he forced himself to say, "You are not Ariana. You are not she."

Bacchus turned from the gruesome display and trudged onward, and still, Ariana's screams raged in the background. He set his jaw and said through clenched teeth, "You're going to have to do better than that."

A shaking hand wiped his wet eyes. Halfway there. He pushed on.

\* \* \* \*

Several more demons had tried to drag him down, some taking the form of friends, some trying to tempt him with sex or drink. Some threatened to kill everyone he loved. Some even tried to take him by force, but he'd managed to repel all of them.

Exhausted, he stood at the base of the cliff wall that led to the hall of souls. Bacchus looked up. Unsure if he had the strength left to make such a climb without a little rest, he sat down and took a swig of water—yes, water. He was that parched.

A rocky outcropping provided him with much needed shade for his respite. Though it wasn't much cooler, the illusory sun no longer beat down on his face and bare chest. He pulled out his shirt and balled it up, tucking it behind his head. No sleep, bad idea to fall asleep here, but he could rest his eyes for a little while before soldiering on.

He knew not how much time passed, an hour or so perhaps, but a soft touch roused him from his slumber.

"Dionysus?" a mellifluous voice asked.

Bacchus's eyes fluttered open. A woman with long bronze hair, clothed in a white stola, stood before him. Gentle creases lined her mouth and eyes. A few gray hairs highlighted the tresses around her triangular face. Her perfect pink lips remained plump, soft. Not a young woman, but definitely not an old one, either. She looked worldly. And how did she know that name?

"Go away, demon." Bacchus waved and hurried to shove his supplies into his pack.

"I knew you'd think that. I didn't want to approach you here, but I had to. I couldn't bear to lose you again."

He ignored the woman or demon or whatever she was.

"You don't recognize me, do you?" she said. "It's me. Semele. You mother, Dionysus."

"Nobody calls me that anymore," he replied without thinking.

"That's right." She nodded. "I heard you go by Bacchus these days. It must've been hard growing up with a name that means 'godling of Zeus' when you really had no relationship with him and no mother to look out for you. Baby, I'm so sorry."

He stood up and shouldered his pack. "Well, it was lovely to see you again, Mommy Dearest, but I have to get going."

Semele reached out and placed a gentle hand on his shoulder. Oh— her touch. Warmth and compassion radiated straight to core, piercing his heart. She gave him a concerned smile. He wanted to shake off her hand, but it felt so damn good.

"You've grown up very handsome." She broadened her smile.

"You are not my mother." He fought the urge to stay with her and turned to begin the long climb ahead of him.

She clutched his hand. "Baby, please, take me with you. I don't want to stay here, lost in the Underworld. Take me with you."

"You're not my mother." He shoved her away and took out his climbing gear. At this point, the rest of the demons had become belligerent or violent, but this one didn't. Tears welled in her eyes, and she hugged herself, arms folded across her chest. Was she really a demon? Why didn't she attack him? What if she were really... Bacchus fought the idea. This was not his mother.

"It's been so hard. I've been trapped here. No way to call to you, no way to let you know I was still here. I watched you grow up as best I could. My baby, the god."

The pride in her eyes shamed him. He said, "I'm not a god anymore."

"How can that be? What happened?" She put an arm around him. "Tell Mother all about it."

The embrace warmed his heart. He was tired—so tired. The humiliation, the struggles to free Ariana, her rejection, and now these trials. Bacchus was too exhausted to carry on. He could stay here with her. With Semele. His mother.

Sobs shook his shoulders, and he buried his face in his mother's soft bosom.

"There, there, love." She stroked his hair.

The storm of tears stretched on forever, though most likely only a few minutes passed. Finally, Bacchus calmed, limp with exhaustion. Could it be true that he'd found his mother at long last? And did he care if she weren't? If he could stay here, just like this, maybe it didn't matter.

His mother wiped his face and pulled out a linen handkerchief for him to blow his nose.

"Thank you, M-mother." The word felt thick in his mouth, foreign and indefinable. He'd never had need to speak it.

Her eyes lit up, and she grinned at the endearment. She smoothed over the bodice of her *stola.* "Now, you have a quest to finish, my son. You can't stay here. You have to keep moving. There are demons in this valley."

See, she wasn't a demon. The demons all begged him to stay, tried to keep him here, but his mother was urging him on. At long last, he'd found his mother.

"You're right." He wiped his nose again. "Will you... Would you like to come with me, Mother?"

"Oh, yes." She clapped her hands. "Do you think you can lift both of us out of here?"

*Cindy Jacks*

"I know I can."

Bacchus rigged a harness that would keep her in tandem and helped her into it. He secured the rope system and boosted her onto his back. A petite woman, she weighed no more than a feather. He'd made it three-quarters of the way up the ravine in no time at all.

"We're almost there, Mother." He looked back at her. "Are you doing all right?"

"Hmm, yes. I am." She squeezed his trapezius muscles. At first, the pressure felt good, but then, the pressure turned to blinding pain. Teeth sunk into his neck and claws ripping his hands away from the safety line. He lost his grip and felt his body float back into mid-air. Then, he began to fall.

Cackles and howls rose up from beneath. Bacchus turned his head to see the demon, who had masqueraded as his mother, tumbling toward the ground with glee. And the ground was coming up fast.

*Stupid, stupid, stupid.* How could he have been so gullible? If he didn't find a way to catch himself, he'd splatter on the dried mud below. He twisted around and reached for the canyon wall. His hands scraped against the brittle rock. Looking down, he saw it. His one chance for salvation—one of the holds he'd driven into the cliff wall. He stretched his arms down and put his hands together. As soon as the metal hit his palms, he clamped his fingers around the peg and held on for dear life.

He jerked to a halt, and his shoulders seared with pain as though they'd been torn from his sockets. Dangling, he bowed his head and battled the urge to vomit.

The demons cackles turned to screams of rage, and Bacchus knew he'd outwitted it. The evil spirit turned into a black vapor and darted up toward him. With all the strength he could muster, he heaved himself up, free climbing up the handholds. His muscles burned, and his shoulders ached for a rest, but he didn't stop. He pulled and wrenched and lugged himself to the top.

One leg straddled the edge as the demon caught him and sunk in its claws. It tore his flesh, but he wrested free. Tumbling onto the dusty ledge, he rolled away from the shrieking phantasm. As if it hit an invisible barrier, the demon evaporated, the last of its obscenities echoing around the chasm.

Bacchus coughed up dust and bile. Pain clutched him, and he lay unable to do anything but quiver. At least he'd made it out of the gorge with his soul intact—as for his sanity, perhaps not.

# Chapter 27

*A Moral Compass*

After a few hours rest, some wine, and bread with cheese, Bacchus felt better able to carry on. He'd made it past Cerberus, bribed Charon to take him across the Styx, labored through the Fields of Fire, and escaped Demon Gorge. The Hall of Souls seemed like a cakewalk in comparison.

"The Hall," Loki said, "is the main reservoir where all newly deceased souls wind up. The longer you spend in the hall, the more you forget who you once were. Preparation for reincarnation."

Apparently, the sorting process worked like this:

Souls ready to move on found their way to enlightenment and therefore passed into the Palace of Light. Those so tainted they were irredeemable were sucked into Hell. But the vast majority of souls milled about aimlessly until they were recycled for another stint on Earth. By the time the spirit was reborn, it had forgotten who it used to be in past lifetimes.

"Do not—I repeat—do not linger too long in the Hall of Souls, or you will forget who you are and why you came there," said Loki. "And you'll need this so you don't get lost."

Loki handed over a silver compass that appeared to be broken since its needle hung limp, stuck somewhere between north and west no matter which direction Bacchus turned.

"It's not broken," Loki snapped. "It's a moral compass. When you get in the hall, if you're worthy, it will show you the way to the Palace of Light."

Though the whole part about "being worthy" gave him pause, Bacchus wondered how he could possibly get lost in a hall? He would march straight through to the Palace gates without dilly-dallying. Now faced with the structure he understood. The 'Hall' of souls wasn't a hall, but a maze. Good thing Bacchus had planned for this eventuality.

From his sack, he pulled the same copy of *Bacchae* he'd read on the plane, and he set his watch to chime every fifteen minutes. He planned to stop and read from the book every time the alarm sounded. Seemed logical he couldn't forget who he was if he constantly reminded himself.

Book, alarm, and compass at the ready, Bacchus entered the Hall of Souls. Despite the fact that it was an enclosed space, a blinding light greeted him inside the maze. It took a few minutes for his eyes to adjust. Everything was white—the walls, the floors, the ceiling. Even his clothes had turned white. He couldn't tell up from down or right from left. Glancing down at the compass, he sighed. The needle swung around wildly without settling on a given direction.

Leave it to Loki to saddle him with a broken moral compass. Perhaps Bacchus's lack of moral direction affected the blasted thing. He'd have to work his way through on his own. Maybe he could find someone to follow.

He walked on for fifteen minutes without encountering another soul. His watch rang, and he stopped and skimmed through the passages off *Bacchae*.

"You are Bacchus, former and future god of intoxication and ecstasy," he said to himself. "You are here to reach the gates of the Palace of Light, meet with the Council of Deities, and gain immortality for the woman you love. Ariana. Who hates you…right."

He picked up and continued to wander deeper into the maze.

After the first three hours, he forgot what he was supposed to do with the compass.

After six hours, he forgot Ariana's name.

By the time he'd spent twelve hours in the maze, he forgot his purpose.

After twenty-four hours, he couldn't remember why he was carrying a book or why his damn watch beeped every fifteen minutes.

Confused, he sat down on the pure white marble floor and chewed his bottom lip. Now why was he here? If only he could remember his name… but that too had escaped him.

# Chapter 28

*Saving Grace*

How long had he been here? Had it been three days or three years? The god…the man… Who he was he couldn't remember. His watch sounded. How did he turn off this infernal thing? And there was something important he was supposed to do, if only he could remember what.

"Help me," he said to no one in particular. If only someone could help him.

A couple other lost souls eyed him up, but none of them had any clue what they were doing. They all wandered around in the whitewashed maze, unaware of what ground they'd covered and what exit they sought.

The confounded traveler had the sense he was supposed to keep going, but why? And to where? He leaned against a wall and bit a worn thumbnail. It'd been worn down to the quick. Had he done that?

A muffled cry resounded off the walls. The traveler checked his own eyes to be sure—No, he wasn't the one crying. He searched around several twists and turns to find a small girl, huddled in a ball in a corner.

He knelt down beside her. "Are you okay, little one?"

She gave a choked squeal and tried to make herself smaller.

"Don't be afraid." He stroked her hair. "I promise, I won't hurt you. I only want to help."

She lifted her head. A fringe of golden bangs grazed her nose. She pushed the hair from her eyes. "I don't know where my mom is."

Something about the phrase sounded familiar to the traveler. Someone he knew had lost his mother too.

"I can help you find her." He held out a hand.

The little girl recoiled and wailed, "I'm not supposed to go with strangers."

"I guess that's good advice." He nodded. But he couldn't leave her here, stranded. He asked, "What happened to your mother?"

"Something bad happened to our car. It crashed. She was holding me... And then I woke up here."

"Oh. I'm sure she must be around here somewhere." He sat down. "Would you like me to wait with you?"

The girl shrugged. "I guess that would be okay."

"What's your name?"

"Grace. What's yours?"

The traveler opened his mouth to answer, but then realized he couldn't answer the question. "This may sound funny, but I can't remember."

Grace wiped her runny nose with the back of her hand and gave a halfhearted giggle. "That is funny."

The traveler's watch sounded.

"What's that for?" asked Grace.

He shook his head. "I don't know."

This time she laughed outright. "What do you know?"

He scratched his temple. "I feel like I'm supposed to find someone too, but I can't remember who."

Grace reached out and took the compass from the traveler's hand. "Is that why you're carrying this?"

"Could be."

The spinning needle slowed and finally pointed to north by northwest. The traveler took back the compass, and the needle reeled in all sorts of crazy directions. He handed it to Grace, and again it pointed north by northwest.

Grace picked herself up, smoothed her wrinkled dress, and held out her free hand. "I think we should follow it."

"Are you sure?"

She leaned over and whispered in his ear, "I'm a Brownie. I know these things." Patting his cheek, she rubbed her fingers over his stubble.

The traveler knew she must be right. He scrambled to his feet and took her hand. "You lead the way," he said.

She took off with trepidation at first, but then gained confidence. Her little feet trotted around each corner with certainty. No matter how many turns they took, the needle remained constant. They'd covered quite a bit of ground in the first hour. So much so, fatigue weighed down her steps.

Grace plopped onto her bottom and looked up at the traveler.

"Tired?" he asked.

She nodded.

The traveler scooped her up and carried her. They kept plodding along until two hours later they reached a long, brighter hallway, no side paths shooting off of it. As soon as the traveler crossed the threshold, a tickle of memory returned to him.

"Bacchus," he said.

"Huh?" asked Grace.

"My name. I think it's Bacchus."

The little girl giggled. "That's a funny name."

Bacchus hugged her. "It is, isn't it? Let's keep going. I think we're close to getting out of here."

Instead of being surrounded by blinding whiteness, the aura of the entire hall changed to a pearly silver. Sparkling flecks dripped onto their skin and clothes. He looked up and saw a river of pure silver rushing overhead. Droplets from the river rained down. Their hair and eyelashes glittered, the flakes stuck to their skin. Abject joy filled Bacchus, though he knew not why. Grace laughed and threw her hands in the air. With each bit of silver touching his skin, Bacchus regained bits of his memory—his tenure as a god, his time on Earth, his beloved Ariana. He remembered the purpose for his quest. He had to save her.

"When you reach the River of a Thousand Tears, you'll emerge at Saint Peter's Gate. From there, anytime you want to get yourself arrested, it's all good. You'll be thrown in the Palace lock-up and brought before the Council for sentencing. Then you say your piece and all that noise. La-dee-da-dee-da." Loki had danced around as he relayed the information.

"We're here, Grace. We made it." Bacchus rushed for the exit. The child clung to him, her quickened breath brushing his cheek.

As soon as they exited the maze, a blue sky and fields of wildflowers greeted them. A set of gates, cast in gold and adorned with sculpted jasmine vines, that somehow still blossomed and perfumed the air, stood in the distance. They opened, and an elderly couple emerged.

"Grammy, Pop Pop," Grace exclaimed.

Bacchus set her down, and she raced to meet her grandparents. They pulled her into a hug.

"Is Mommy here?" she asked.

Her grandmother brushed a lock of hair from Grace's forehead. "Baby, it's not time for Mommy to join us yet."

"Can I see her?"

"Yes." Her grandfather handed her a mirror. "Anytime you want to see Mommy, look in here."

Grace gave a soft smile. "This is my friend, Bacchus. He saved me."

Bacchus knelt in front of her. "No, little one. You saved me."

"Here's your compass back." She held out her hand.

"You keep it." He planted a kiss on top of her head. "Looks like you're in good hands now."

The gates swung open, and her grandparents motioned to them. "Time to go, baby."

Grace nodded and turned back toward Bacchus. "Can you come with us?"

Bacchus shook his head. "No, love. I have to stay here. But all the milk and cookies you can eat are waiting for you inside those gates."

"Even chocolate milk?"

He gave a chuckle. "Even chocolate milk."

She encircled his neck and gave him a full body hug. "Thank you, Bacchus."

He rubbed her back. "Thank you, Grace. Now, go on. The gates won't stay open forever."

She took her grandparents hands and walked through with them. Warm and pure white light enveloped her, and then the gates swung closed.

Bacchus opened his pack and pulled out a package of balloons and his wineskin. Time to get arrested.

# Chapter 29

*Redemption*

*Thwack. Sploosh.*
*Thwack. Sploosh.*
Using a slingshot and water balloons filled with wine, Bacchus pelted the guard tower of the Pearly Gates. As expected, Saint Peter trotted out to check on the commotion.

"What in the name of Mother Mary—" The white bearded cleric studied the sullied tower.

*Twack. Sploosh.* Yes. Right on target. Bacchus had managed to hit Peter square in the face. Marvelously accurate weapon for having cost only five dollars.

Peter sputtered and called upon the archangels. Michael descended in a burst of heaven's fire. Bacchus squeezed his eyes shut to avoid being blinded or disfigured. Poor Moses and his goat's horns.

Manifesting in his human-like form, Michael stood eight feet tall with the baby smooth skin of, well, an angel. His long, blazing red hair hung between his wings, down his muscled back in a long braid. He wore only a loincloth and his sword belt. His hard, marble-like skin needed no armor for protection. It could not be pierced by any implement, mortal or divine. It could, however, break a water-balloon.

Bacchus took aim and let a projectile fly.

*Thwack. Sploosh.* A direct hit of Merlot stained one of Michael's snowy, white wings.

"What the fu—" the archangel began, but Peter interceded.

"Language, Michael."

Instead of finishing his expletive, Michael turned his steely gaze on the cloud cover around the gates. He easily spotted Bacchus who hadn't tried all that hard to camouflage himself.

"Bacchus? Is that you?" the archangel asked, storming out to snatch up his foe, sword drawn.

The fallen god jumped up and dropped his latex arsenal. He put his hands over his head. "I don't want to fight."

"You shoulda thought of that before you hit me with a wine grenade, huh?" Michael grabbed Bacchus by the shirt and hoisted him up.

"Take it easy, now, Michael. It was just a joke."

"Not a very funny one."

"Clearly."

Michael dropped Bacchus and pulled out a golden strand of rope from his sword belt. Not that he was stupid enough to resist an archangel in Bacchus's current limited form, but Michael secured Bacchus's hands anyway. The angel grunted and gestured toward the tunnel off to the side of the Pearly Gates. Bacchus trudged toward the Palace of Light's jail entrance.

The inside of the Palace prison looked more like a day spa than a jail, but considering the prestigious inmates that had been inside these walls, certain luxuries were required to prevent rebellion. Not designed for serious law-breakers, Strawberry Fields—as it was nicknamed—never saw the likes of infamous outlaws such as Kronos or Lucifer. It had held Loki more than once, and even Bacchus after a particularly eventful bender. It was nice to see the place with a clear head.

A short hallway adorned with an intricate floral mural led to cells with invisible walls. Each prisoner had their own fountain of nectar and buffet of ambrosia. Along with nourishment, there were velvet divans, hot tubs, and garden spaces available for use by inmates. At first glance, the prisoners looked as though they were attending a cocktail party rather than awaiting judgment by the Council.

"We've had a busy day," Michael said, "so you'll have to share a cell."

Bacchus shrugged. "That's okay."

"I wasn't asking permission."

Right.

The archangel placed a hand against the ether around each cell. A small opening appeared and Michael pushed Bacchus through it.

"Enjoy your stay." Michael turned to leave.

"Oh Mikey, how long will I be here before the Council summons me?"

Michael's angular face broke into a menacing smile. "God only knows."

"Ha ha."

So much for the right to a speedy trial. Silly earthly concept. But considering an outcast god had breached the Underworld, made it through Hell—literally—and had made it as far as the Pearly Gates without prior detection, the Council would probably want to have a chat with him as soon as possible. Bacchus took a seat on a divan and made himself comfortable.

The ornate sofa disappeared and dumped him on his back against the cold marble floor. A cackle reverberated around the cell. The Egyptian god Set materialized.

"Little help?" Bacchus held out a hand.

Still snickering, Set pulled him up. "Bacchus, how are you, friend?"

"I've had better days." He rubbed his backside.

"All in good fun." Set strolled over to the buffet and popped a strawberry into his mouth. Shy of seven feet tall, the trickster cut an impressive figure. Though he'd been blessed with gorgeous locks of jet-black hair, he wore it shorn except for a topknot. Cinnamon skin and golden eyes gave the god an ethereal glow. A tunic of spun silver draped over his sculpted body.

"What are you in for?" Bacchus asked.

"I cut up my brother Osiris again and fed him to some crocs along the Nile. I don't know why the Council always gets their loincloths in a knot. He never stays dead."

Bacchus gave an uneasy chuckle. "I know, right?"

"Not to be rude, but I heard you'd been banished."

"Not to put too fine a point on it, Set. Yeah, I was banished, but I'm here to argue for the immortality of another. I broke in through the Underworld."

"Oh, ho, ho. You're here for the same reason I am, then."

"What do you mean?"

"A female, correct?"

Setting his jaw, Bacchus nodded. "And she hates me."

"But you love her, and you'd do anything to have her. Even murder your own brother."

"Well, not exactly, but just about anything else."

Set sank into the reappeared divan. "And they never appreciate it. 'Osiris, Osiris, Osiris,' that's all I ever hear from Isis. But has he bothered to slice me into pieces for her? No. I think they like this ridiculous game."

"Then, why do you play it?"

A glazed look came over the storm god's face. "Because the little bit of time I get to spend with Isis makes it worth all the hoops, all the trials—all the darkness I endure on her behalf."

Bacchus stroked his scratchy chin. Food for thought. By devoting himself to Ariana, would Bacchus trap himself in a cycle of devotion and rejection from which he'd be unwilling to break free? It was a chance he was willing to take.

Michael descended outside the cell, golden bindings at the ready. "It's your lucky day, Bacchus. The Council would like to see you. Immediately."

"But Set was here first. He should be allowed to plead his case."

Set shook his head and gave Bacchus a nudge. "I know my fate, friend. Go find out yours and plead for your lady love."

Bacchus shook Set's large, warm hand. "Thank you. I shall do my best."

Releasing Bacchus's hand, Set reclined on the divan and closed his eyes. The storm god hummed, *Strawberry Fields Forever*.

\* \* \* \*

"What are you doing here, Bacchus?" The Father's voice boomed, a thunderous echo throughout the hall.

Bacchus dropped to his knees, though not of his own accord. The shock waves from the Father's shout had knocked him down. "My lord, I have witnessed injustice, and I cannot let it stand without doing everything in my power—"

"Your power?" The Father seethed, clenching his fists. "You have no power."

The Mother placed a hand on her husband's arm and gave him a look. *The* look. With a wrinkle of his upper lip and eye roll, the Father fell silent.

"Please rise, child," the Mother told Bacchus.

He complied, his whole body trembling. This had to work. They had to listen. He wouldn't leave until they did. Even if they struck him down, he would haunt these halls and beg for Ariana's life.

"Speak," she said.

Bacchus cleared his throat, peeling his tongue off the roof of his mouth. The words wouldn't come, but he forced them out. "As I was saying, I've witnessed an injustice, and I'd like to plead with the Council to set it right.

"I was cast down to Earth because I—I didn't take my responsibilities seriously. I don't even think I understood what those responsibilities were, but this woman, my Ariana. I set out to help her, but that's not how it turned out. I mean, I think I've improved her life. I hope I have, but this much I do know. She helped me. She showed me how inadequate a god I was, what an inadequate being I have been."

Discordia glared, oozing hatred. "And for this you think you deserve to be reinstated? So you can skip along like you used to with your head up your ass?"

"No, madam. I didn't come here today to plead for my divinity. I don't deserve it, and I'm not sure I ever did." Bacchus shifted to face the Father and the Mother. "I came to ask for the redemption of another. During the trials I undertook to help myself, I was lucky enough to know an enlightened spirit. I'm here today to ask that you elevate Ariana. Release her from the cycle of death and rebirth. She is truly worthy of your gifts."

The Father waved away Bacchus's words. "Why should we favor one average, insignificant human? She's not even the best example of her kind. There are far worthier individuals who will require at least one or two more rounds of reincarnation before they are ready to join us."

"I don't argue that point." Bacchus clasped his hands together as if in prayer. "She may not have negotiated a peace treaty or devoted her life to sick children in India, but she is enlightened, and she sacrificed years of her own misery so that her father might be released from his. If that isn't noble, then I don't know what is. To her father, I'd dare say, she is far from insignificant. And she's far from insignificant to me as well."

He waited for a response, but saw only blank stares and Discordia's penetrating gaze.

Wiping the sweat from his forehead, he walked closer to the Council, Bacchus placed his hand to his chest. His heartbeat pounded against his fingertips. "She taught me the real meaning of love. She taught me the error of my ways. Though there may be more accomplished souls on Earth, there is none any finer. And yet, in your ultimate wisdom, you've chosen to cut her life short, give her this terrifying condition that will at best haunt her for the rest of her days and at worst—" Emotion clutched his throat, but he pushed himself to go on. "And you wonder? How many times have I heard each one of you voice bewilderment that the beings we preside over often forsake us? Why do they turn away? I couldn't answer the question during my time as a god, but I can say now, with all certainty, that it is you who have turned your backs on them. They feel it as surely as I do. The coldness and darkness chases them, and yet, they still find the strength to rise and struggle and work their way back into the light. And that—that is the true miracle."

Silence. He studied the passive faces of his former peers. Not one moved to speak or acknowledge the truth in what he'd said. Their apathy disgusted him, twisting a knife in his gut. He spat. Casting Ariana's sorrows box on the floor of the Great Hall, he didn't wait to be excused to take his leave.

"Halt." Two voices rose in unison. The Father and The Mother spoke as one.

With fear as much as reverence, Bacchus stopped his retreat and turned to face them. This would be his end. Every fiber of his being vibrated with dread, but he struggled to remain calm.

Their bodies bloated and intertwined, resembling an enormous yin and yang symbol. Their voices continued to thunder through the entire palace. "You have shown more growth than anyone could have expected from a god of your youth. We will not command you return to your former post. Instead, we will embrace humility, embrace our folly, and request that you rejoin our ranks. Ariana's fate rests now in your more than capable hands."

Bacchus bent in a deep bow, one knee genuflected, his forehead a hair's breadth from the floor. "My lord and my lady, your humble servant accepts."

# Chapter 30

*Humble Pie*

If his palms could've sweated at this particular moment, they would've. Since Bacchus's reinstatement as a divine being, he no longer experienced the physical side effects of emotion. However, the emotions themselves became permanent remnants of his time on Earth. Anxiety clutched his spirit. Would she agree to see him? Raising an uncertain hand, he willed himself to ring the doorbell.

A few excruciating minutes ticked by, but finally, the locks rattled, and she opened the door.

"Hi." She croaked out the word. Her gaze darted from his face to the floor and back again.

"Ariana. I'm so glad to find you well." He raked a hand through his thick curls. "May I come in?"

She stepped aside and motioned for him to enter.

"Thank you." His arm grazed hers as he passed through the entryway, sending a shiver through him. He looked around his former home, the mark of the new owner evident. The furnishings and décor softened by her presence. Small touches like printed throws and vases of flowers. And all those angel figurines. His gaze fell upon the erroneous depiction of Michael—all goodness and light—and Bacchus smiled.

"What are you doing here?" Lips pursed, she regarded him askance.

The chill in her voice broke over him, heightening his already rampant panic. "I had to see you."

She crossed her arms over her chest. "I thought we'd said all there was to say."

"That's not quite true." He shook his head. "You said your piece. I'm afraid I didn't do a very good job of defending my position. I didn't mean to startle you that night. You must know I would never hurt you."

She nodded, but remained silent, and the silence frightened Bacchus more than any harsh words could. At least if she were talking—even arguing—he would have hope that he could smooth over her anger. But in quietude, what could he do?

Rushing to close the distance between them, he gathered her in his arms and pressed her body against his. "Please, Ariana. Please. I cannot bear another moment without you. Don't condemn me to an eternity of morose pining. I don't want to wind up like Set, forever bound to a woman who despises me. Please, my love."

She wrangled free and gave him a playful shove. "Oh my God, you drama king. 'An eternity of morose pining?' There you go with the fruity language again."

Though she tried to remain aloof, the hint of a smile flirted at the edge of her lips, and the corners of her eyes crinkled. Warmth spread through his chest. He was winning her over. "I know you don't owe me a thing, but please, can we talk? Can I explain to you that I know what an idiot I was?"

With her sigh, he was sure he'd broken through. Hands pressed to his lips, he waited. The reply he desired would come, he had to be patient.

Another annoyed exhalation and she relented. "Fine. I was going to get something to eat, anyway."

Bacchus threw his arms around her again, and her breath quickened. She asked, "You're a god again, aren't you?"

"How did you know?" He inhaled the sweet scent of her hair, his lips against the crown of her head.

"You feel different."

"Different how?"

She tilted her head up to meet his gaze. "It's hard to explain. Your scent, your body heat, your skin. It's all different. Overwhelming."

"Is that bad?"

She extricated herself again. "I'm not sure."

"Ariana, I am so very sorry—"

She put a finger to his lips and nodded toward the door. "*Vamonos.*"

They took the stairwell down to the streets of South Beach. In the darkness of the Underworld, Bacchus had forgotten how empowering sunlight could be. The heat kissed his face and arms. He reached out for her hand. After a moment's hesitation, she gave it, but broke free of his grasp a few seconds later.

They walked without haste or conversation to a cafe near Eliseo. The hostess seated them on the patio so Bacchus could continue to soak up the sun. He adjusted the table's umbrella to shade Ariana.

"Thank you." She lowered her gaze.

"My pleasure."

A waitress stopped by to take their order. Ariana requested a *cafe Cubano* and a *pastelito de guayaba*. Determined to enjoy all the Earthly pleasures he could during this visit, Bacchus ordered a mimosa and a slice of key lime pie. The gods only knew when he'd return to this realm.

Ariana wrinkled her nose. "I'm not sure about that combination. Or does everything taste good when you're a god?"

"I suppose, I never really thought about it." He shrugged off the question. He wasn't here to compare and contrast the different states of being he'd experienced.

She pursed her lips. "Why am I not surprised?"

The venom in her words stung. She was angry. She had every right to be. He'd not treated her with the care and concern she deserved. On the other hand, how could she be upset he wanted to give her eternal life? A lot of good all his power and glory were. Ariana had leveled him with a few unkind words.

"I don't understand," he mumbled more to the napkin on his lap than to her.

"I know you don't."

"Will you explain, then?"

She narrowed her eyes and studied his face. He reached for her hand, but she demurred. "I don't know if I can."

"Why?"

Instead of answering, she looked toward the ocean and took a deep breath. He stared at her willing her to speak. Why did this have to be so hard?

Finally, she looked at him again. "You don't understand why I don't want you to save me."

"No, I really don't." He reached for her but stopped short of touching her hands.

She pressed her lips together and then whispered, "When I'm around you, I feel weak."

"No." He furrowed his brow. "No. You have so much strength. I only want to help."

"What happens when you're aren't around to help anymore, and I still can't take care of myself?"

"Why wouldn't I be around? I'm immortal again, love."

"I don't know." She stroked her chin. "I'm just saying…what if?"

He shrugged. "I can't answer that question. It's not a contingency you need to plan for."

"But what if?" She pounded a fist on the table.

The force of her objection startled him, and many of the cafe patrons stared at her. Unwanted attention be damned, Bacchus smoothed one of her stray curls and tucked it behind her ear. "What if Apollo fails to tow the sun across the sky? What if Earth spins backward on its axis? What if I'm cast out of the heavens again? The ways in which life can suddenly change are infinite. But we are here. Now. How can you think yourself weak when you've survived so much? Most of it before you ever met me."

Closing her eyes, she shook her head. When she opened them again, she sighed. "I can't get my brain around all of this. I mean, if I told anyone else, they'd think I was crazy. A cast out god took an interest in me and liberated me from an abusive piece of shit boyfriend. Then, I finally had hope for a different life and even that was taken away because there's a blood bubble in my brain ready to pop at any second." She wagged her head back and forth. "I'm tired of being afraid."

"I—"

"Let me finish." She held up a hand. "Please."

Bacchus swallowed the words straining to leave his lips. Though he'd come here to have his say, she needed him to listen and listen he would.

Ariana sat back in her chair. "You never asked me if I wanted to be saved. And you assume I want to be by your side forever. Not that I don't appreciate everything you've done, but you never once asked me if you could meddle in my life the way you have. You made the decisions because they seem logical. It makes sense I'd want to be saved. It makes sense I should want you to take this aneurysm from me. Yeah, I should want to live forever. I should want the most insanely attractive man I've ever met—or god—whatever you are." She paused to wipe away a tear. "But you still should've asked. It's my life. My choice to make, not yours."

The full weight of his own insensitivity pushed down on him. Bacchus ran his palm across his forehead. She was right. Of course she was. She was the only being in the entire Cosmos who could correct the course of his rudderless ship.

He nodded, wishing he still had the capacity to break down into tears. What a blessed release that would've been. "I'm sorry, my love. I truly am. I didn't see it before, but you are right. I'm not used to thinking of anyone but myself. I really thought… I thought I was thinking of you."

"I know that."

He floundered, lost in a sea of words he longed to offer her, none of which would make any difference. The flat line of her lips, the blankness of her eyes, left him adrift on waves of despair. He turned toward the beach with an unseeing gaze. Perhaps she'd been right. Perhaps there was nothing more to say.

"For what it's worth"—he shifted, facing her again—"I really am sorry."

She chewed her lip and then hiccupped a sob. "And you really aren't very bright."

"What?" His eyes grew wide, and he froze. Had she no mercy? This exchange of emotions, all this discussion of feelings, he was poorly equipped for all of it. He spent barely a couple years as a mortal, and he had no clue what she wanted of him.

Finally, she broke down. "Why don't you ask me, stupid?"

Her meaning dawned on him as the sun emerged from behind a cloud, and he felt as though Thor had hammered him on the head. "Oh…ohh."

The God of Intoxication and Ecstasy scooted out of his chair and dropped to his knees before the only woman—the only being he'd ever truly loved. He took her delicate hands in one of his and brushed away her tears with the other. "Ariana, will you spend forever with this insanely attractive, but very stupid deity?"

She laughed through the tears streaming down her face. "Yes, my insanely attractive but very stupid deity. I will."

Not bothering to rise, he hugged her waist, and she smoothed his hair with her cheek. He turned his face upward and pressed his mouth against hers. The sweet taste of her lips soothed the ache that had been a fixture in his chest since she'd cast him aside. His tongue laved hers, and he pressed closer, cradling her body. Nothing could tear him away from this moment. Her warmth, the pleasing wetness of her mouth. And in that moment of clarity, he knew this woman was his alpha and his omega. His beginning and his end.

As the kissed ended, he opened his eyes and studied her black lashes and caramel skin, her red lips still moist and parted.

"I love you," he whispered.

She kissed his cheek and snuggled her nose against his hairline. "I love you, too."

A smattering of applause went up from the wait staff, who had apparently been watching the couple from afar. That they had an audience snapped Ariana and Bacchus back to reality. Her cheeks flushed bright pink, but used to being the center of attention, Bacchus scrambled to his feet and gave a short bow.

Once he was seated again, he brushed his unruly locks from his face and dusted off his pants. The waitress brought their breakfast, a smug grin on her face.

"Could you also bring us your finest bottle of champagne?" asked Bacchus.

The young lady nodded. "On the house, congratulations."

He shoveled a forkful of pie into his mouth. "By the gods." He spoke through clenched teeth. "You have to try this."

Ariana chuckled and shook her head. "It's all very simple in your world, isn't it?"

"It is." He caressed her cheek. "Something either feels good or it doesn't."

"Do I feel good to you?" She arched one brow.

Bacchus took her hand and kissed her fingers. "Simply the best, love."

# Chapter 31

*The Crown*

Holding open a burgundy velvet curtain, Bacchus peeked out at the gathering festivities. Scores of cherubim strummed lyres and played pipes as they fluttered across the gilded dome ceiling. Vines covered in jewel-toned blossoms curled around every marble column, explosions of color like fireworks frozen midair. The hall brimmed with gods, goddesses, demi-deities, angels, and even a few minor devils, all turned out in their finery. Divine beings from all realms had come to celebrate his wedding to Ariana.

He let the curtain fall back into place and turned toward a full size mirror made of crystal and liquid mercury. His reflection brought a smile to his face. So long it'd been since he'd donned a proper *chiton*, one made of the finest snowy white linen trimmed in blood red and gold. The downy fabric caressed his skin, draped from his thick collarbone, and fell in graceful folds to brush the tops of his muscular thighs. Golden sandals crisscrossed his feet and calves. A wreath of grapes leaves, forged of wafer thin gold perched atop his head. Thick cinnamon locks curled around his regal crown. Despite his confidence in his extraordinary looks, waves of nervous anticipation rolled around his taut belly. He hoped Ariana would find him handsome in the attire befitting a god. And he eagerly awaited the moment he would turn to watch his bride approach him. Speaking of which, it was time for Bacchus to head to the altar.

His father, Zeus, stood at the head of the Great Hall, resplendent as ever at the top of the marble steps that lead to Bacchus's regained throne. Bacchus trotted up the stairs and greeted the god who had given birth to him.

He bowed deeply, *"Pateras."*

"Arise my son, for you are the star of this glorious day." Zeus's silvery hair cascaded around his broad shoulders. His patrician nose held high, the god looked over his son with an air of appraisal. "It seems your time on Earth agreed with you."

"Yes, *Pateras*." Bacchus turned to face the crowd. Looking upon the beauty of his estranged father ran a knife through his chest. Had Zeus been one of the Council members who agreed to strip his own son of his divine status?

As if Zeus sensed Bacchus's thoughts—which he probably had—he said, "I have a great many powers, but dissuading the Father is not one of them. I did try...dear boy."

The last two words Zeus spoke sounded to Bacchus like an afterthought. No matter. He wouldn't let his father's strange and unpredictable affections distress him today as it had for eons. Today would be a celebration of the greatest love Bacchus had ever known. A love that bound him at last to another being. His dark beauty. His Ariana. Bacchus could not contain his jubilation at the very thought. He took a sip from his wineskin to calm his nerves.

Trumpet blasts announced the arrival of his bride to the entrance of the Great Hall. The very sight of her inspired him to drop to his knees, but somehow, he maintained his erect posture. She glowed, literally glowed, surrounded by firelight faeries, dressed in the finest spun silver. A veil of white gossamer covered her face, but he could make out the deep brown of her almond eyes and her rouged lips. Her hair tumbled around her neck, its ebony color in stark contrast to the cream-colored jasmine woven into each curl. Mouth agape, the god waited for his wedding gift to his exquisite bride to arrive.

At her side appeared a man and woman, each bearing a marked resemblance to Ariana, and her mouth fell open.

"M-Mami? Papi?" She dropped her bouquet. The firelight faeries hurried to catch it before the crystalline flowers shattered. Ariana sank to the floor and clutched her beloved parents' hands. Her mother and father joined her, the family knelt together weeping, and embraced.

"But how?" Her question echoed around the silent hall.

Ariana's mother wiped the tears from her daughter's face. "*Tu amorcito*. He arranged our crossover from the Hall of Souls for this blessed occasion. *Te quiero, mi'ja. Te quiero mucho.*"

Ariana turned her gaze toward Bacchus, and he blew her a soft kiss. A smile lit up her face; her eyes glittered. Never had he seen her so happy. His heart swelled to the point of bursting. He could fade from existence right here and now and still consider himself the luckiest god that ever was.

After taking a moment to collect herself, she stood, with the help of her parents, and righted her gown. The faeries placed the bouquet to her fingers, and she clutched onto it as if for dear life. With a deep breath, she took her parents arms and nodded to the Cherubim. They began the wedding march to signify the bride's approach to the altar. Faltering steps took Bacchus's ladylove to the base of the altar.

Zeus cleared his throat, sending a ripple of thunder through the air. "As is the custom on Earth, I now ask who gives this woman to be wed in blessed matrimony?"

Ariana's father answered, "Her mother and I do."

Her mother gave her a hug and a gentle kiss. She and her husband took their seats at the top of the altar. Bacchus extended his arm and escorted Ariana to his side on the first riser.

"I love you," she murmured and laced her fingers into his.

"I love you, too." He gave her hand a gentle squeeze.

Zeus plucked a quicksilver ribbon from the ether and wrapped it around Bacchus and Ariana's joined hands.

His free hand slipped beneath her veil. Bacchus caressed Ariana's face. "*Ubi tu Gaia, ego Gaius.*" Where you are Gaia, I am Gaius.

"*Ubi tu Gaius—*" Her voice broke and a tear slipped down her cheek.

Bacchus caught the teardrop with his thumb and brushed it away. He'd hardly gotten the words out himself. Not that he didn't long to speak them with every fiber of his being, but the gravity of what they meant—the promise to be her world and embrace her as his world—the moment overwhelmed him, and he was a god. He stroked her neck and gave her a nod of encouragement.

She closed her eyes and swallowed. "*Porque tu eres Gaius, soy Gaia.*"

His heart beat faster. She'd found a way to make the vow her own. Zeus cradled the newlyweds' heads in his mammoth hands and planted kisses on their cheeks. A jolt of electricity passed through Bacchus, and Ariana shivered. The quicksilver absorbed into their skin, leaving the mark of marriage snaked around their left wrists and blossoming into Bacchus's grape leaf crest on the backs of their hands.

Lifting her veil to reveal his wife to the wedding guests, he pulled Ariana to him. Eyes heavy lidded, she gazed at him, her heartbeat pounding at the base of her throat. He dipped his head, breathing the warmth of her exhalations. Their faces a hairbreadth apart, he paused. He wanted to live in this moment as long as he could. Closing her eyes, she pursed her lips, bridging the smallest of gaps. The warmth of her mouth, the sweetness of her body pressed to his, time stopped. He could feed only on the taste of her lips for the rest of his days. Fingers tangled in his hair, she drew him closer, deepening the kiss.

Zeus cleared his throat, shaking the ground beneath them. Time had not stopped after all. Breaking free, Bacchus peered down at his wife. A blush gave her cheeks a rosy glow, and she struggled to catch her breath.

A gasp went up from the crowd as he released her. A diadem of sapphires appeared above her brow. The crown. Her crown. And Bacchus knew exactly what he was meant to do with it.

He carefully removed the diadem and placed the jewels into the heavens. The new constellation of stars blazed to the side of Heracles's grouping, rewriting all of space and time. The *Corona Borealis* always had been and always would be. Bacchus sealed Ariana's immortality and divinity. His new bride would be his for eternity.

\* \* \* \*

Lounging on a down-filled chaise of velvet, Bacchus held Ariana to his chest. Courtiers fed the couple grapes and replenished their goblets from never-ending wineskins. He took in the splendor surrounding him and his wife.

Nymphs in diaphanous gowns pirouetted to the music played by the symphony of Cherubim. Faeries and pixies flitted around the hall, keeping the flowers in bloom and adding extra sparkle to the bubbling stream coursing through the foliage. The receiving line of gods and goddesses had dwindled, and the guests reclined on chaises and pillows while sampling the ambrosia. Satyrs and centaurs displayed their incomparable wrestling skills in a center ring, trying to keep the exhibition good-natured. No small task for the hybrids. Bacchus breathed in scent of the jasmine in Ariana's hair. The wedding feast was in full swing.

The revelry went on for the equivalent of three Earth days, but one by one, the party guests departed, leaving him alone with his new bride. Where he most wanted to be.

Ariana gave him a look—a look he knew all too well. The wedding was over, time for the honeymoon to begin.

One fingertip tracing her shoulder, he slipped the dress down her waist and let it fall to the ground. He stripped off his *chiton* and then embraced his beautiful wife. The heat of her bare skin against his bare skin took him higher than any vintage wine ever could. As their lips met, Bacchus knew he would forever dwell in heaven as long as Ariana ruled at his side.

# Epilogue

Bacchus reviewed his appearance in a floor to ceiling mirror. The white linen tunic glittered with the golden threads woven into the cloth. It hung over his broad shoulders with a regal drape. A diadem encircled his head, dark locks of hair curled around it. Despite the familiarity of the outfit, an unfamiliar anxiety clutched his abdomen.

"First day back on the job?" Ariana moved in behind him and put her arms around him.

"It is. And I'm nervous. How absurd is that?" He smoothed the back of his hair.

"Not absurd at all, but you'll be fine. I'm sure it's like riding a bicycle."

He faced his wife and shook his head. "But I don't know how to ride a bicycle."

With a gentle laugh and kiss, she dismissed his fears. "Now, go rule your domain, you sexy god you."

God. The word filled him with joy. Almost as much joy as Ariana's smile gave him. Almost, but not quite. He took a deep breath, inhaling the scent of tuberose braided into her long hair, and collected himself. He would savor every moment of his reinstated reign and rule with renewed purpose, but first, he had one little errand to take care of. After kissing his wife good-bye, he headed for the West Wing of the palace.

Bacchus peered into the Hall of Earthly Gifts and watched the elderly Pandora sort out new gifts from various gods and goddesses. From Itzamna, a clean burning, renewable fuel source. From Toth, a portable reading device that allowed humans to take hundreds of electronic books with them everywhere they once would've taken a paperback. From Victoria, a miraculous new swimsuit design that she claimed could help even a mere mortal win at least eight gold medals at the Summer Olympics. Bacchus wasn't so sure about Victoria's claims. Eight gold medals in one Olympics for a single athlete? No way.

He tapped on the door to avoid startling her. "Do you have a moment Madame Pandora?"

"Bacchus, I'm so glad you're back." Her face brightened.

"Me too, love. And I have something I want to share with you." He took a seat next to her and held her hand in his. "You're never going to guess what helped me save my bride from the sorrows and certain death."

She placed a wrinkled hand to her mouth in thought then shook her head. "I've no idea. What?"

"Apple strudel."

Pandora clapped her hands and gleeful laughter echoed around the salon.

"With streusel?" she asked.

Bacchus planted a kiss on top of her graying head. "Yes, my lady. With streusel."

\* \* \* \*

Steam hissed from the cracks along fault lines and the scent of sulfur-tainted the air. Belches of lava boiled around his throne made of the bones of evil men—all once bringers of war and death in their own right. That he sat on Tomas de Torquemada's fleshless face every day amused the outcast angel. What a wonderful servant the Grand Inquisitor had been.

He held the box in his hands and turned it around and around, studying it. Such a tiny thing, but what a big difference it would make. Tucking a lock of golden hair behind his ear, he picked up a sack of gold coins and tossed them to the awaiting mercenary.

"Thank you for your service, Loki," said Lucifer.

"Any time, my lord." Loki bowed and took his leave.

Discordia emerged from behind a black velvet drapery and took a seat on the arm of Lucifer's throne. Rubbing his chest, she asked, "Shall we open it, my lord?"

They'd waited centuries for the Council to oust the foolish Bacchus and the two years it had taken the fool to stumble across his destiny in the form of his wife. The god of intoxication was so stupid and self-absorbed he'd forgotten all about the master-less sorrows box Loki had stolen. And it'd been all too easy for the trickster to steal it back under the guise of lending Bacchus a helping hand. A little while longer and the entire prophecy would be realized.

A cruel grin parted the Prince of Darkness's lips. "All in good time, my dear. All in good time."

# Meet the Author

Prior to becoming a writer of romantic and erotic fiction, Cindy went to college at the University of Hawaii at Manoa and graduated with a BFA in Art. After a brief attempt at an art career, she decided the 'starving artist' life wasn't for her. She worked for ten years in the corporate arena, but now spends her days as a full time author.

Her first published work was inspired by a collection of short stories she wrote to entertain her best friend. Since then she's explored her inner bad girl, producing books full of humor and packed with real emotion.

When not chained to her laptop, she enjoys belly dancing, international cooking, and making jewelry. She and her family make their home in the Washington, DC area.

www.ingramcontent.com/pod-product-compliance
Lightning Source LLC
Chambersburg PA
CBHW050732250626

47155CB00005B/1769